ANYTHING FOR YOU

BRITTNEY LAUREN

Author's Note

Anything For You is a work of fiction and while it's a romance first and foremost there are some serious elements that I'd like to make note of before you take a trip into Fairvale. Content includes death of a spouse, alcoholism, anxiety, and implied childhood neglect. This story includes open-door romance, meaning there is on page sexual contact intended for mature readers only.

If any of these could be a trigger for you this may not be the book for you and that's okay.

Xo - Brittney

For my over active imagination.
Who knew you'd be good for something other than causing my anxiety.

It's normal, not to forget your first love.
- The Notebook, Nicholas Sparks

The Playlist

1. Memory Lane – Haley Joelle

2. Too Damn You – Julie Roberts

3. Religiously – Bailey Zimmerman

4. Unknown/Nth – Hozier

5. Always Been You – Jessie Murph

6. Shelter – from the room below – Sleep Token

7. Let Me Love the Lonely – James Arthur

8. i am not who i was – Chance Peña

9. Jaws – Sleep Token

10. Everything Has Changed – Taylor Swift, Ed Sheeran

11. Must Be Doing Something Right – Billy Currington

12. Quietly Yours – Birdy

13. Afterglow – Taylor Swift

14. Everywhere, Everything – Noah Kahan, Gracie Abrams

Listen on Spotify

ONE

Lennon

WHEN THEY LOWERED MY husband's casket into the ground, I screamed. The gut-wrenching noise echoed out into the chilly afternoon and would reverberate in my mind until the end of time. The moment his casket sank into the ground, every ounce of happiness I ever experienced evaporated like it never existed. In its wake, pain made its home in my heart, burrowing deep enough that I knew it would be impossible to remove.

Heartbreak was supposed to be a metaphor, an unspoken step in the process of grief that you worked through in your mind. That statement no longer held any weight, since my heart was sitting in the bottom of my chest, torn into pieces. The pain rippled through me, forcing my body forward in my chair. Every part of me, from my limbs to my skin to the very atoms I was made of, writhed in agony.

No one moved, all too stunned by my sudden outburst to help. This was the first sign of any emotion from me since I received the call that my husband, my Camden, was dead.

For three weeks, I had been devoid of all feelings. Numbness was my only companion. It followed me like a ghost with every step I took and lingered around corners, waiting to remind me that he was gone. I had built what seemed to be a thousand layers of protection around me to help me through this day. Then his casket slipped past the horizon of his grave and it all came crashing down around me.

My hands clawed at my throat as I struggled to breathe. Tears clouded my vision as I twisted myself around in my seat, searching for refuge in anyone around me. Why was no one helping? Why was no one stopping what was happening in front of us? Why was my husband being lowered into the ground?

I didn't understand.

I screamed again and again.

My sister materialized before me, taking my face in her hands. "Lennon! Lennon!" she said, her voice full of panic. Abigail shook me, trying to snap me out of the psychosis that was continuing to set it. Her hands dug into my upper arms as my eyes focused on her through the blurriness. For a second, I was grateful, her frame blocked my view of the hole that was no longer empty.

"Help me," I choked out between ragged breaths. If I could count on anyone to get me out of this situation, it would be her. A realization slammed into me like a freight train. She's one of the only people I had left. Her and Carina, the only other friend I truly had.

Nothing worked.

My brain couldn't seem to tell my legs to move, and everything was numb. Abigail had to physically pull me to my feet before I latched onto her to step away from the site. We walked hand in hand along the paved roads that circled around the cemetery. There were no words that I could find to fill the space around us. Instead, I silently broke into pieces in front of her. The grief was overwhelming, and with each moment that passed, I fell deeper and deeper into an endless pit of agony.

Clouds hung low in the sky as the air whipped around us. Icy as it sliced over my skin, a picture-perfect funeral if there ever was one. November was always a cruel month, gray skies that seemed to stretch on for forever and an endless amount of rain.

When the first drops fell, I tilted my head back, hoping they'd wash away the hurt that was simmering under my skin. But when they hit my skin, I felt nothing, like someone had scooped out everything that made me, me and left only an empty shell.

There was an endless loop of memories playing in my head. The type of memories you wouldn't think to treasure when they were happening, but now, they were the only thing I had left. The simple way he would walk through the door after work, his voice in the shower shouting for a towel, or how his fingertips would mindlessly drag across my skin as we sat on the couch. Everything was coming to me in flashes, and I was trying desperately to grasp onto them to safely lock them away.

I couldn't possibly begin to wrap my mind around that this was all I had left of him—brief moments that would only exist in my memories.

"What can I do?" Abigail pleaded with me as anguish flashed in her eyes. Her long chestnut colored hair billowed in the wind as I contemplated what she was trying to ask me.

Could she turn back time and give me one more day with him? Could she make it so that at the very least I could've been there when he passed? Could she bring him back?

That was all impossible, so no, there was nothing she could do for me.

Another wave of sobs erupted from my chest as I clutched my arms around my black clothed torso to hold myself together. I turned towards Abigail as grief continued its assault on my soul. I didn't want to be here, and I did not want to be doing this.

He was gone.

The man I was supposed to spend my life with. The man I vowed to love for all of eternity was dead, and I was left alone, a widow at thirty-three. This wasn't part of the plan we had for our life together. Surely this was some cruel mistake the universe was playing. I was going to wake up any second and this would all be a bad dream; that could be the only logical explanation.

"Abby," my voice sounded weak and I could barely form the words. "What am I supposed to do now?" Tears cascaded down my face without pause. I was convinced I would die drowning in them.

The wind swept my auburn curls through the air, leaving strands clinging to my damp cheeks. Abigail pulled me in and enclosed me in a suffocating hug. Bunching the fabric of her black dress, I held onto her. She stroked my hair softly and replied, "You will get through this, I promise. You are not alone; whatever it takes, I will get you through this." Her voice broke over the words. Her tears fell freely, wetting the fabric around my shoulder, as we stood among the headstones grieving under the clouds.

My eyes scanned the lawn from over her shoulder, headstone after headstone lined the perfectly manicured cemetery. Some held wilted flowers, others were overflowing with lush, fresh bouquets. Every plot contained somebody's loved one. I took little comfort in knowing I'm not alone in my grief.

Burying your loved one is one of times oldest traditions, a cathartic action of closure, but one that never got easier. Throughout millenniums and across cultures, it's the one thing we all had in common—no one escaped death. We were all born to die. The hope was that the time between our first breath and our last was filled with more joy than sadness.

Everything about this was wrong. Burying Camden wasn't bringing me closure, only heartache and doubt that there was something better after this life. Anger burned through my veins that he was no longer here. I wanted to curse the sky and God and everything that was good in this world that he was taken from me too soon. Much too soon. How was I supposed to move my way through life without his hand in mine, without his light to guide me and brighten the darkness that always seemed to follow me?

I thought that if I could stuff it down far enough, I could make it through today and face it all tomorrow. It was stupid to hope when, all day, I couldn't take a step without someone offering their condolences.

'He's in a better place,' or the equally stupid, 'he had a good life,' or 'he was so happy with you.'

It was all filler conversation people felt compelled to say while they looked at me with eyes full of sorrow. A better place would be a world with Camden alive and with me. A good life would have been a long life together. Anything less than the life we had planned was clearly a mistake, and they had been reminding me constantly.

This had to be a mistake.

I softened my grip on Abigail's dress, dropping my head onto her shoulder. My breathing steadied as I stood there, unmoving, as she rubbed small circles on my back. Before I pulled myself away, the words "What's the point anymore?" fell from my lips so softly that I was sure Abigail didn't hear me. She regarded me with careful eyes as I pulled myself upright and brushed my tear-stained cheeks with the back of my hands. A weak smile tugged at my lips, but my eyes didn't crinkle like it used to, and I didn't think they ever would.

I drew in a steading breath and again stuffed everything back down. "Let's get the rest of this day over with," I said and started back to her car after taking note that our friends and family were gone from the gravesite and likely on their way back to my house. I squeezed my eyes shut and took another deep breath.

Just a few more hours and it would all be over, and I could go back to—not normal, but something other than whatever this was.

"I love you," Abigail called out, causing me to turn back and face her.

Her appearance matched my own. Even in my damaged state, there was still a pull in my chest to comfort my younger sister. "I love you, too," I replied. A simple statement of fact, but not one we often spoke aloud. It didn't matter how many years passed, there were still times I looked at her and saw the small girl I spent my life protecting. She slipped her hand into my outstretched one without a second thought. Our heels clicked against the pavement as we walked in sync toward the car.

Nothing about me would be the same after this.

How could it be?

Camden blew into my life during a time when nothing in this world seemed to go my way. He was the light that illuminated every dark crevasse that carved its way through my body. With him gone, I was a black hole devouring even the smallest beams of light, until I was left blind and in the dark. I would never be able to get back what I lost in Camden.

After all the people left, food filled my refrigerator, and I stopped experiencing feelings hours prior. I was drained of what little energy I had left. My sister and our closest friend Carina were the only ones who remained in my home. They found me sitting on the edge of my bed, too exhausted to even remove my dress, as I stared blankly at the wall in front of me. Together, they gently tucked me under my covers and crawled in beside me. The chill that had been permeating my bones, threatening to freeze me from the inside out, lessened as they wrapped me in their arms and whispered promises of survival.

TWO

Lennon

MY CEILING FAN NEEDED to be dusted. I had been lying on my bed staring at the blades while they slowly turned in circles for the past hour when the front door creaked open. "Good morning!" A voice shouted out from the entryway. My arm stretched out over the empty space next to me and gripped the blankets that laid undisturbed on the side of the bed he used to occupy. If I could fall back asleep I would, I would do anything to get this day over with.

It didn't take a psychic to know that my sister was going to show up today, but that didn't stop me from being annoyed by it. A groan escaped as I tossed the covers over my face. It had been two years to the day since Camden died.

Two years, and my heart still sat in my chest, cleaved into pieces. Every day, I missed him. Every day, I woke up hoping this had all been a dream. And every day, dread took up space in the pit of my stomach when I remembered that this, in fact, was my real life.

"Lennon?" Abigail's voice carried down the hallway as I waited for the squeak of her sneakers to get closer.

"I'm in here. It's eight in the morning. Where else would I be?" My voice was muffled by the thick blanket covering my face. I could sense her lingering in my doorway, likely taking in the shape of my covered body.

"What are you doing?" she laughed.

"Clearly wallowing in self-pity, Abby," I snapped, and the bed dipped as she joined me. I didn't really mean for the words to sound as harsh as they did, but honestly, what type of answer was she looking for? Abigail drew the blanket down to look at me with a raised brow.

"I'm just trying to figure out what type of situation I'm going to be dealing with today." I couldn't place the emotion in her voice; it was a mix of amusement and something I couldn't quite decipher. Pity maybe?

"Remember, this doesn't have to be a bad day. We can do anything you'd like to do."

Definitely pity, it's always pity.

On the first anniversary of Camden being gone, I had myself quite the party when I secluded myself in my home that I shared with no one but my cat. It started with a champagne breakfast and ended with a vodka dinner. The day had passed in a drunken blur as I cried more times than I could count while looking over a photo montage that had inconveniently generated itself on my phone of

Camden and me. I vaguely remembered Abigail showing up to tuck me into bed at some point after all her calls and texts had gone unanswered.

"I don't have any plans, and I don't anticipate a repeat performance of last year. The hangover alone was enough to make me never want to drink again." I nearly gagged thinking of the memory.

We laid side by side in silence for a little while longer as Abigail's eyes scanned the room. Nothing had changed in the past two years. Our wedding photo still sat on the shelf and Camden's clothes still hung in the closet. His nightstand still held the watch I bought him for his last birthday, and the dish that had collected his day's change still had exactly two dollars and seventy-three cents. I hadn't been able to bring myself to move anything; it was as if the room was in a standstill.

On days when loneliness crept in too far, I could pretend I was expecting him to return home and climb into bed with me at the end of the day.

I was living in a time capsule, and I didn't know how to get out. I didn't even know if I wanted out.

"Do you want to go shopping?" Abigail questioned.

I rolled over so that we were face to face. "Nope," I said, popping the sound for flare.

"Okay, okay." Abigail held up her hands in defense. "I was just asking. I thought it might be a good time for a fresh start."

No, no, no. This was not what I wanted to be doing. I wasn't ready, and she knew it, too.

I sat up and threw the covers off and headed for the bathroom. "Give me twenty minutes and we can go to breakfast." I closed the door behind me and collapsed back against the frame. I would not cry today, I thought to myself.

The water ran while I stood in the bathroom, looking back at myself in the mirror. Two years had changed everything about who I was, down to the very thoughts that floated around in my head. I couldn't stop the hurt from consuming me at every turn as much as I wished I could.

One step at a time, though.

I wish I could express how much I appreciated her showing up today. Or really every day since Camden died, but I had never been good with words. My sister had been my saving grace and a sounding board against the grief that I'd let isolate me during this period in my life. Abigail never wavered, never left. She stood by me, picking up my broken pieces, slowly helping me put my life back together.

"You can do this. You can do hard things, you can do uncomfortable things," I said to my reflection, with no one else around but me to hear. I wanted to start by not shutting everyone out. It was the least I could do.

We sat in our usual window seat at Wake Up Café. The plastic booth seat crinkled under me as I let the sun sink into my skin.

We had been coming here for over a decade, seeking solace from heartaches and hangovers over the years.

I brought my coffee mug to my lips and let the aroma linger before taking a sip. I glanced up over the cup to meet Abigail's eyes. We stared at each other briefly, refusing to blink.

It's the one feature we shared, our eyes, dark blue that we inherited from our mother. Otherwise, we were complete opposites, and barely even look related. My tall and curvier figure to Abigail's shorter and naturally thin body. But as opposite as we were, there was no mistaking that the bond we shared was significant and unbreakable.

Sisters, best friends, soul mates. Even when we're locked in a stalemate, she would always be the best thing in my life.

"So, how's work been going?" Abigail asked, breaking the silence that we had been sitting in.

I rolled my eyes. "Really, work? That's what we're going to talk about?" Coffee sloshed over the rim of my mug as I set my drink down with more forced than needed. I shoveled food into my mouth to avoid another outburst.

It shouldn't be this hard, I thought. I shouldn't have to work to have a conversation with my own sister without my short fuse exploding. Abigail sat back in the booth, glowering at me. "We can talk about whatever you want to, Lennon. I didn't come here to just sit and watch you eat."

Touché.

"Work is work. I get up, I walk to my office, and for the next eight hours, I sit in front of a computer. It's mindless. That's how it's going." I really did enjoy my job; it was simple enough customer service work, and being able to work from home was a luxury I didn't think I could ever give up.

After Camden died, I took a short sabbatical. I had to. When even the simplest daily tasks were overwhelming, work was out of the question. It took months before I was able to return, but I knew it meant I could still hide within the walls of the home we shared. One of the only redeeming features.

"Have you given any more thought to the trip?" Abigail's eyes danced as she asked. She was on one today and putting her best effort into pushing all my buttons. I squeezed my eyes shut for a second. If I tried hard enough, maybe this would be a daydream, and I would still be in bed. My eyes opened to Abigail, still staring back at me.

At least I tried.

I snorted into the coffee cup as I took another drink. "No, I can't just take that much time off work to run around the Scottish Highlands like a fairy book princess, as much as I would like to. I have bills to pay."

That was only partly true; I had the money to keep myself afloat, even if I decided to take a year off work, let alone a few weeks. It was the work aspect I couldn't work out. Granted, I hadn't even approached my boss with the idea of getting a few weeks off, but taking time off seemed like it would only leave more work for me when I returned than I wanted to deal with, so I scratched the idea before it even got off the ground.

That was the easy reason I placated Abigail with, at least.

In reality, I shot down the idea of this trip because I couldn't fathom having to take a vacation alone that was originally supposed to be for Camden and me. We had agreed that our ten-year anniversary deserved a big celebration, and Scotland was chosen specifically for me.

My fascination with the history of the country ran deep. Its lush green spaces, lochs and castle ruins had occupied my mind for years. Camden couldn't have cared less about where we went. "As long as we are together, we could go anywhere," he would say, and he had always had an overwhelming desire to make me happy. If Scotland could do that for me, then that's where we would go. Camden would have followed me anywhere in the world if it would bring even the smallest of smiles to my face.

Our anniversary came and went earlier this year, yet another reminder that he was gone from my life.

"Come on, we can go together. It could be fun." The shine in Abby's eyes quickly dissipated as I shook my head back and forth.

"He would have wanted you to go, you know."

I shot her a look that was more internalized pain than a warning. I was not far from giving up altogether and crawling back under my covers until it was the next day. My face pinched as I let out a sigh.

"We don't know that."

"Yes, we do."

"Abigail, no, we don't. Listen, I know you're trying to help, but I would rather spend the day at home and not force myself to put on a brave face for the public." I started to gather my stuff. I needed to get out of the restaurant, and fast. My throat constricted and tears pricked my waterline.

"And that includes being brave for you."

I stood up from the booth, but Abigail snatched my wrist and pulled me back before I could get too far. "Don't push me, Lennon. I know you're hurting, but you don't get to be rude." I yanked my arm back out of my sister's grasp and stalked toward the door. It wasn't supposed to be like this. She should be the last person I fought with.

All I wanted was to be alone, in my cold and empty home.

Day in and day out, my life was more like a battle and I was constantly at war with myself. I was being pulled between who I was before Camden's death—carefree and full of life—and the woman I needed to learn how to be without him in order to get past the heartbreak. But I didn't know how to be that person and I was scared to be someone new. New meant Camden was in the past and that wasn't a reality I wanted to live in yet.

When I arrived home, I headed straight to the bedroom and crawled underneath the covers. I pulled the pillow that belonged to Camden close to my face. It had long since lost the scent of him, and that realization broke my heart all over again.

I wanted it back. I wanted him back.

Longing coursed through me as the memories of him played in my head. There was a time when we would lie together, a tangled mess of limbs under the sheets, and I would relish in the warmth of him. Nothing could compare to the way I felt in his arms.

I was safe. Loved. Wanted.

As I grasped the pillow tightly to my body, a sob escaped my throat, reminding me that I was cold and hollow. I choked out the words, "I miss you," and it echoed out into the empty room. The only other sound was the quiet purr of my cat, who had pounced up onto the bed. He was a gift from Camden and the last thing he ever gave me. I reached out to stroke his orange and white fur. "It's just you and me, Anakin."

There's a place I liked to escape to right before sleep would fully take me under. It's a small space that could only be found in between my dreams and reality, but it's the only place he existed anymore. I closed my heavy eyes and let myself drift off to sleep, happy for the brief interruption in my agony and I hoped that he was waiting for me.

THREE

Lennon

WEEKS PASSED, AND I hadn't heard from Abigail since I left her sitting in front of our unfinished breakfast. It's not lost on me that I acted like a petulant child who had been told 'no' for the first time. It was unlike Abigail to not reach out. She had always been the better one to bridge the gap after a disagreement. I must have hurt her feelings more than I realized. I would cave first this time. It's the least I could do, and I had no patience to wait out her cold shoulder.

> I'm sorry

> I know

The quick reply chimed from my phone. This apology was obviously going to be harder to earn than a simple "I'm sorry" My feet carried me back and forth the length of my living room. I knew I was at fault. I just needed to show Abigail that.

It didn't take long after my failed breakfast with Abby to realize that maybe she was right. Maybe what I needed was time away from the mundane life I had created for myself. I spent hours upon hours scouring the internet researching flights and hotels or rentals in Scotland. I immersed myself in blog after blog about people's experiences and ones I wanted for myself. I convinced myself that this was the right choice after the second website I visited and the new accounts I followed on social media, my feed was flooded with the breathtaking landscapes.

My time off was approved, and as long as I didn't chicken out, I would be in Scotland in a few short months. Telling Abigail would be easy, but having to tell her I wanted to go alone, that would be the difficult part. I had been using Abigail as a crutch for far longer than I should have been, and I needed to start relying on myself. How could I move forward if I relied on other people to hold me up? It might be a long shot, but I had the thing to apologize to Abigail with, and hopefully, soften the blow that she wouldn't be joining me on the trip.

The front door swung open precisely ten minutes later. Abigail waltzed in, making her way to the back bedroom. "You ready." A statement more than a question.

What I loved most about my sister was her ability to forgive, mainly her ability to forgive me for quite literally everything. The years we spent growing up sharing a room had spawned so many fights between us that it was second nature to not be on speaking terms. It would never last long, though, and like a flip of a switch, it was as if the fight never happened.

Today was no exception, and I was grateful.

After what seemed to be hours of aimlessly wandering down aisle after aisle, we returned to the house, bags in tow. I pulled out the new pillows and a throw blanket I had purchased and shuffled back to the living room. I didn't even really want these, but Abigail was pushing for more drastic changes, and this was all I could manage.

I had spent the whole shopping trip going back and forth with how to tell Abigail that I decided to go but that she couldn't come. I knew she wasn't going to like it, and I wouldn't be able to explain the need inside me that said I should go alone.

Expressing myself comes through with my actions, not words, and this was something that had to be said; it was going to suck. I silently prayed that I could get my point across without completely upsetting her or stumbling over my words.

Fiddling with the tassels on the pillow, I tried to work up the nerve. I took a deep breath and began. "So, I'm going to do it." Abigail whipped around from where she stood in the kitchen.

"Do what?" Her eyebrows knitted together in slight confusion. An inpatient clicking sound escaped my mouth.

She knew exactly what I was talking about.

"Scotland. I'm going to go." Maybe my subtle use of the phrase "I'm" would be enough for her to get the hint, and I didn't actually have to tell her, 'no you can't come with me'.

"That's great. When are you thinking of going? I'll have to put in a request for time off soon, but whatever dates you have should work." I could see the way her face lit up as she spoke, and my next sentence was hard to get out.

"This will be so fun. We haven't gone anywhere together in a—"

I cut her off. "No, I'm going to Scotland. Just me." I wanted, no needed, to get this conversation over with as soon as possible.

Abigail's face contorted. "By yourself? Why?"

How could I explain that this was something I felt in my bones that I needed to do alone?

I dropped my head back and stared at the ceiling for a brief moment. Walking into the kitchen, I confronted Abigail.

"It's not that I don't want you with me; I do." I began to fiddle with the wedding ring on my hand. "I do." I repeated as I slipped the thick band up and down my finger. It had been sitting on my left hand for the past ten years, making what I had always assumed would be a permanent indentation. I knew that I would have to remove it at some point, but I hadn't been able to yet.

"I just…" I searched for the words, stuttering slightly as my lips trembled. "You were right. Camden would have wanted me to do this, and I think by going alone, it will allow me to start moving forward." I looked up to meet my sister's gaze. She didn't look hurt, but my pulse thrummed inside my chest, regardless.

"I don't expect you to understand. I barely understand." Pacing around the island, I ran my hands along the countertop. The marble was cool under my fingertips, grounding me to the present conversation. Stopping mid-way so that we were on opposite sides of the counter. I reminded myself that doing what I thought was best for me was a good thing, that expressing what I wanted would help me move forward.

For two years, I'd been hiding—from everyone around me and from myself. Something needed to change, and it had to start with me.

I was going to start doing things that could bring me joy, and this could be it.

"I think that by going alone, I can prove to myself that being alone isn't the worst thing I can be." I had been selfishly keeping everyone out since Camden died, and I was living barely half a life. It was time to start living again and putting myself out there.

"Maybe going out into the world alone will allow me to find the parts of myself I've lost. It has to be better than what I have been doing, which is nothing." I confessed, as my hand gripped the edge of the counter. My sister observed me with eyes that held some unknown emotion.

"I've been reading about the area. It's safe for single travelers. And I've already got the whole trip planned out. I'll only be gone for two weeks, and I'll keep in touch with you the whole time, so no one gets worried." My statement ran together as I tried to get all the information out as quickly as possible.

My heartbeat sped up as Abigail continued to stare at me before she spoke. Her eyes darted around my face. "You don't have to do this alone. You know that, right?" I reached across the space between us for her hand. "I know, but I want to. I have to see what I'm still capable of." She squeezed my hand, and my anxiety lessened at her touch.

I floundered through the past two years of my life and, by the skin of my teeth, I barely scraped by. The first few months were the worst. Days and weeks were spent nearly catatonic, following Camden's death, allowing only Abigail and Carina to see how truly bad things got for me.

It took everything I had in me to not leave this world behind to be with Camden. I was ashamed that I even had those thoughts. It wouldn't have solved anything; it would've only pass my grief onto everyone I left behind. I know that now.

It was Abigail who had been with me through the sleepless nights that seemed to bleed into each other, and the days when I could barely get out of bed. She plastered herself to my side, begging and pleading with me to eat some days.

I owed it to her and to myself to be better.

She clapped her hands together, the worry gone from her eyes. "Okay then, how can I help?" We sat at the table as I pulled out my computer and began to lay out my trip.

"I'll fly into Edinburgh and spend a few days there before taking the train to Glasgow, then up to Inverness and back down through St. Andrews." My voice was bright, and I could see the smile that Abigail attempted to hide. I don't think I had shown this much excitement for anything in a long time.

We went back and forth for the rest of the night, planning out my itinerary. I had two weeks to fill, and it wouldn't be nearly enough time to see everything. I wanted to spend my time overseas exploring the cities, the ruins of forgotten castles, and roaming the vast rugged highlands, feeding my empty soul with the open spaces.

I had no one to answer to, and I could do whatever I wanted, whenever I wanted. Something inside me stirred. It stretched itself out slowly, unfurling from its two-year hibernation. Hope was blooming, and I would not take it for granted.

FOUR

Lennon

The next three months were spent meticulously combing through the details of my trip. The flight was booked, hotels set up, and I found the most dream-like cottage in Inverness to stay at. Located on a local estate surrounded by highland wilderness, exactly what I had envisioned for my stay. It was all approaching so quickly, causing my nerves to twist themselves in doubt.

Two weeks completely on my own sparked an unknown fear within. No Abigail to call when the darkness lurked its way out of parts of my mind. No work to distract myself from the empty home that used to be so full of love.

More than that, there would be no Camden.

When I first started to plan this trip for Camden and myself, I had envisioned us wandering hand in hand amongst the rolling hills or tucked away together in some small café a thousand times over. Every imagined scenario involved him, and now I was headed halfway across the globe without him. There wasn't a spot on Earth that I could go where the absence of Camden wouldn't be noticed. Even my hometown felt smaller and smaller each day that passed without him.

Everywhere I looked, there was some reminder of him and my heart would break all over.

Camden and I met a few years after I was out of high school. The decision for me to stay local to attend university was easy. I needed to in order to stay close to Abigail, who was still in high school. Our mother lacked the empathy one needed to be a decent mother. Hell, even a decent human. I couldn't bear to leave Abby alone with her.

My path first crossed with Camden when I was in my second year. Camden was a year older when we first met. I had been in the library finishing a paper when he walked in. I barely looked up from the table when he found his way over and slid into the chair across from me.

I remembered the brightness of his voice as he greeted me. It caused my head to snap up, and our eyes met for the first time. Time stalled as I sat there, staring into his deep brown irises before I caught myself. There was a lazy smile splashed across his face. His black hair curled and fell just above his eyebrows; all it took was a moment, and he seemed to steal the very air from my lungs.

"Do you mind?" he said as he gestured toward the table. He flung his bag on top without waiting for an answer and began removing his computer, making himself comfortable.

"Uh, yeah, I guess, but you know there are plenty of open tables in here."

Our eyes locked as he said, "I know, but none of them have you." He held my gaze, and heat began crawling up the back of my neck and my cheeks burned with a blush.

I had never met someone who was so direct. I squirmed under the boldness of his obvious flirtation. He extended his hand across the table. "I'm Camden." I swore to this day that electricity shot up my arm from the initial touch. "I'm Lennon."

"Lennon," he repeated. "That's beautiful." A few simple words from a stranger and I was hooked. A second with this person, and my body was on fire. I hadn't felt anything like it in however how long. It had been years since anyone had caught my attention, not since high school, but I refused to think about him.

We began meeting every week at that same table. Some days we sat in comfortable silence as we poured over our work, others everything fell to the wayside as we lost ourselves in conversation. Weeks bled into months as we fell in love amongst the books, our days in the library turned into late night dinners and early morning coffees. Camden brought fire and excitement into my life, and in turn, I brought him balance and dependability.

We were married by the time I turned twenty-five. In a small church ceremony, we vowed to love each other through this life and the next and any lifetime that followed. You couldn't find two people more devoted to each other, two souls that had been created together in the beginning, destined to live out every timeline interlaced.

Then, in some cruel twist of fate, all of this came crashing down around me the day he died. Even knowing how it all ended, I wouldn't change a single moment.

The piercing ring of a phone pulled me from the past, and I glanced at the name that appeared across the top of the screen—Charlotte. I answered on the next ring, knowing the woman would keep calling. "Hi, Charlotte." My mother-in-law was truly a wonderful person, warm and caring. She lost her only son and still found it in her to check in on me. Countless times, I would find myself in her arms as grief would take over. She would hold me while I cried and promise that it would get easier with time. All I needed was time.

"Hello darling, how are you?" Her voice was light and reassuring. It had been a few weeks since we last spoke. It wasn't on purpose, but had happened nonetheless, an unconscious separation between myself and his family. Whatever the cause, nothing would stop Charlotte from continuing to keep up with me; even in death, I was still her daughter.

"I am actually in the middle of packing. I'll be out of the country for a few weeks." I grimaced slightly. I didn't understand why, but it seemed like I was lying by not telling her sooner. That soon passed as I heard a squeal of laughter coming from the other end of the line.

"How wonderful! Where are you going? No, wait, let me guess." She had the unique ability to pull excitement out of me.

Charlotte was the rarest of mothers-in-laws. She loved me with such conviction I often forgot she was Camden's mother and not my own. From the moment Camden had introduced us, there wasn't a moment that I didn't feel welcomed or loved. She doted on us both. No birthday went unnoticed, no job promotion gone uncelebrated; she left much to be desired in my own mother.

She prattled off a few countries before I cut in. "Belarus?! No, what?" Laughing while shaking my head. "It's Scotland, Charlotte." Giving her the answer.

"Oh, how wonderful, dear. You must be so excited! Are you leaving soon?" I knew that her interest was genuine, but there was a nagging pull in my chest that she was only keeping me close so she could hang on to some small part of Camden. It wasn't fair for me to think this way about a woman who would drop everything to help me in my time of need, but it didn't stop the doubt from creeping into my consciousness.

"I fly out tomorrow and will be there for two weeks." I was almost done packing, but I still didn't want to linger on the phone.

"And is Abby going with you?" My head dipped backwards as I shut my eyes.

I inhaled deeply. "Uh, no, I am going on my own."

There was a heavy pause that was only broken by Charlotte's quiet, "Hmm, I see."

I stood from the bed where I had been organizing my suitcases and stepped in front of the mirror. "I'm just hoping to start living my life again, and I figured why not start off strong with a once in a lifetime trip?" Maybe if I said it enough times out loud, it would be true.

"Well, I think it's about time. You are an incredible person, Lennon. You deserve to be happy. Camden would be so proud of you." I smiled at my reflection. I almost believed it this time.

"Ooh," she continued. "Who knows? Maybe it will be like one of those Hallmark movies and you'll meet a millionaire who will sweep you off your feet." My laugh echoed throughout the room.

"I... that's not why... oh wow, that's too good, Charlotte." I gasped out in between breaths while my heartbeat thumped in my chest at even the thought of being with someone new.

"Hmm, you never know. Well, I love you, dear, and I'd love to hear from you when you're back." I could picture the smug look that would've been plastered on Charlotte's face if I could see her.

"Of course. Once I get back, we'll do dinner, and I love you, too." I really did. Charlotte was one of the strongest and most upbeat people I knew, and I was grateful for the family I had in her. The passing of her only son should have extinguished the spark that kept her going, but it had only damped it. She continued to have a positive outlook on life and lived every day to the fullest.

"Lennon, remember that you are still here, and you deserve to continue to live your life. I would never want to push you in a direction you are not comfortable with, but I hate to see you so unhappy. I know you love him, and I could never thank you enough for the time you spent with my son and the happiness you brought him, but I would also love to see you enjoy your life again. Even if that means finding someone new."

My mind raced as my eyebrows pinched together. This was not the way I thought this call would go. "I'll keep that in mind,

Charlotte, and I'll call you when I'm back." I hung up the call and threw the phone onto the bed.

I paced the room, as I frowned at the ground as her last sentence echoed through my head. "Even if that means finding someone new." I didn't want to find someone new. Spending time trying to get to know someone sounded tedious. I wouldn't even know where to start if it was what I wanted.

Camden knew me like the back of his hand. He could anticipate my moods and knew how to handle me in a way that could never be replicated, and I doubted it existed outside of our marriage. There's a small part of me that thought maybe having someone to spend time with wouldn't be all that bad. There was no replacing Camden, and I wouldn't even try to, but maybe finding someone to share parts of myself wouldn't be the worst thing.

"Maybe she's right." A statement heard by no one, but for me, it was a promise to myself. Scotland would be just the thing I needed to, not start over, but to move forward at the very least.

FIVE

Lennon

MY PHONE CHIMED WITH Abigail's message, saying she was pulling up to the house. I gathered my suitcases and dragged them outside to meet her while the wheels scraped against the concrete driveway, kicking up loose pebbles. Her smile widened while she waved from the front seat and for a split second, I wanted to change my mind and tell her to come with me. The words never left my head as I reminded myself that I could do this on my own. I could do hard things, I could do uncomfortable things.

"You're leaving for two weeks, and you only have two suitcases!" she yelled out from the driver's seat. She shook her head and threw her hands up in disbelief.

I rolled my eyes and knocked on the back window for her to open the trunk. "Ya, ya, ya," I quipped, brushing off her comment. I was nothing if not over prepared; everything was planned, down to which socks and jewelry to wear on which day. And there was no way I was paying those extra baggage fees.

My seatbelt clicked into place and I pulled a deep breath in as we backed away from my house. This was what I wanted, to break out of the stagnant life I had settled into, but the farther I got from the safety of my home, the more I began to doubt myself.

Within forty-five minutes, we arrived at the departure drop off. I stepped out onto the curb and went to grab my bags. Abigail met me around the back of the car with a prominent worry line between her eyes.

"Please call if anything happens or, you know, if you just miss me." She pulled me into a hug, and I was immediately uncomfortable with the amount of affection going on. "I'm still pissed I'm not going. You will have so much fun, I know it." Her tight squeeze around my shoulder eased the tension that was building.

"I will call you every night to recap my day. How's that?" I said. I was not a hugger or a touchy feely type of person. This type of closeness usually caused my stomach to turn, but I fought the urge to slink away and hugged her a bit tighter. She had been too good to me not to.

"You better."

We released each other, and I gathered my bags and started towards the airport doors. I couldn't believe that I was really going through with this. Months of planning led to this moment, and there was excitement alongside the fear coursing through my veins.

I hadn't been so far from home on my own since before Cam, and even then, I wasn't the type of person struck with wanderlust. I was content in my small town and with my husband, who worked to give me the world within the four walls of the home we built together.

There was a wave of calmness that fell over me. It crashed through the jitters that had been plaguing me and forced them to still, telling me this was exactly where I needed to be.

This is what I'd been searching for, a chance to reset and start moving forward. With one last look back at Abigail, I stepped further into the building with a smile plastered on my face.

My body was screaming at me by the time the plane touched down in Edinburgh. Eighteen-hours of travel did nothing but make me question why I ever decided to leave home. With every step I took towards baggage claim, my muscles ached, everything hurt, and was crying out for a long soak in a bath.

All of this melted away as the taxi sped through Edinburgh, and I was suddenly speechless. I grew up in a beautiful town, full of lush foliage and trees that seemed to go on forever. My neighborhood overlooked Orange Grove River and the buildings on Main Street, I knew beautiful scenery. But this town was breathtaking in a way I found hard to describe, cobblestone roads wove through the city and architecture that was centuries old. Everything was full of ancient beauty, unlike anything I could experience at home.

I stepped out of the cab in front of the hotel, my senses drinking in the atmosphere. I couldn't take in the sights fast enough, and I was a second away from giving myself whiplash from trying to see everything I could just outside the hotel as fast as possible. My eyes finally fell on the reason I was here—Castle Edinburgh.

It seemed silly to be a grown woman still fascinated by castles, but we all had our quirks, right? Castles happened to be mine, though I gave up on the fairytales a while ago.

In Edinburgh, there was only one place to stay to have the best view of Scotland's most notorious castle. The Caledonian situated itself below Edinburgh Castle. It provided an unmatched view of the castle that had me desperate for morning so I could finally see her in all her glory.

My fascination with castles started early in life. Like most children of the 90s, princesses ruled the movies that I watched and were the focus of all my attention. Girls who got to rush through the halls of beautiful castles while wearing flowing ball gowns were what my dreams were made of growing up, and even now, if I was being honest. I just couldn't find a way to fit a ball gown in my suitcase.

As I grew older, the fairytales faded away, but my love for the castles stayed as I became more engrossed with the history of the stoic buildings. These were once houses of kings and queens across the globe that had fallen into either dilapidated mounds of stones or museums. To be able to walk the halls of the fortresses that had been standing for hundreds of years, and would be here long after my lifetime, made my space in this world minuscule, but in the best way possible.

I couldn't explain it, but there was something about this country and its history that called to me. Despite the red hair, I'm not Scottish, so there's no familial history that connects me, but it didn't matter. My heart was set on this place, and I wasn't going to let anyone talk me out of it. That included Camden, Scotland was nowhere near the top of his list.

"Haven't you ever connected with a place, even if you've never been?" I said to Camden one night. The side-eyed glance he shot me answered my question before he even spoke. A soft chuckle escaped his lips. "No."

"Hmm." I was already frustrated with trying to explain why I wanted to go. "I don't understand it either, really. I just..." My sentence trailed off unfinished as Camden spoke up.

"If it's what you want, then let's go. I'll take you to every castle the world has to offer if it makes you happy." Statements like that melted my insides, no matter how often I heard them, and any frustration I had was instantly gone. I squealed out a laugh and threw my arms around him, peppering his face with as many kisses as I could muster.

The memory faded away as I walked through the hotel lobby. By the time I reached my door, there was a tightness in my throat, threatening to turn into tears. I missed him a little more than normal today. Camden's loyalty and pledge to keep me happy was unmatched. He would bring the heavens down to Earth and lay them at my feet if it was what I asked for. I knew he would be proud of the steps I was making to move forward, but I wished it didn't hurt my heart so much.

No expense was spared on this trip, and when I stepped into the room, it proved that the splurge was all going to be worth it. Abandoning my bags by the door, I walked toward the window, and there it was. Edinburgh Castle perched upon Castle Rock itself, looming over the city. A grin spread across my face as I gazed out into the night. There was a weight that had been stuck in my chest for the past few years, but being here, it seemed to unravel ever so slightly.

As I crawled under the fluffy duvet of the king-sized bed, I drifted to sleep, and for the first time in years, I was filled with hope and excitement for the next day.

SIX

Lennon

WHEN MY ALARM WENT off the next morning, I had already been up for hours. Too anxious and excited to sleep any longer, I sat curled up by the window waiting for the sun to rise. The mug of coffee warmed my hands as the sun struggled to peek out from the morning gray clouds.

I dressed for the day in black jeans and my favorite oversized forest green sweater that had once belonged to my husband. Before heading out the door, I slipped on my favorite dainty gold jewelry, which included a plain wedding band for my left hand.

Camden had proposed with a beautiful emerald-cut diamond; I still remembered the way it had sparkled from the velvet box as he looked up at me from his bent knee. The memory of that day had been ingrained in my mind ever since. It wasn't until after Camden passed that I tucked that ring away and replaced it with his wedding band that I had resized to fit. I twirled it around my finger while staring back at myself in the mirror.

I wondered if I looked as different as I felt on the inside. My dark reddish curls framed my round face in an erratic fashion, impossible to tame, and had been since I was young. My skin was pale from the winter I escaped and was only marked by a dusting of light brown freckles across my nose and the tops of my cheeks. Nothing really looked that different to me until I got to my eyes.

They were always his favorite feature on me, a deep blue that reminded him of the sun shining on the ocean. Or so he said. But as I looked at them now, they were full of nothing. No longer shining the way they once did when I would look at him. The spark had died with Camden, or at least I thought it had.

If I looked close enough, there was a faint shimmering of something. Hope, excitement—whatever it was, it was enough.

"You got this," I muttered to my reflection. "You can do hard things. You can do uncomfortable things." I say it once and then again for it to sink in.

I practically stumbled out the hotel door and onto the street. The brisk morning air filled my lungs as the foggy mist kissed my skin. It was still early enough that the sun hadn't made its way through the clouds, but the overcast day suited my mood. I darted between the early risers and people rushing on their way to work and stopped at the nearest café for much needed caffeine.

The streets wove around Castle Rock, and I was finally on my way toward Edinburgh Castle. I stopped at the base, gazing upward as the grassy slope met the cobblestone of the building.

Walking through the archways was a surreal experience, one I never thought I would get. I took my time as I wandered through the open space of the castle that looked out onto Edinburgh itself.

Imagining the people that walked these same streets for more years than I could wrap my head around. Fending off attacks from the unwanted and warding their internal treasures, they would lock themselves down at the first sign of trouble and become impenetrable.

It's not lost on me that I had been doing the same with myself. I had been on guard for the past two years, refusing to let anyone closer than I was comfortable with, which wasn't close at all. If I did, they would see how broken I was, how undeserving I was.

I had my great love story, which was more than some people could say, and the type of connection I had with Camden was a once in a lifetime occurrence. He went out of his way to ensure I didn't shrink away from life and pulled me to the light when all I wanted was to keep myself secluded in the darkness.

Happiness never came naturally for me. It took hard work, dedication—and lots of therapy—to keep myself upright, and Camden was a driving force behind my commitment to be better. With him gone, it had been harder and harder to keep up with all the work I put into myself.

I only scheduled a few days in this city in order to make the most of it. I spent the rest of the day exploring Victoria Street, visiting the Scott Monument, and finished my day at Calton Hill during sunset. It had been everything I had hoped it would be, the perfect start to my trip. I tucked myself into bed that night and was out before my head hit the pillow.

The next day started much the same. I dressed quickly and muttered my mantras to myself in the mirror. I laced up my sneakers and snatched the tour books I had picked up the day before and then headed out. I didn't want to miss a thing and needed to ensure that I had all the information and history available to me while I wandered the city.

As I left the hotel, I pulled out one of the books I stashed in my bag and started down the street with no real destination in mind this early in the day. I should have known better than to walk with my nose stuck in a book because the next thing I knew, my body collided into what seemed to be a solid wall. It sent my book flying and my bag crashing to the ground.

"Shoot!" I exclaimed, stumbling backward from the collision.

My feet were quicker than the rest of me and I caught myself before I looked like a complete fool. Avoiding any eye contact with the person that I mistook for a stack of bricks, I bent down quickly to retrieve my bag.

"I am so, so sorry. I wasn't looking where I was walking." I didn't dare to look up as I apologized, out of sheer embarrassment. My hand stretched out toward one of the books that was lying open a foot away from my feet.

"Lenny?" A voice washed over me, causing me to stop mid reach.

I hated nicknames, or rather I really liked my full name, to the point that I never allowed anyone to shorten it. It was the one good thing my mother gave me, even if it had no big significant meaning.

It was mine, and I loved it. Everyone from my friends to Camden called me Lennon.

I was always just Lennon, except at one point in my life.

There was only one person on Earth that had ever got away with calling me anything other than my full name. The voice tugged at a string that tied a box full of memories closed and forced them to spill out of the dusty corner of my mind where I stashed it all those years ago. They unraveled before me, flashing scene after scene, like I was holding one of those viewfinder toys.

Visions of my eighteen-year-old self and the first boy I ever loved were locked away after he left me, and my broken heart stranded on the sidewalk. Now, they were the only thing occupying my thoughts. I hadn't even confirmed it was him as I let my past run wild through my head.

Taking a deep breath in, my senses were flooded with a faint scent of home. Fresh, bright, and like all of my favorite forgotten memories. My eyes flicked upward through my lashes for a glimpse of the man standing above me.

It was him, alright, but not exactly how I remembered. He wasn't the same boy I expected to see, with a lopsided grin and shaggy brown hair. In his place stood a man with the same tan skin and kind eyes, but who had gone through what I could only assume was a late in life growth spurt because he loomed over me. Even under his jacket, my eyes fixed on the way his light blue button up strained over his chest, with the top two buttons flicked open.

He filled the entire space around us, so all I could see was him, and all the air seemed to vanish. At record speed, I gathered my dropped books and shot up to face him. Forcing myself not to blink, I held his gaze, in case he was an apparition that would disappear the second my eyes closed.

At eighteen, I thought Theodore Beckett hung the moon and stars and that he did it for my own personal benefit. He was kind and funny, the type of boy that could make you feel important by looking at you, and he loved me fiercely.

Until he didn't.

We had spent most of our high school years attached at the hip, swearing to anyone that asked that we were only friends. Until the summer before our Junior year, we were working together at a local ice cream shop, and somewhere between the closing shifts and warm nights, I fell for him as the heat rolled through the town. It was easy to do when he spent his time doting on me even though we were "just friends". When I mustered up the courage to admit that I had feelings for him, he pulled me into his arms, surprising me with one simple word. "Finally."

There was a faint chuckle that escaped present day Theo, bringing my focus back to him. My mind was completely blank. "Theodore," I breathed, as all other words escaped me. I was stammering over my next sentence.

How was this even possible?

I hadn't seen him in seventeen years, if my quick mental math served me right. How was it that he was in front of me and halfway across the globe, no less?

"I... How..." Maybe if I shook my head fast enough, it would erase away the figure of him like an Etch a Sketch. A smile broke out across his face, lighting up the area.

"Lennon." The deep timber of his voice was drenched in nostalgia. I returned his smile with a small one of my own.

"It's been a long time." For some reason, the words came out in barely more than a whisper.

"Seventeen years too long, if you ask me," he quipped.

My math was right.

He stepped forward as if to reach out for a hug, but stopped suddenly. I didn't mean to flinch, but he dropped his hands back to his side at the sight of my recoil. "If I knew it only took me coming halfway around the world to see you again, I would have been here a lot sooner," he said, as his eyes filled with humor.

A surprising blush crawled its way up the back of my neck. "Well, I just got here, so it would have been a waste of time." I scrunched my nose up at him. The easy banter flowed out of me as if it never dried up and left. He threw his head back as a deep laugh burst through his lips, causing his eyes to crinkle shut. My smile widened as the sound enveloped my senses, and for a moment, I let the warmth of his laugh wash over me.

"Good to know. What are you doing here?" His eyes bored into me, shining like a clover covered field in the morning sun. He was so much the same and yet someone I hardly recognized.

A sharp jawline replaced the familiar boyish roundness, with just a shadow of a beard and high cheekbones. He no longer had the shaggy brown hair that I used to push back out of his eyes;

instead, his hair was cropped shorter and swept off his forehead. Every feature had grown up with him, everything but his eyes. The kindest green eyes I had ever encountered.

I chewed the inside of my lip before answering, "No reason; it's good to travel. You know, see the sights outside of our hometown." Definitely not trying to get my life back together after my husband died, of course.

There was a slight raise in his eyebrow, and I was worried he could see right through my words. I wondered if he knew I had been married or that I'm a widow.

A beat passed before he asked the logical next question, the type of question that had my heart pounding in my chest. "That's great. Who are you here with?" It was like a knife was plunged into my heart.

"It's just me." My voice was flat and lacked any emotion. I couldn't even fake it for strangers. Or even strangers that I once knew it seemed.

We were still on the sidewalk, people weaved around us and shot off looks since we blocked most of the path. I ignored the glares while he glanced down at his watch.

"Shoot." The word left his lips, breaking me out of my thoughts. "Lennon, I'm running late for a meeting." I opened my mouth to apologize for keeping him, and I moved to the side, allowing him to leave without even giving it a second thought.

He's not here for you. You're wasting his time. My mind chanted the words at me in a quick succession.

"But you said you're here by yourself. Are you free for dinner, then? Tonight?" The hopefulness of his voice was laced throughout the words. My gut pushed me to say no, a knee jerk reaction to keep everyone away, but I'm here to be better.

I accepted this was a solo trip that would be filled with dinners for one and lonely conversations with myself in the mirror. There was no amount of preparation I could have done that would get me ready for a dinner with Theo after seventeen years of no contact.

"Oh, I don't want to mess up any plans you may have. I'm... I'm sure you're busy." The words rushed out of me. The morning air breezed around us as a shiver rolled its way up my spine, but I wasn't entirely sure if it was from the cold.

"Lennon, please have dinner with me. I would love to catch up with you." His gentle words coaxed me into acceptance. "I also want to hear why you're all the way over here by yourself. I never thought I'd ever see you go so far without at least Abby." A playful smile pulled at the corner of his lips. I forgot how well he once knew me, as that would have been the right answer up until recently.

I drew my bottom lip between my teeth as I wrestled with my emotions. He wasn't exactly a stranger, and while I didn't know who he was now, at one point, he was the secret keeper of all my hopes and dreams. He was the person I turned to for comfort, and I couldn't fathom he would be so far removed from the boy I once knew.

"Okay, only if you're sure it won't interfere with anything else you have going on."

"I'm sure." He glanced down at his watch again. "Can you meet me at about seven o'clock at Vittoria?"

"Yeah, okay. That sounds good." I had no idea what I was getting myself into, but the prospect of not spending the night in solitary was worth it. Theo drew himself to his full height as he maneuvered his way around me and onto the rest of his day. I peered up at him, tracking his movements with my eyes, wondering what else had changed about him.

Before passing me fully, he stopped, eyes bright and trained on my face. "I didn't believe in fate before today, but I sure as hell do now. I'll see you at seven, Lenny."

He marched forward down the street, while I remained stuck to the pavement. "What the hell just happened?" I muttered to myself. Seventeen years I've gone without seeing Theo or even giving him a second thought. Now, suddenly, I had dinner plans with him halfway across the globe.

Fate seemed to be the right word.

SEVEN

Theo

SEVENTEEN YEARS LATER AND she was still as captivating as I remembered. I wasn't lying when I said I didn't believe in fate. Hell, I didn't even know if I believed in a higher power. But seeing her today, in this place, would be enough to turn even the most devout atheist to the light.

After graduation, I made a decision that likely saved my life. But in order to do so, I had to rip apart the heart of the one person I loved most in this world. We were young but I was more in love with her than with any woman that followed her. She deserved a life that was better than what I could have gave her. It was a harsh reality that I had to talk myself into believing, but one that was true.

Long before we got together in high school, and for far too long after I left her standing on the sidewalk of my parents' old house, Lennon was the center of everything I was. I was going nowhere, and fast, so when my parents sold their house to move across the country, I went with them. Staying would have been easier and I wouldn't have had to give her up, but I would have ruined her life. I would have ruined her.

The day I left might have been full of sunshine, but there wasn't an ounce of happiness found in either of us. Every part of me screamed in protest, and even if I knew it was for the better, there was a lingering sensation that I was ruining both our lives instead of trying to save my own. Nothing about that goodbye felt right.

My parents packed the remaining boxes into the car while I stood with her on the sidewalk outside my house. I forced my eyes to memorize her face, her hair, the way she smelled, anything that would keep her alive in my head once I left. To this day, I could still picture the way her lashes stuck to each other and how her sapphire eyes darkened to near black from the tears. Even the way she had chewed her perfectly pink lips to a raw sort of red.

Her face fit between my hands as my voice cracked over the hardest goodbye I had ever said. "It doesn't matter where I am or how long we're apart, I will always love you." Each word sat in my throat as jagged pieces of a broken promise, ripping me to shreds from the inside out.

She pleaded with me over and over to not forget her and how she didn't understand why I had to leave. And even as she begged for answers, I couldn't find the words to explain why I had to go. Forgetting her, that was an impossible notion, when my heart already carried her name like a tattoo.

"Anything for you." It was the last thing I said to her. I kissed her goodbye and climbed into my parent's car. My eyes never left hers as my dad pulled the car away from the house.

In that moment, I was sure she would never forgive me, but if I was ever given a second chance, nothing would keep me from her.

It took me more time than I thought it would, but I finally got my life on track. After leaving Lennon, I threw myself into photography. At first it was only a hobby, then I took a few courses at a community college and really started honing my skills, and in it, I could channel all the hurt and longing that had been building inside of me.

During a student gallery exposition, some of my photos were picked up for a spread in some magazine I couldn't remember the name, and had been freelancing ever since.

I strolled down the final street before arriving at the set of office buildings that held the Europe Division of Castle Architecture Magazine. There was a smile that hadn't left my face since I left her standing there on the sidewalk. Very reminiscent of that last day we had together and maybe not my best move, but I really did have a meeting I couldn't be late for. It was the whole reason I was here to begin with.

I walked through the doors of the editor's office at exactly eight o'clock. "Theo, good to see you. Please sit." Archie Fraser waved me to the seat across the desk from him. Large framed glasses slid down his nose as he bent over to examine the photos in front of him. I sat for a few minutes, my foot shaking impatiently while it rested on the opposite leg before he finally looked up.

"These are good. Exactly what we were looking for from Château Gaillard." I nodded my head in thanks.

He started again, "I know you think Scotland is a bit redundant, but they want to dedicate the 25th anniversary issue next quarter to the country." I would have rolled my eyes, but I suddenly had a vested interest in staying here.

"It's no problem. I understand the interest and the list of spots that are needed was easy to work with." It consisted of the tourist heavy sites, but what I loved most about this job was the amount of freedom it came with. If what they asked for was included, I could add in the lesser-known spots. The ruins that intrigued me and the estates that were still housing the same families hundreds of years later.

Archie provided me with the deadline for the photos, and within the hour, I was out of the office and back to my hotel to grab my gear. I had been a professional photographer for over ten years now; blending into the background to catch authentic moments of nature that surrounded us had been my passion.

Today I was starting with Edinburgh Castle. I had photographed the historic site in the past, and I knew the sheer size of it would take most of the afternoon to capture. Anything to keep me busy and stop me from tracking Lennon down to see her face again.

By ten o'clock, I was trudging up the castle steps to start my work. As I peered through the lens that was fixed on the Gatehouse entrance, the memory of the first time I had held a camera in my hands drifted in unannounced. All at once it was like I could be something, and I owed it all to her.

It was my birthday and I was finally an adult.

The social pressure was weighing on me, that at eighteen you needed to know what you wanted to do with your life. It was getting heavier and heavier by the day, and I was beginning to feel trapped.

Lennon had been acting weird, or weirder than normal, all week, and it was putting me on edge. She suddenly burst through my bedroom door and had all but shoved a gift onto my lap. She sat by my side as I began to unwrap the present, her body buzzed with excitement next to me. When I pulled the final piece of tissue paper out and my eyes snapped to hers as she watched me with careful eyes, chewing on her bottom lip.

"What did you do, Lenny?" I whispered as I carefully removed the camera from the box, cradling it like it was a newborn.

Lennon and I had been wandering down Main Street one day when I saw it sitting in the window of one of the consignment stores and I knew I wanted it. No rhyme or reason, but it felt like it was calling to me. For the last six months, I put every dollar I earned aside to save up for a Pentax 67 camera; it was all I talked about.

It was the most expensive item someone had ever given me outside of my parents, and it all started to make sense. Lennon picking up extra shifts, the odd jobs I would find her doing when calling to see if she could hang out. She had been saving just as I had been, to purchase something that I had desperately wanted.

Tears pricked my eyes as I pulled her in close and wrapped her in my arms. I buried my face in her curls, breathing deep in an attempt to control my emotions.

"Thank you," I said, as my voice cracked with emotion.

I came back to the forgotten camera, turning it over in my hands, still in utter disbelief that this was actually mine. Standing from the bed, I placed it on my shelf not wanting to accidentally break it and turned to see her lay back on the bed. Her wild curls fanned out around her head as she smiled up at me. She was beautiful, and she was mine.

There was no way I could ever repay her for this, but I knew I would spend my life trying to.

I crawled over her body and peered down at her, sweeping my eyes over her face. "One day, I'll take you all over the world. I'll get to take photos while you explore all those castles you like." For whatever reason, it was all she talked about, castles and fairytales. We spent more time watching happily ever after movies than anything else.

"You'd do that for me?" she asked. She pulled me down to her and held me tight, and I spoke the only words that meant something to either of us.

"Anything for you."

I brought my focus back to my task, thinking of the memory. That one phrase had been everything to the both of us at one point. I told her I'd do anything for her before I told her I loved her. Not much sooner, but it did come first.

It was a simple phrase that we would exchange, and often it outweighed a declaration of love. For us, 'I love you' was a given—the words resonated every day. But it was the abundance of sheer devotion we shared that morphed into the phrase 'anything for you'. Simple, but everything to us. To me.

The Lennon I remembered was like a bright summer morning—she radiated happiness and warmth. I sought any excuse to be near her, anything that would allow me to bask in her rays of light. She was the sun and the center of everything I was. Seeing her today was like waking up and realizing my dreams of her have only kept me halfway satisfied.

Turned out everything I thought I remembered, I had forgotten. Like the precise shade of blue her eyes were in the morning or the way the wind would tinge her cheeks a dark pink when it's cold. If I had remembered everything, I don't think I could've stayed away from her for so long.

Years passed us, but I had always kept her close in some way or another. Not in a creepy, I'm stalking you type of way, but social media made it so simple to keep up with someone's life when you're stuck on the outside.

The rest of the afternoon seemed to drag on. It was odd the amount of emotions that swirled inside of me as I walked through the city to meet Lennon for dinner. Excitement at being able to lay my eyes on her again, fear of maybe having nothing in common with her at this stage in our lives, and this dinner ended up being the last that I'd see her. I'd be lying if I didn't mention the desire that sat at the base of my heart.

The one that surprised me the most, though, was the guilt. I knew that she was married and that her husband had died only a couple of years ago. The way her eyes dulled when I asked who she was here with wasn't lost on me, but I saw an opportunity to spend more time with her and I took it without a second thought. It was selfish, but worth the risk.

It was that thought that had my stomach churning as I waited in front of the restaurant for her. Being early was a mistake; every minute that passed, doubt began to creep in that she wouldn't show or that maybe I hallucinated her this morning.

I was a few moments away from scheduling a doctor's visit to have my head checked when I saw her. She powered her way down the street, her face set with determination as she weaved in and out of people. God, she was breathtaking. Her dark hair fell in waves around her face and down the white sweater she wore. And the jeans, even from a distance, I could tell that they are practically molded to her legs.

I gulped down the nerves, the sudden lust and the indescribable feeling that this was the first day of the rest of my life.

Catching her line of sight snapped me out of the haze that was spreading through my head from the sudden onset of too many emotions. I popped off the wall I was leaning against to meet her as she crossed the street.

"You came. I was beginning to think I had conjured you up like a dream this morning." I tried to cover the relief in my voice, and it was nice to see the way her body relaxed once she was standing in front of me. Then she smiled, and I knew I was already willing putty in her hands.

"Not a dream, just me, Theodore."

There was a sudden urge to tell her that they were one and the same, but I bit back the words. I was trying not to be a creep and that, while true, would toe the line.

She turned her head towards the restaurant and her eyes widened slightly at the signage. If I knew one thing about Lennon that would never change, it was that she loved pizza. The second the question left my mouth this morning to ask her to dinner, I knew exactly where to take her.

"Oh, they have pizza," she exclaimed.

"Some things never change, do they?" I smirked as Lennon rolled her eyes, and we walked into the restaurant and the waitress led us to our table.

Lennon rocked from side to side in her seat before she peered over her menu at me. Her eyes roamed over my face, the small movement sent flames up my spine. I would've given anything to know what was going through her head.

Was she nervous? Did she wish she never said yes to dinner? Maybe she was picking out the differences that time notched in my face. A small smile pulled at the corner of her lips as a wistful sigh escaped her mouth.

Maybe it was my wishful thinking, but it sounded like remembrance.

"So, tell me, Theo, what have you been up to all these years?" She leaned back in her chair, lifting her eyebrows in question.

I recounted my life since I left, from the couple years of community college on the East Coast to the job I landed with Castle Architecture Magazine as a freelance photographer. I described all the countries I had been sent to over the past ten years as Lennon sat with her face in her hands, her attention never straying. I pulled up some of my work from various social media accounts to show her, a part of me screaming internally, "It was all because of you. Don't you see?"

"These are beautiful, Theo. Is that why you're here in Scotland, for the magazine?" Our food was finished, and we sat together, talking over her wineglass and my empty water. We had slipped into a comfortable cadence of conversation. Any doubt that had crossed my mind when we first sat down evaporated.

"Yes," I exclaimed. It had been so long since someone had been this interested in my work, I could've keep her late into the night, just talking. "Did you know that Scotland has more than a thousand castles? The next quarter's issue will be dedicated strictly to the country. I won't be able to visit all of them, obviously, but I'm here for the next few weeks and will try to get to as many as possible." When I finished my rant, I found her smiling at me, it was bright and blinding. I couldn't tear my eyes away from her.

She laughed as she shook her head. "You said it was fate this morning, and I think I'm beginning to agree." I cocked my head at her statement as she continued to laugh. She leaned forward, beckoning me in, and I had no choice but to obey.

"You're here for castles? That's exactly what I'm here for."

"Is that so?"

The playfulness she was exuding seemed to vanish a second later. She sat back in her seat and took a deep breath. "Did you know that I was married?" she asked. I nodded yes, and her smile dropped slightly. "And did you know that he died two years ago?"

"I did." If I surprised her with my honesty, she didn't show it.

"We would have been married ten years this year, and before he died, we started to plan this trip." She took a long sip from her wineglass before continuing, and I kept quiet. There was no surprise how easy it was for me to fall back into habits I had when I was with Lennon. I knew she talked more when you left her with the room to keep speaking, and all I wanted was to know was everything about her.

"I have been... lost, I guess you can say, since Camden died. I haven't been interested in moving on or forward in any way until recently. Abby encouraged me to take this trip as a start, saying it's something Camden would have wanted for me, and she was right. So here I am. By myself, hoping that it will help push me in the right direction to start living my life again."

She stared into her glass as she dragged her finger slowly along the rim. She was so much the same and yet so vastly different. I reached across the table and placed my hand on top of hers.

She jumped slightly at the intrusion, and before I could snatch my hand back, cursing my stupidity, she turned her palm upwards and gave my hand a slight squeeze before she returned hers to her lap. My stomach flipped back and forth at her touch, and time seemed to lurch around us. It came to a halt and picked up at light speed all in the matter of seconds. Before I could stop myself, words poured out of my mouth in the most reckless manner.

"Lenny, what if we went together?" It was a dirty play, but I used her nickname on purpose and her face softened, just like I knew it would. My heart thundered in my chest, threatening to break free and expose itself to her.

She looked panicked. The waitress had come and gone with the check as we stood to step back outside.

This was it, the last time I would see her, and my heart already missed her. Of course, she didn't want to spend two weeks with someone she didn't really know—anymore, at least.

I was an idiot.

"I'm sure you have your trip planned out and say no if you really do not want to, but like you said, we are both here for the castles. I have a loose itinerary; we can fit in exactly what you want to see, and it's likely the same spots I was headed, anyway. I also have a few places that I was able to get special access to that the public normally does not get to go that I think you would enjoy." I was terrified that I scared her off entirely.

"I know it sounds crazy, but you don't have to be here alone if you don't want to."

"I don't know, Theo, you're going for work. Wouldn't I be in the way?" She fiddled with the strap of her purse, looking anywhere but my face.

"No, not at all. Honestly, it would be nice. Normally, I do these trips by myself. Having someone to share it with who is interested in the sites would be a nice change. You don't have to decide right now, but I would like you to come. Here, take my number." I pulled my phone out, and we exchanged numbers. She pulled her bottom lip between her teeth as she contemplated the option I had presented to her.

"Let me think about it and I'll text you. I still have another day for my stay here in Edinburgh that I would like to finish." The night surrounded us as Lennon tilted her head up to meet my gaze. The cold wrapped around us as our breaths came out in smoke-like puffs.

Dreams couldn't compare to the sight of her standing in front of me and I pleaded with whatever force that would listen that she would say yes.

"Theo, I had a really great time tonight. Will you be in Edinburgh much longer?" Her voice was soft and reassuring.

"I'm seeing a few local places tomorrow, and then I'll be in Glasgow for a few days."

She made a noncommittal sound before replying. "I will call you tomorrow if that's alright."

"Of course. It was good to see you—I mean it."

"Goodnight Theodore."

"Goodnight Lennon." She didn't reach for me, but offered a soft smile before she turned her back to me. As she walked away, I silently hoped that this wasn't the last time I would see her.

EIGHT

Lennon

THEO'S QUESTION WRESTLED WITH what I had accepted for this trip, and I was conflicted. None of what happened was what I had planned for or how I had envisioned moving through this country. I pictured the solitude of roaming through ruins to help piece together the rubble that was my life and my heart. But new pictures were forming, ones that included a man who was not my husband, and I was ashamed that there was a part of me that wanted to say yes.

The cold air did little to help clear my mind on the walk back to the hotel. As I approached the door, I stopped outside and tipped my head toward the stars. The wind moved around me as more of the far-off lights came into focus, and I did little to stop the chill that was settling deep into my bones.

Warmth had been absent since the day my husband's casket lowered into the ground, as if all the heat inside me was buried n the ground along with him. But seeing Theo was so unexpected and thrilling, I couldn't deny that I wanted to agree to two weeks with him in the highlands, but the guilt was overwhelming.

"Tell me what to do, Camden," I whispered to the sky with a voice that begged the wind to carry the message to him.

A tear slipped down my cheek and clung to my skin as a reminder of why I was on this trip alone. With a final inhale of the icy night, I walked inside and resolved to make the decision in the morning, but first I needed to talk to Abby.

I paced in front of the window, looking out at Castle Edinburgh as I called my sister.

She answered on the first ring. "I was wondering when you would call. How was your day?" There was a slightly annoyed tone in her voice that I had no patience to deal with.

"I ran into Theo." I blurted the words out, nothing else. No 'hello, it's going great,' just straight to the point. My nerves had been on overdrive since morning and I had no patience for small talk.

The dead airwaves crackled on the phone before Abigail answered. "Theo?"

I flopped backwards onto the bed, my breath huffed out of my lungs. "Theo, Abigail, The-o." My voice jumped two octaves as I sounded out his name.

One of my favorite things about Theo had been that he treated Abigail like a sister and loved her almost as much as I did. Abigail was the most important person to me back then, and even more so now. I would never let anyone come between us, and when I was with Theo, I never had to choose.

"Shut up," was Abigail's only response as it finally clicked who I was talking about.

"I know." I sighed and then launched into recanting the encounter to Abigail, who chimed in for follow-up questions at the right parts and pried for all the details about what Theo looked like now.

I could picture the reaction Abigail was about to have to the final part of the story before I even told her. "He also asked me to spend the rest of the trip with him." I winced preemptively as Abigail's shriek pierced through the phone.

"Are you going to say 'yes'?"

"No. I don't know. Maybe?"

"What's stopping you? If it's true and you were going to the same places, wouldn't you be able to enjoy it more if you weren't alone during it?'

Silence passed between the airwaves. "I want to say yes, but just thinking about it makes me feel like I'm doing something wrong, like I'm not allowed to be alone with him. That it's an insult to Camden to do so."

"Oh, Lennon." Abby's voice floated through the speaker. "You are allowed to have adventures, you are allowed to live. Being out in the world does not mean you are going to forget him, it means you are honoring him. He wouldn't want you to be stagnant; he would want you out there creating memories."

Tears gathered before they cascaded outwards. "I know." I wished it was easier.

Missing him was like living in a world that was speeding by me while someone had pressed the pause button on my life. Everything was a blur, and yet, I remained the same—never moving, never changing.

"Say yes, Lennon. And if, for some reason, it doesn't work out, you can still move on with the rest of your trip without him. If you say no, you will wonder what could have happened if you didn't go."

She was right, of course.

I can do hard things, I reminded myself internally, and this was hard on my heart.

"So, tell me. What does he look like now?" I could hear the smile in her voice.

"Ugggh. Perfect, of course. He's taller somehow, his hair isn't long anymore. He looks like such a man, its weird." I was not blind. Theo was incredibly good looking, he always was. Time had done nothing but good things to his appearance. He had the type of look that people noticed, especially the girls at our school. Golden skin and a smile that would brighten even my darkest moments. It really was unfair.

I wasn't unattractive, but I had my moments with self-image, as most teenage girls did, and being with Theo sometimes heightened my insecurity and the lingering thoughts of "why was he with me". But it was all on me. He never entertained the notion that I was anything less than perfect. The boy called me beautiful like it was my God given name.

Abby and I said our goodbyes as I tucked myself into bed and I willed sleep not to evade me tonight.

It was a useless request, I didn't sleep at all that night. It was spent tossing and turning as my dreams replayed memories of Theo alongside my life with Camden. I woke up confused and I had never felt more alone.

Thoughts volleyed in my head, ricocheting from wanting to say 'yes' to guilt for wanting to spend time with him. It didn't matter that I wasn't thinking of Theo romantically, but spending time with another man felt like a betrayal. The love I had for Camden ran deep within my veins. It was the type of love that could easily overwhelm someone, but I thrived under the out-pour of affection that came from Camden. He cared with his whole heart and never let a day go by without reminding me that I was his, and he was wholly and without a doubt mine.

The months following his death were unbearable. I stopped eating, I never left my bed, refused to speak, and it went on for longer than I cared to admit or remember. There are days where it's blank when I try to think back, as if my mind was trying to protect me from myself.

It was Abigail and Carina who helped pull me out of the hole that I spent my time digging, and while I never fully recovered from the darkness that shrouded my mind, it was enough to keep me moving.

I had come a long way in the past two years. I put in the work, and with patience, I was beginning to see the other side of my life. One where I could see myself happy, even if it meant a life that was just me.

But a life that was just for me didn't mean I couldn't expand on friendships.

This could be good for me.

I spoke the words aloud before placing the call to Theo. He answered on the first ring, and I practically yelled out my answer before he managed a hello. I couldn't give myself the opportunity to back out.

"What?" a shocked voice replied back to me.

"Yes, if you really don't mind an extra person, I would love to join you for the trip." Slow and steady, I relayed the words back to him.

"Lenny! That's great." I could hear the smile in his voice, easing the tightness that had built up in my chest. I was one of those people who, even if someone was explicitly clear with their plans that involved me, I would still find a way to convince myself that it was not something they truly wanted. That they only agreed to plans with me out of pity or a twisted sense of humor. The anxiety that I experienced had always made it hard for me to form connections with people over the years. It kept my circle small, but I preferred it that way.

I had my suspicions, but I believed that Theo remembered. His reassurance of his excitement that I would be accompanying him was refreshing.

We went over the details of our newly combined trip, each city we would stay in, and I gave him the list of the different castles I had my heart set on seeing. Theo wasn't lying, our lists were almost identical in the stops that we had planned. My only request was to keep the stop at Inverness, so I wouldn't have to give up the cottage I booked.

We agreed to meet in Glasgow the next day at our hotel. We both rearranged our bookings so that we were staying in the same building; not only that, but now, instead of taking the train, I would tag along with Theo since he had rented a car.

The next day I waited for him outside the hotel, bouncing with excitement. He met me on the sidewalk in the morning sun, and like someone flipping a switch, I was flooded with memories of our time together, and not the innocent hand holding that went on. I was looking at him and realizing that I had slept with this man before, he had seen me—all of me. He caught my gaze and I quickly looked away. I was flaming hot and wondered what I had gotten myself into.

NINE

Theo

THE FIRST WEEK IN Scotland with Lennon was... interesting. Without any problems, we managed to make it to all the agreed upon stops from Glasgow to Inverness. I got some great shots of Buchanan and Knockderry Castle so far.

Each day, we would meet in the lobby of whatever hotel we were staying at, and Lennon would trail behind me as I lugged my gear around the sites before wandering off. I would catch glimpses of her as she strolled around the properties, her arms wrapped around herself as she peered around towers, and the way she would trail her hand along the stonework. It was as if she was asking for the memories they held in between their bricks.

Today shouldn't be any different.

"Inveraray Castle is still a family home," I explained, as we pulled into our next destination and drove across the grounds. The sun had yet to rise fully and the dense clouds were slowly rolling through the sky, but this place was made for the fog and dreariness that Scotland was known for.

Lennon pulled her jacket tighter to fight against the mist once we got out of the car, and I was beginning to think this morning shoot might not have been the best idea, but she hadn't complained once. "The family has been in this area since the 1200s; it's truly incredible." I figured the more facts I could ply her with, the more it would keep me from bombarding her with all the questions I still had about her life.

She was closed off, which I guess was to be expected. I was not much more than a stranger to her, but I wanted to know everything she'd been doing since I left, and she was reluctant to offer anything. That first dinner after running into each other, I got what I figured were the basics, but I wanted it all.

I was sure that it would come off a bit creepy, and the last thing I wanted to do was push her. So, for now, I stuck to the safe space we'd created in the castles and their history. It was our common ground, and I'd take whatever I could get.

There was something about her need for information that got my heart beating a little faster. It had been a while since I'd been with someone who was as interested in the sites that I visit as I was. She hummed at my facts beside me, as I took out my equipment, then she handed over one of my smaller totes that she insisted on carrying.

"You don't have to help me carry anything, you know. You can do your own thing. Don't worry about me," I said lightly, but really, it was usually the highlight of my day. Every day when we had a site to visit, she insisted on helping me pack the car and unload once we got to the site. And even when I told her not to help, she'd usually already slung a bag over her shoulder and asked me where to first. Within an hour, though, she ended up trailing off to another part of the castle we were in or out on to the grounds to look around.

"Maybe I'm just hoping to get my name in the magazine. Photo by Theodore Beckett, assistant Lennon Arden. Sounds good, doesn't it?" She threw her head back in laughter, and her breath mingled with the mist in the air. We were here before dawn in order for me to get the shots I wanted, and it was close to freezing. She didn't complain, but the way her teeth chattered said otherwise.

I shrugged out of my outer jacket and walked over to the edge of the bridge where she was currently sitting. I draped the jacket over her shoulders and pulled the front closed around her. Her eyes flicked up to meet mine, causing my heart to jump into my throat, and I noticed that even after all these years, the blue of her eyes was still my favorite color.

"Thank you," she whispered and offered me a small smile.

"I should have warned you, this early in the morning is usually freezing," I murmured, then turned back to finish setting up my camera. She stayed in her spot as I shot from the bridge on the estate, with the castle looming in the distance through the misty clouds.

This wasn't my first visit to this castle, but I could already tell my photos from this trip would be my favorite. I took a few steps backward to get a better view and brought my camera back up to my eye, but it still wasn't quite right. I took one more step back, without realizing how close I already was to the edge, and fumbled slightly as my legs hit the edge of the bridge. My hands were full and for a second, I thought I was going to flip over the edge before I caught my balance and my ass hit the wall's edge. Lennon jerked out of her spot and shouted my name at the same time I started falling. She darted over to me, eyes wild and frantic, and grabbed onto my shoulders.

"Jesus, Theo. You need to be careful." Her voice was full of worry as her hands dropped from my shoulders and turned away quickly to look over the edge of the bridge. It wasn't a far drop into the river, but yeah, it definitely would have hurt.

Her shoulders were moving in an erratic motion as I stepped closer to her, and I could hear her attempt to regulate her breathing. She jumped at my touch and turned to me with glassy eyes.

"Hey, are you okay?"

She brushed a stray tear from her eye and apologized before stepping back. "Yeah, I'm fine. I'm sorry, that was a silly reaction. I-I don't know what that was," she said as she pulled my jacket off her shoulders and handed it over to me.

"I'm going to go wait in the car until the tour of the castle starts. I'll see you later." She didn't wait for my reply before she turned on her heel and started back to the castle. The moment she disappeared, the surrounding air suddenly felt colder. I wanted to go after her, but my common sense kept me planted.

The rest of the day passed in a blur, and I didn't even see her until I was packing up. She appeared out of nowhere before I had a chance to call and see where she was. Her hair was windswept, and her cheeks were tinged pink from the spring wind; she made it hard for me to focus.

There was no intention on my part to fall for her again, but looking at her pulled feelings from the depths of my heart that I never thought I would see again.

After I had left Lennon, I stuffed everything about her in a box, then tucked it away under lock and key. Every touch, every kiss, every time she'd look at me with those deep blue eyes had to be kept hidden away. But now, it was impossible to keep the lid closed. She was everywhere, and I only had myself to blame.

What was I expecting to happen, asking her to come on this trip with me? That I could be around her twenty-four seven, with no consequences?

She was worth it, consequences or not.

"How was the tour today?"

"It was good," she said, tight-lipped. She slid into the car as I threw the last of my stuff into the back. The sun had finally broken through the clouds, but I was sure it would be short lived, rain clouds gathered in the distance.

We were headed to Inverness today, but the way she was closed off was making me want to detour a bit, and I had the perfect place to take her.

"It's still early. Do you mind if we detour? I have somewhere I'd like to take you."

She agreed, but she was still so quiet. We spoke a while about sites we'd seen the past few days. Polite conversation was all that

I got from her; it was almost as if she was scared to be left alone around me. So, we tiptoed around each other throughout the days, and at night, I would lie in bed alone, my dreams filled with images of her.

She was made for this country, it seemed, her auburn hair would billow in the wind, and her eyes were bright as she wandered her way around the grounds of each new place. It was hard to focus, so I did what I do best and turned my camera on her. I wasn't sure she even noticed that she was my subject, but I was drawn to her, pulled in a way that I didn't care to fight.

It was another silent drive as we drove out of the grounds, Lennon reading silently in the passenger seat. After about an hour, she closed her book and turned to me.

"Where are we going?" she questioned, as her eyes scanned the landscape we were passing through.

"It's a surprise," I said and threw her a wink as she groaned and flopped back into her seat. It only took us about two hours before we got to our destination. Lennon kept flashing me skeptical eyes throughout the drive.

When we pulled into the lot, it was already showing signs that it would be busy. I unbuckled and leaned onto the console to tap her book. "We have about a twenty-minute walk from here."

By the look on her face it felt like she was about a half second away from running, maybe not all surprises are good. "You didn't bring me here to kill me, did you? Cause that would really put a damper on my trip," she asked half-heartedly, as I reached for my door handle. There was a smile that pulled at the corners of her lips.

I got out and jogged over to her side of the car before she reached for the handle. Leaning on the open door, I held out my hand for her to take and pulled her out.

I must have pulled a little too hard because suddenly she was entirely too close. She stumbled slightly as her hands braced themselves on my chest. A tiny "oh" fell from her lips, but all I could focus on was the heat of her hands on me. We both paused, frozen in this position. Her head tilted up slightly and I met her stare. Her pupils dilated as they pinged between mine like they were searching for something. My hands buzzed with anticipation. She must have hit the play button. I blinked and she moved quickly to the side and let me shut the door.

"It would really ruin my trip, too, so no," I said with a lazy smile that earned me an eye roll.

We weren't really in the middle of nowhere, the parking lot nearly full, and we'd passed enough people on the trail that I could sense her relaxing beside me. We followed the river and the signs that pointed for the Viaduct Trail, and I could tell she still had no idea where we were, which was more exciting for me. My heart thumped in my chest at the anticipation, and I kept stealing glances of her as she walked beside me. We finally got through to the view-point, and there were small crowds of people gathered around, all waiting for the afternoon passing. It took about a minute before I heard a small gasp from her.

"You didn't!" she exclaimed as her hands gripped onto my arm. There was pure excitement radiating from her; it was tangible as it wove through the air. This was the Lennon I remembered, and that box that I had been keeping closed flew open and everything I had ever loved about her came pouring out. There was no point in trying to stuff her back in, I was doomed to fall again from the beginning.

She let go of my arm, and I was dying to reach back out for her again. I pulled my camera out and snapped a few pictures until she turned back for me with her hand outstretched. Snapping one last photo, I let my camera hand fall from its leather strap and walked toward her. Without a second thought, I placed my hand in hers.

It was warm and familiar, and I wondered what it would be like if I never had to let go.

She tugged, and we walked farther into the space before us. Glenfinnan Viaduct was stunning in itself, but it was the Jacobite train that drew in the crowds. Twice a day during this time of year, it rolled its way over the viaduct.

Like most people our age, the magical book series roped us in and the movies brought it all to life. I had hoped bringing Lennon here would bring a spark from the past back, and it looked like I was right.

She kept her eyes fixed on the landscape as I stepped up behind her. "The train should pass in about five minutes." I breathed her in, letting the subtle scent of flowers envelop me. It launched me back in time and I was lost in it until she leaned backwards, hitting my chest. There was a good chance my heartbeat was echoing in her chest.

There was a pull inside me that had me fighting the urge to wrap my arms around her and press her into me tighter. Instead, I allowed myself to let this be enough; if all I got was her a fraction of a heartbeat away, then this trip was worth it.

The steam from the train was the first thing we could see, and as if on cue, everyone's phones rose in anticipation, including Lennon's. I slipped my camera out from under my arm and snapped my finger against the shutter button. She might not be looking at me, but I could sense the smile on her face as she watched the train sped by quicker than we all would have liked. When she finally turned back around, the smile stayed on her face, and I took one last picture of her just for me.

"Thank you for bringing me here." She looked around while shaking her head back and forth slightly. "This was everything." Her voice was a whisper that I could barely hear over the crowds starting back to their cars.

The words formed like second nature as they knocked at my throat and demanded to be said, 'anything for you'. In a past life, they would have spilled out at the smallest of interactions between us, and they would light our world.

I doubted they would have the same effect now, but when she looked up at me, there was a pull inside of me that said give up everything and take her anywhere that would keep that smile on her face.

Ten

Theo

"Wait till you see this place, Theo. It. Is. Everything. It's not fancy and it's in the middle of nowhere, but it's perfect." *There she is*, I thought. Life had been breathed back into her. She spoke non-stop as we finished our drive to Inverness. She talked about her sister and what she had done with her life and the job she's had for the past few years. I drank it all in like a man that was on the brink of debilitating thirst. I wanted to know everything.

She told me how she never moved from our hometown, that she always wanted a house close to the river and that dream came true a little after she was married. Oddly enough, she mentioned nothing about Camden in any of the stories. I knew he was by her side for most of what she was talking about, but she skirted around his involvement. Not even a mention of his name.

I knew nothing about him, apart from they were married and then he died. Even his death was still a mystery.

"Oh, and the best part: it's close to Loch Ness." Her eyebrows were in her hairline as she beamed at me.

"As in the Loch Ness Monster?"

"Yep. Nessie herself." Her laugh carried out of the window, a sound I could listen to forever.

We pulled into the cottage that Lennon had booked before we joined our trips together around noon. It was a quaint cottage crafted entirely out of stone, older than we could guess. Dreary bushes and shrubs encircled the home and a wooden gate sat in front of the entrance. It looked as if it would fall apart the second you touched it. She was right, it was perfect, and a much needed break from the endless amount of stark hotels.

Lennon threw her bag into the closest room she saw when we walked in, and then headed straight out the door to explore the grounds. The house was small, our rooms just off the dining room, with our doors across from each other.

Being close to her for an extended amount of time proved to be difficult for me. My body didn't quite seem to register that she was still grieving the loss of her husband.

She bounded around in outfits that, while covering everything, had me thinking of only what's beneath it, and it hurt to know that I once knew. I wanted nothing more than to reach out and touch her. I wanted to run my fingers through her hair to see if her curls would still tangle in my hands. To be able to wrap my hands around her hips and see if she felt as soft as she looked.

If the devil appeared before me, I would sign on the dotted line for even the smallest touch.

But I wouldn't, not that she gave away any inkling that she would welcome anything I was desperate to offer. I couldn't say I understood where she was at; I had never lost anyone relatively close to me, thankfully, but she had lost her husband, for Christ's sake.

Of course, she wouldn't welcome any advances, and I didn't blame her. I'd seen photos of them together throughout the years, and they looked happy, perfect even. My heart soared and ached at the same time.

I never expected Lennon to wait for me, I never asked, and it wasn't implied when I left. But there was always a small part of me that wished she had or that I had never left. I tried to move on. I dated some women, casually slept with more, but whether I knew I was doing it or not, I compared them all to her. Her wit was unmatched, her laugh infectious, and the way she loved me could never be replicated, so I never found my way to the end of an aisle.

When Lennon came back to the cottage a few hours later, the sun was beginning to sink into the horizon and I was setting the table for the simple dinner I threw together. She came through the house like an angel after her fall from the heavens, with her face tinged pink from the frigid spring air.

She stopped midway through the threshold of the backdoor and I couldn't quite place the look on her face. Her eyes had widened before she rolled her bottom lip in between her teeth.

"What's all this?"

"Dinner, Lenny. We can't all live off of cookies and candy on this trip."

"But I like living off cookies and candy, Theodore. You didn't have to make me dinner, you know." Now I was worried I had overstepped some sort of invisible boundary. Out of all our dinners, this would be our first alone—no restaurant full of people or a quick meal in a car while driving to a new site.

"Come sit. Everything's ready and it's nothing crazy." She approached the table like she expected to find it set with a trap. Her body lowered into the chair across from me and she slid the filled wine glass towards her. She pulled in a generous first sip before setting it back down on the wooden table. Her eyes never strayed from mine. What I wouldn't give to know what she was thinking.

My mind was going a million miles a minute.

The dinner passed without Lennon giving too much away as to her inner thoughts. I wanted to keep her talking. About anything, it didn't matter. But there were only so many times we could discuss the Scottish weather.

Without thinking, I asked the one thing that had been on my mind. "If it's not too much, can I ask what happened to Camden?" I glanced up from where I was pouring us both a fresh glass of wine in time to see pain flare in her eyes.

"If you don't want to tell me, you don't have to," I quickly added.

This was a bad idea. I was a fucking idiot; my curiosity got the best of me, and the rest of the trip was down the drain because I couldn't keep myself in check.

"No, it's fine," she assured. The inside of her cheek must be chewed raw at this point. Anytime she was lost in her thoughts, her teeth would immediately toy with the soft flesh.

She pulled in a deep breath through her nose and rolled her shoulders back, the movements had regret brewing in the pit of my stomach. She was physically getting herself together before answering, knowing that speaking the words would cause her pain.

"It was an aneurysm." She swallowed loudly before continuing. "He had been out of town for work and was staying in a hotel. The cleaners came in to turn over the room and found him dead."

I blinked once, then again. "I don't know what I was expecting, but it wasn't that." My mind was telling me maybe it was some sort of fall that occurred; it would explain why she was so panicked when I nearly fell off the bridge.

"You and me both." She leaned in closer, setting her elbows up on the table to rest her chin on to her hands. With how small the table was, she was close enough that I could see the different colors that made up the freckles that were sprinkled across her nose. I traced the patterns with my eyes, hoping the constellations I had once memorized were still there.

"I think that's why I'm still so angry; it was nothing anyone could have predicted or prepared for. He was here one second and just gone the next." Her hand came down on the table in a smack while her words were drenched in heartache and sorrow, but the next phrase had my throat contorting with unknown emotions.

"And I wasn't even there." It came out as a shaky whisper. I expected her to clam up and protect herself from further harm, but she took another breath and kept talking.

"Maybe if he had been sick, I could work through all these emotions easier. I would have been able to anticipate the loss at least, you know. Nothing in the world could have prepared me for the call I got, saying he was dead," she said as her eyes drifted closed and her dark eyelashes held back tears. I was entranced as my heart longed to reach out to hers. Of course she was still angry, but with no one to pin it on, it had stayed within her, festering until she could feel nothing but the pain and loss.

The dam she built to keep everything inside broke and the words came pouring out of her. "Ever since I was little, I have been enamored with fairytales. Obsessed really." A snort escaped into her glass as she brought it up to her lips for a taste.

"I remember." It slipped out, but she just laughed in response and her eyes closed again.

"I wanted the castles and the knights in shining armor to fall in love with. I wanted the magic that came from the stories. Camden was the closest thing to magic I found," she said, as a small smile pulled at her lips. Her eyes drifted open, but she kept them cast downward toward the table between us. Her voice trembled as she tried to keep the emotions tucked away.

"He was the very best person I knew, and he loved me unconditionally, regardless of my flaws and, trust me, there are many," she added before I could protest her negative comment. "Loving him was the easiest thing I have ever done, and I count myself incredibly lucky that he chose to spend his life with me." Tears threatened her waterline by the end of her sentence.

I sat unmoving, taking in the weight of her words. I tried to think back and remember if I had ever loved someone that strongly, but nothing came even close. The only person that came to mind was Lennon and the love we had for each other all those years ago.

"You must miss him." An obvious statement, but I lacked the words to convey my racing thoughts.

A huffed laugh escaped from the back of her throat. "More than you can imagine. It's like I've been living without air since he's been gone." Her white knuckled grip strained the glass stem. "I am homesick constantly, and I would give anything to have him back."

"I just feel so alone." Our eyes met across the table as a single tear streaked down her face.

An overwhelming urge bubbled up in my chest to reach out and brush it from her face. One I didn't fight. My arm extended across the rickety table and I skimmed my thumb gently through the lone tear. She leaned her head into my hand as the smallest of sighs escaped her throat.

Fuck.

Since our trip started, I spent hours losing myself in my imagination trying to remember exactly what she felt like in my hands. No surprise that it was better than anything I had conjured up. My fingertips trembled as they skimmed her soft cheek in slow, torturous circles. I wouldn't be the one to break this.

A tense air surrounded us as the silence lingered after her confession. Seeing her like this sparked a fire within my chest. I wanted to pull her close, chase the darkness from her, and to show her she didn't have to do any of this by herself.

She didn't have to weather her storm alone.

Lennon shifted in her seat once her tears had dried. I dropped my hand from her face and suddenly I was cold. "Theo, I... " her voice trailed off.

"It's getting late. I'm going to head to bed," she stated as she stood and began to stride from the room. As she approached the doorway, she paused and glanced back at the table where I still sat. "Goodnight, Theodore." Her voice was low as it floated through the air.

"Goodnight, Lennon." I held her gaze before she disappeared into her room, and for a fleeting moment, a thought crossed my mind.

What I wouldn't give to be loved by Lennon again.

Suddenly, it all clicked. I realized why none of my past relationships worked. Why they all seemed to fizzle out before anything became too serious.

It was her. There was always a before her, a small part of my life that I barely remembered. And I know now, without a doubt, that there would never be an after her.

It would always be her for me.

ELEVEN

Lennon

I WAS KICKING MYSELF as I shut the door to my room after leaving Theo in the kitchen. The uncomfortable itchiness of the honesty I shared was crawling over my skin. It wasn't like me to share my innermost thoughts, especially the ones about Camden. I kept those for myself, knowing my memories of him were the only thing keeping him alive.

The heat of Theo's touch lingered, burning into my skin as a scar I'll carry around forever. It had been years since any man had touched me, and the first one that did, I couldn't help but lean into it.

I sulked about my room as I got ready for bed. My attempt to read failed as I rolled over to turn off the lights. I could not stop thinking about dinner. I may be embarrassed, but I was seen for the first time in forever. He listened when I talked, and when I was overrun by my emotions, he moved to comfort me. I was thinking about what would have happened if he leaned in closer, or if his hand had drifted from my face.

Heat began to move through my lower abdomen as my thoughts got carried away, and by the time I acknowledged it, guilt poured over me, extinguishing any fire that was building.

This was not what I came here for.

The faint sound of dishes clinking together where Theo was cleaning up echoed softly in my room. His footsteps started picking up as he walked around locking up until he crept down the hallway.

The soft light outside my room illuminated the underside of my door. His shadow appeared between our rooms and lingered there for a moment, facing my door. My breath caught in my throat as I waited, but I didn't know what for - a light knock or the slight turn of my door knob, maybe. My heart thrummed inside my chest as I sat up from my bed.

Honestly, I didn't know what I would say if he appeared in my room. Could I do it? Could I put Camden out of my mind long enough to allow someone else to warm my bed?

Every part of me seemed to come alive as I waited. As my hands trembled as I gripped the worn quilt covering my body. It wasn't nerves that were lighting me up; it was the subtle pin pricks of anticipation. I wanted him.

Then, the switch flipped, plunging my body back into the darkness as his feet turned back to his door, and he disappeared into his room.

Memories of Camden seemed to flood my senses once I laid back down. A hint of pine floated through the back of my mind, his contagious laugh echoed in my ears, and the image of his deep oak-colored eyes lingered in the forefront of my mind.

He had consumed every single part of me, down to my very thoughts, day and night, for years. He had been my life vest in an unkind world, my safe haven. Without Camden I was untethered and alone, like a small raft in the middle of a dark and wild ocean.

All I wanted was for someone to notice how tired I was of fighting the choppy waters and throw me a lifeline. I thought of Theo and wondered if he could be the one to drag me back to shore.

I spent the rest of our remaining week actively avoiding Theo, and he knew it. He'd catch my eye and move to say something, and I'd take that as my cue to turn abruptly and leave whatever I had been doing. It was childish, I was aware, but I had no idea how to handle this situation, and I did not trust myself around him now. I was liable to snake my hand through his hair, pull his mouth to mine, and—*what was wrong with me?*

Even though I'd been skating around him, he had gone out of his way to keep my attention as much as possible. We also went back to nights with restaurant dinners that only made me wish we were alone again. Most of the time he looked at me like he was on the verge of pouring his secrets out to me.

Today was my last full day with Theo, and I really, really, didn't want it to end. Two weeks was not enough time here, but had left me closer to myself, which was exactly what I was looking for on this trip.

We were at St. Andrews Cathedral today—ruins, to be accurate. Theo stood behind his camera in the courtyard, laser focused on the stoic archways and rubble in front of him. A wave of sadness ran through me; I didn't want to think about the end of this trip, so I hadn't asked yet. I wished he was coming back home with me, or better yet that I was going wherever he was off to next. There was a push inside of me to be closer to him, so I walked to where he was currently bent over, staring into the viewfinder.

"I can't wait to see how these turn out. When will the issue come out, so I can make sure to order a copy?" Lighthearted conversation was all I could handle as he stood to his full height. My head needed to tilt backwards to look up at him. I still didn't know when he gained the extra height, but I wasn't mad at it.

He smiled at me. He was always smiling, even when I avoided him or didn't talk. And it was always for me. "I'll do some editing on these for about two weeks before I turn them in, then the issue should come out in about six months, I think."

"Where will you be when you do all the editing?" He was going to see right through me.

"I'll be here. I like to stay close to where I have been shooting, just in case I need more content."

"Hmm, makes sense." My hands dropped from my jacket pockets and hung limp by my side. The sadness working its way through me was a surprise. I knew leaving Scotland would be hard. It wasn't the knowledge that I would soon be back behind my computer for eight hours a day and spending my nights alone that had me upset. It was the thought that I might never see him again after this. That this was all we would have, these two weeks, and another seventeen years would pass us and we would be strangers once again.

"Want to try?" he asked as he stepped away from his camera and ushered me behind it, knocking the creeping feeling of loneliness out of my system. He took his time walking me through the different parts of his craft, while excitement poured out of him.

"These are going to be no good." I laughed after a few moments of what felt like clicking.

"Wait here. Let me grab something." Theo jogged over to where his bag was and pulled out what appeared to be another camera. "Doesn't matter what camera; I just don't have the talent, Theo," I yelled out as he made his way back to me.

He stopped in front of me and a sly smile crept up on his lips. My heart sped up as I glanced at his hands to see what he had brought over. "A little trip down memory lane for our last day seems fitting." My eyes shot up to meet his. His throat worked to swallow his remaining words as his eyebrows pulled together slightly.

My eyes darted back down to see in his hands sat a weathered-looking Pentax 67 camera. My hands reached out and ghosted over it, I couldn't believe what I was seeing. It was a used camera when I first purchased it for him almost twenty years ago. I'm surprised it's still in working order.

Why would he have this with him, and did he take it to all the countries he visited? The thought that he's kept the one thing I worked so hard to give him caused my body temperature to spike.

"You still have it." My throat was constricting, which was fine because I had no other words.

I was still looking downward at the camera when his soft laugh reached my ears. Slowly, he moved and planted himself directly behind me. For a moment, he stood there, hovering but not touching, then maneuvered the camera in front of us. Every sense I had faded away and was replaced with him. My heartbeat kicked up again. It hammered in my chest, threatening to expose me.

Memories of every kiss, his arms around me when I cried, and the way his body pressed against mine flooded my mind. His breath skated up my neck, causing the soft curls to flutter against my skin as he flicked open the finder of the camera. I couldn't focus with him so close.

"Tell me, Lennon—" *Anything*, my brain shouted at me. "—Is everything in frame for the shot?" Not what I thought he was going to say.

I cleared my throat. "Yes." He pressed the shutter, capturing the sight before us.

We stayed there for a moment, hovering but not touching. "I can't believe you still have this thing."

He pushed the hair off my shoulder, letting his hand tangle in my curls briefly. His head lowered so his mouth was outside the shell of my ear.

"Well, I couldn't keep you." My breath hitched. There were warning signs flashing in my head, but I couldn't figure out what they were trying to tell me.

It doesn't seem to matter because, without thinking, I turned to face him.

He kept his arms low around my waist as I tilted my head back to look up at him. Everything was heavy around us, like gravity had doubled. Then he pulled me in closer and my spine melted away as his hand grazed over the sliver of skin exposed on my lower back.

It was easier here; I didn't feel like a widow or like a woman who was lost and alone. I could be somebody who was more than the shell of a person I had once been, and that Theo could be more than somebody from my past. And for the first time, guilt was nowhere to be found.

His green eyes beckoned me in and before I could panic my way out of this moment, I reached up onto my toes and placed a delicate kiss on his lips. Years have passed since the last time we did this, but the moment our lips met I couldn't help but think how easy it would be to fall back into what we had before.

Before I lost myself completely in the moment, he pulled back. I was thankful for his smile as it eased the tense knot that began to form in my stomach. The wind picked up and sent my hair flying around us as the sun began to sink into the horizon. He tucked a wild strand behind my ear, sending shivers down my spine that had little to do with the weather.

"Lennon, these past few weeks with you have been better than anything I could have dreamed of, I'm..." He swallowed whatever he had been about to say next and took a step back. "We should get you back to your hotel. You have a long day tomorrow back to the States," he said, finishing his sentence with a statement he was definitely not about to say.

I watched him carefully as he gathered up his gear, and I was desperate to hear what he had been about to say.

"Theo," I called out to him. He turned back, and against the dropping sun, he looked like a dream I willed to life. "I thought that this was something I had to do alone. I'm grateful I had someone to share it with, that I had you." I choked over the words, grateful didn't even begin to cover what I was feeling. I didn't want to leave; real life was going to be so boring after this trip.

"If you're ever back home, you'll call me, right?" I asked without bothering to stop myself from looking too eager.

"Right."

"Thank you, Theo, for everything." How could I repay someone for opening my eyes to so much I was missing out on? The two weeks I spent here had opened a door to a new life. It was so close I could taste it and all it had to offer. It had me straddling the threshold of who I was and who I could be.

"Anything for you, Lennon," he replied with a smile that said he'd been waiting a lifetime to say those words again.

That phrase, three words, and everything changed. For years, my heart beat to the rhythm of my grief, but with those words, it seemed to change and beat to the tune of hope.

TWELVE

Theo

I WAS A WRECK. Two weeks was all it took, and I was a hopeless fool for Lennon.

Again.

The kiss had been playing on a loop in my head since she walked through the doors of the airport terminal. She was so close for so long that her scent had seeped into my skin, making it impossible to remove. I couldn't do anything without it pulling me into the past.

After she left, I started looking for a reason to bring us back together. It was proving hard to do without coming off like a super creep. All she needed was some guy following her home from across the globe.

But I wasn't just some guy. Right?

God, I hoped I wasn't just some guy.

I was deadline meeting with Archie was set, and I was going to ask for an assignment on the west coast somewhere. It was odd that a magazine about castles had a North America division, but today I was grateful. All I had to do was make it through another week and I would finally be on my way back to her.

The final edits were great; I sent a few to Lennon. We'd texted a few times since she left—niceties only. Nothing about the kiss, nothing that screamed, 'I miss you, come back to me.' But I was holding out hope that I didn't fabricate the magnetic pull between us.

Much like the first day I saw her, I strolled into the meeting with Archie first thing in the morning. And again, Lennon was the only thing on my mind. "Ahh, Theo. Great to see you again." I swear Archie had some sort of non-official uniform going on, because every time I was here, he looked the same. Black-rimmed glasses and all.

"Your trip went well by the looks of these photos. I've marked the ones for production with the green tabs."

There were dozens marked green, causing my chest to swell with pride. This was one of my favorite parts, having them comb through the photos for the best shots. Knowing that someone else believed in my work was always a high that I never wanted to come down from.

"Well, my boy, where to next? We have a few options that might interest you—Bavaria, Vienna—to name a few."

"I was hoping to pick up some work back in America, on the West Coast, by chance?"

"America? You never take jobs there." He narrowed his enlarged eyes at me from behind his glasses. He saw right through me, I was sure of it.

"What's in America Theo?" There it was.

I couldn't help but laugh. We had been working together for years; this job kept me moving, and he was the closest thing I had to a steady friend. It didn't matter that he had about two decades on me. "If I give you the truth, will you give me California?" His shoulders rose, then dropped to his sides nonchalantly at my request, while waving his hand at my question.

"A few weeks ago, I ran into an old friend here. She was on her trip alone, so I invited her to stay with me while I worked on the itinerary. She lives in California."

"And now you're following her back there?" The look he gave me had amusement written all over it.

"It won't be following her if I have work there."

That's what I was telling myself, at least, anything to seem the least creepy as possible.

He continued to stare at me. "If you say so. There are a few places on the West Coast that we can send you. You can take them all, and it will keep you over there for about six months or so." He swiveled in his chair to face his computer and started plucking away at the keys to draw up the list for me.

"That sounds perfect. Thank you, Archie. I appreciate it."

Six months. I could work with six months. I didn't know what my end goal was. I knew I needed to be near her, in whatever capacity she would have me. I would also be lying if I didn't acknowledge that there was a part of me that hoped I didn't end up in the friend zone.

Once the meeting ended, I was back at my hotel trying to find anything to occupy my mind. For years I had lived out of suitcases, never staying in one place long enough to put down roots or to have a place of my own. I enjoyed the freedom I found in my career. Not having to think about anyone before disappearing to a new country. Behind a camera, I could lose myself and capture some of the most beautiful sites this world offered. Besides my equipment, there was nothing else to show that I existed. Normally, that was something I never thought twice about, but now, as I look around the empty room, doubt crept in.

Deep down, I knew that I'd been running away from the life I fell into, the one that I had forced myself to give up even though it meant I had to give her up too. I never had a reason to go back home. This could be the biggest mistake of my life. She could turn me away the second I turn up and this would all be for nothing. But if I didn't go back to her now, I would spend the rest of my life wishing I had taken the chance.

It had been years since I even stepped foot in the states, and there was no way I could step on American soil without calling the only family I had. After a few rings, the line picked up.

"Hi, Ma."

"Theo. Oh, it's so good to hear from you. How are you, son?" My mother was the best kind of person. She was kind, warm, and nurturing. She loved me without condition, despite the hell I put her through in my younger years.

She and my dad had been married for forty years this year, and they spent their time in New England, at the beach and playing cards with their friends. Honestly, I didn't know much about what they did, which was my fault. I'd been too wrapped up in my own world to remember there were people who still cared about me. But I knew that I missed them.

"I've been really good lately, Ma. Real good."

"That's wonderful, dear, and what country are you in now?"

"Scotland, but that's why I was calling. I'm picking up work on the West Coast and thought I might stop by to see you and Dad first before making my way over."

"Well, it's good you called. We have some news, as well. Your dad and I are moving back to Fairvale!" I could hear my dad whoop in excitement in the background as my mom laughed.

If I could have anything in life, it would be to have what they have. A partnership that had only been strengthened by time. My parents were soul mates, which was not something most people could say about their parents. A sharp laugh escaped from me; fate was working overtime at my expense, and I did not intend to mess this up.

"That's great Mom. It will be nice to see you both more often."

"You too, son. What else is new? Meet anyone new in your life?" I may get along with my mom, but she was still a mom and frequently reminded me that I was alone.

"No, no one new." Not technically a lie. If I mentioned Lennon, a million more questions would have followed. None of which

I had the capacity to answer, and I wanted to keep Lennon to myself.

"You should get out there more, Theodore. You're a catch, and any woman would be lucky to be by your side."

"Okay Ma. I love you and I'll see you soon, okay?"

"I love you, too, son."

She meant well, but I didn't know how she would react if she found out that I wasn't tied down to anyone because of Lennon. Whether I knew it or not, I had been comparing everyone to her. Honestly, my mom wouldn't be all that surprised. Lennon was everything to me back then and just because I left didn't mean my world stopped evolving around her, at least not at first. My mother was the one that helped pick up the mess I had made with my life. She was well versed in the depths of my feelings for her.

I had one more call to make, one that had my stomach in knots. It wasn't someone I talked to often, but we'd kept in touch throughout the years. She was the only person who could help me with my Lennon situation, and she was the best person I could have in my arsenal.

She answered on the first ring. "Well, well, well. I've been wondering how long it would take for you to call me." Her voice mocked me through the receiver.

"What's up, Abigail?"

THIRTEEN

Lennon

By the time five o'clock rolled around, I was halfway through a mental breakdown at work and wishing I could frisbee my laptop out the window. I had been in a slump since my trip nearly three weeks ago, and I couldn't seem to find my way out of the post-vacation depression hole I was in.

Within the hour, I was slipping into a worn plastic booth next to Abby. The smell of spices and hot peppers assaulted my senses, and I wouldn't want to be anywhere else. The waitress dropped off chips and salsa, and I didn't hesitate to reach for the basket.

Abby had launched into a re-telling of my trip to our friend and if my mouth was full, I wouldn't be put on the spot to answer, hopefully. Luckily, I never told Abby about the kiss or the tension filled dinner, so it was all pretty harmless.

"So, you're telling me that you spent two weeks alone with a gorgeous photographer in a foreign country and did what? Nothing? Talk?" Carina said as she tossed her hands up in front of her. Carina was as straightforward as they came and had no problem saying exactly what was on her mind.

After Camden died, I pulled away from everyone, but Carina did what she does best and kept bullying her way into my life. Even when I fought her, she showed up, and kept showing up until I accepted the help she was offering. It was a quality that I would always be grateful for. But now, if she kept pushing, I was liable to spill everything that did happen, and I was not ready to unpack those feelings in front of other people.

"How do you know he's gorgeous? He could be ugly for all you know."

"I know things."

"You know things."

"He's a photographer," she said with an eye roll. "Obviously, he has social media, and obviously I looked him up the second I found out you spent two weeks alone with him."

I shoveled another chip into my mouth and shrugged as she narrowed her eyes in my direction. I couldn't help the smirk playing on my lips before I burst out laughing.

"It was a great trip, but nothing happened, okay?"

"But why not?"

"Because, Carina," I shouted, causing the people at the next table over to glance over at us.

There was a tightness forming in the middle of my chest, and I absentmindedly reached my hand up to rub the spot. I didn't want to talk about how much I wanted to do more, but at the same time, even the thought of being with anyone other than Camden sent me into a spiral.

The issue was maybe I was reading into Theo too much when we were together, that maybe want that was bubbling up inside me was solely one sided. Even if it wasn't, what could we possibly expect to do when he bounced from one country to another while I hadn't moved from our hometown?

There was also a part of me, an echo in the back of my mind, that said no one would ever want a woman with so much baggage. A dead husband must be one of the top reasons not to date a woman, I would assume.

The conversation was steered away from me and on to Carina's latest conquest—she was perpetually single and preferred it that way. The waitress, who was dropping off our third round of margaritas, was blushing from the tail end of Carina's story when an older couple walked by our table on their way to the door.

I was pulling the straw up to my lips, trying to stifle a laugh, as I glanced up out of habit and caught the eye of the woman. Her eyes widened as she stopped in front of our table as I continued to gape at her. "Lennon Faulkner." My maiden name rolled off her tongue so quickly I didn't realize she was talking about me until I registered who she was.

I forgot how much Theo looked like his mom—same brown hair, striking green eyes, and that smile. She beamed at me as I finally remembered to close my mouth. I wiped my hands down the front of my jeans to rid myself of the sudden onset of sweat.

My heart dropped a little when I did a quick scan of the restaurant. Theo wasn't with them.

Although, I guessed that was a good thing. He would have told me that he would be in town.

"Mr. and Mrs. Beckett, hi. Wow, it's good to see you." My eyes flicked back to the table as both Abby and Carina watched me nervously interact with the older woman. I stood and gave her a brief hug. I assumed they still lived out of the area, so what were they doing here in Fairvale? I had no idea if she knew that I had spent two weeks with her son on vacation and I was not going to be the first to offer that information.

"Lennon, you look great and so grown up, I can't believe it." She had both of my hands still and gave them a little squeeze.

"Thank you, Mrs. Beckett."

"Oh, enough of that. You're not a teenager anymore. Please call me Melanie." Her kindness radiated off of her in waves. The same kindness she instilled in Theo that I longed to be around.

"Melanie, you look great as well. What... What are you guys doing in town?" I didn't know why I was nervous, but I felt like I was keeping a secret, like the time Theo and I snuck out. I only wanted to see the stars, but when you're eighteen and get caught sneaking around by your parents, they're not too inclined to believe you.

"Paul and I just moved back to the area. Oh, I can't wait until Theo gets here. I'll be sure to tell him we ran into each other. I'm sure he would love to see you." Well, that answered one question and opened up a pandora's box worth more.

"Theo? He's coming here? To visit you guys?" Subtlety was never my strong suit, but I needed answers faster than she was giving them. My gaze bounced back over to Abby at the table, where she was watching us like a movie.

"Yes, and no. I'm not sure if you know, but he's a photographer, and has been in Europe for years now. Well, now he's doing some work here and is moving back. It will be so good to have him..." Her sentence trailed off as I lost focus, and blood rushed in my ears.

He was coming here.

He was coming here and hadn't said anything to me.

I wasn't his keeper, and he didn't owe me anything, but I thought I would get at least a text that we would be in the same country, let alone the same city. Our city. My heart was in my stomach as I swallowed back the insecurity forming in my throat.

This was what I deserved. I knew it was too much to ask for someone to come into my life who might understand me. I was so stupid for thinking it was anything more than pity that drove him to invite me to spend the trip together. Even more stupid for the number of times I had texted first to see how his day was or would call to hear the sound of his voice. He was probably kicking himself for even allowing me easy access to him.

The tightness in my chest returned. I hated every part of this.

I came back to the conversation and cut her off. "I don't want to keep you two. It was great to see you." It was harsher than it needed to be, but I wanted out of this interaction. Luckily, she didn't pick up on the urgency of my exit, and waved at my sister before she left.

Abby was looking at me with an expression I couldn't quite place as I sat back down. The silence was broken by Carina's question. "Scotland man's mom, I presume?" I sucked down the entire drink that I had in front of me and flopped backward into the back of the booth with a heavy exhale. There was a tingling sensation crawling up the back of my neck, making it hard for me to sit still.

"He hasn't said anything to me about moving back here," I said with such a small voice that I was surprised they heard me at all. They were both watching me with careful eyes as I twisted my hands around themselves in my lap. Abby scooted closer across the booth and placed her hand on top of mine, stopping my restlessness.

"I'm sure he was going to. Maybe he was busy with the move." She offered a perfectly reasonable answer, but that didn't mean it would help.

"Or maybe he's just been a waste of my time." We flagged down the waitress for the check, and I left them both outside the restaurant with promises that I was tired and needed to get home.

I paced my house, and allowed the hurt and my anxiety to spiral out of control. The emotions bubbling over only added to my spiraling. I had no idea how attached I became. Which was ridiculous. There was no expectation that I would see him again. So why did it feel like he betrayed me somehow by not telling me right away that he was coming back?

He was moving back home and didn't tell me.

Or hadn't told me. Either way, I felt as if I had been left out of something. It was like I was twelve all over again, when I would try to make plans with my friends only to find out they were already going to be busy doing something together and I wasn't invited.

I felt unwanted by a man I wasn't even in a relationship with. A man that didn't even live on the same continent as me. Pitiful.

The next day consisted of me fighting the urge to call Theo. Every time I picked up the phone, though, I lost my nerve. And it was a little crazy, even for me. Abby, on the other hand, had been hounding me non-stop about if I had talked to him, and every time my answer remained the same—no, I hadn't. It got to the point where I wondered why she cared so much; she had nothing vested in what would happen if he ended up here. Yet she remained adamant that moving took time, let alone moving his life to a different country—he was probably overwhelmed.

No one was too busy for a text nowadays.

There was a sense of defeat lodged in my chest that I couldn't shake, and I was missing Camden more than ever now. If he was alive, this wouldn't be an issue. If he was alive, I would've felt wanted and I wouldn't have tied up my sense of worth in the first man who showed me an ounce of interest. I put myself out there. Maybe it wasn't as far as I hoped I would get, but it was something, and it wasn't worth it.

I sought solace in the one place that had always brought me comfort. On the days when my mother would scream at me to leave, when Camden died, and even when Theo left, I always ended up in the same place. Pushing the large door open, I stepped into Nevermore Used Books, and I was greeted with the comforting smell of aged paper. The sunlight beamed into the room through the large front window, casting bright rays onto the large leather chairs pushed into the corner. Time stopped every time I came here, picked up a book, and stepped into a new story.

My hand trailed along the bookcases as I wandered through the aisles, shelves with more stories than I could ever have time to read. Stacks of books were overflowing on tables that were strewn about the space, spilling onto the floor and littering the ground, and I loved every part of it. The store was run by an older couple who had seen me in more seasons of life than I cared to remember. The wife, who I only knew by Mrs. Andrews, waved at me from the back of the store, where she kept the boxes of donated books, as I meandered over to the romance section.

If I was destined to live the rest of my life in cold solitude, then I would live through the stories of others and find a way to be content.

Mrs. Andrews approached me while I attempted to balance more books than I needed in one hand. "How are you Lennon?" her soft voice asked me. Turning to look at her, I'm met with eyes that witnessed me grow up. She's seen me walk through the doors with tears in my eyes on more than one occasion and never has she treated me with anything less than kindness.

"I'm okay Mrs. Andrews." Our relationship doesn't exist outside these walls, but that doesn't stop her from knowing when something was bothering me. Her soft hand reached out to give mine a quick squeeze.

"Actually, I have a list of some books I'm looking for. Can I leave it here with you to watch for them when donations come in?" I dug around my purse for the loose piece of paper I had written on.

When I was younger, money of my own was hard to come by that I could spend on books, so I bought them all second hand. That meant sometimes I had to wait longer than others for the book I wanted to come through this store in a donation pile. Which was where the list came in. I had been leaving titles of books I wanted and if she sees them she would set them aside so the next time I'm here I could pick them up.

"Of course, Lennon, I'll leave it behind the desk." She took the paper from my hands and shuffled towards the counter.

As I was sifting through the latest donated Danielle Steele novels, my phone chirped from my bag with a new message. A second chirp rang out, immediately followed by a third, causing me to stop and rifle through my purse for my phone. My lips pursed as Theo's name lit up my screen, but then I read the messages he had sent.

Hey!

> I've been so busy and feel like I haven't had a chance to talk to you. But I have great news that I can't wait to share with you.

> I took some assignments in California and I'm moving back to Fairvale. I'll be home on Friday and I would like to take you to dinner.

I clutched the phone to my chest as a smile tugged at my lips and a fluttering started in my stomach as I read the words over again. Maybe my spiraling was a little bit extreme, because all I could think about was Friday and being able to see him again.

FOURTEEN

Lennon

I'd been rifling through my closet for over an hour searching for an outfit that said this wasn't a date, but I'm so happy to see you, platonically, of course. Nothing jumped out at me, so I settled on comfort clothes as I pulled my jeans up my legs and hopped around a few times to get them past my hips to button them.

The heat had been steadily climbing, and I knew it would be too warm for the sweater I wanted to throw on even if it was night. The bulky sweater would have been enough to hide the parts of my stomach and love handles that spilled out over my jeans. Which is what I would normally gravitate to and I would have felt safe. Instead, I pulled out my favorite rust colored blouse. The sleeves were still long, but they billowed out at the wrist and the light material wouldn't suffocate or overheat me. The neckline dipped in the front slightly, but was still high enough to remind me that this was not a date.

I'd always been pretty confident in my own body. It wasn't perfect, it was softer in spots than I would like, there wasn't a gap between my thighs that constantly rubbed against each other, but it was the only one I had to carry me through life. I tried to be kind to it. My favorite asset, though, was, well, my ass; it tended to draw attention whether I wanted it to or not, and tonight it was living its best life in these jeans. My reflection stared back at me as I shifted from left to right. I bit into my cheek as I tried to hype myself up for this not date.

The nerves in my stomach reminded me a lot of our first dinner, but there was the fact that I had kissed him lingering between us. I didn't regret it, not in the slightest. I wanted more, he was the one to stop. Which was a moment that would haunt me for the rest of time. But where did we go from there? Was he here for a short time, or was he settling down more permanently? Would I even be able to allow myself the chance to get close to him if I knew he was leaving soon? Probably not.

The turmoil was raging inside of me. Did I really even want to move on with anyone? A few months ago, the immediate answer would be no, absolutely not. Camden was my person, love of my life, soulmate or whatever other cliché saying there is. People walk through this life without ever encountering the type of bond I had with Camden; the likelihood that I came across that again in my lifetime was miniscule.

And if I ever found myself in a relationship again and that man didn't bring down the stars to light up the room I was in, call me difficult, but I didn't want it.

By the time I made it to the restaurant, I had chanted, 'this was not a date, you are just friends,' more times than I could count. I walked through the door and didn't see him in the waiting area by the hostess stand or at any of the tables near the front of the restaurant. Panic started setting in, and my hands were sweaty again.

Did I get the date wrong? Did I miss a text saying he was canceling? There were a million scenarios playing out in my head as I gave the hostess Theo's name. She smiled brightly at me and led me toward a booth in the back because, of course, he didn't cancel.

He was here early.

He stood from his seat and waited for me to approach the table. It had only been a month, but I somehow forgot how utterly breathtaking he was. My eyes dragged up his fitted dark jeans to his black knit long sleeve shirt. Stopping to admire the way he pushed his sleeves up, leaving his forearms bare. What a sight he was, even in this dimly lit restaurant. We stood there, looking at each other, before I remembered to sit.

Fairvale was on the smaller side, with not many places to eat, and Riverside House was the nicest place we had for dinner. Celebrating—Riverside House, Prom—Riverside House, need a nice place to take your wife to dinner since you made her mad earlier—Riverside House—you get it. We'd been in this exact place before, and I wondered if he was remembering the same night that I was.

Theo and I had been dating for a few months when he said he wanted to do something special, and for two seventeen-year-olds, this was the place. My face heated up as I remembered the rest of the night, when he had stripped us of our clothes and laid me down in the backseat of the car. It wasn't picture perfect, but I knew I was loved in a way that would follow me for a lifetime, and that was everything I could have hoped for.

His throat bobbed as he took a sip of his water. Even that slight movement had me blushing. I couldn't tell if I welcomed the heat, as everything about him set my nerve endings on fire.

Get a hold of yourself, Lennon.

Every time I tried to think of something to say, my brain would go fuzzy. My fingertips rubbed against the white cotton tablecloth that was draped across our table as my eyes roamed the area around us. The river flowed gently below us, breaking only where it hit large rocks along the shore and trees lined the edge for as far as I could see. A candle sat in the middle of the table. The flickering light mocked my lack of words. My gaze flicked up, only to be met with Theo already looking back at me.

Then he smiled. It was like the tension inside me wound tighter and lessened at the same time.

I snatched up my menu to give my hands something to do and skimmed over the words in front of me while I tried to come up with something to say. "Your mom seems really excited to be living in Fairvale again." I peered at him from over my menu in time to see his brows pull inward and his head shift backwards a bit. "My mom, when did you see her?" His head cocked to the side, and there was a ghost of a smile on his lips.

I smiled as I bit into my straw before answering. "Last week. I was at dinner with Abby and a friend when she and your dad were leaving the restaurant. She came by to say hi and let me in on your secret that you were coming back to town. I was surprised she even remembered me, let alone what I look like.”

“You are unforgettable, Lennon. That, and they were subject to eighteen-year-old me whose favorite subject was you.” The comment fell off his tongue with little effort. As if it’s a known fact to anyone that would listen.

How does he do that? It was always the simplest sentences that sent me reeling once they left his mouth. Every word was sincere and had this ability to relax and heighten my anxiety all at once, but I wouldn’t deny that roller coasters have always been my favorite.

We ordered dinner and the rest of the evening passed in a blur filled with laughter and way too much wine for me. It wasn’t until we were about to ask for the check that I realized I hadn’t thought of Camden once. It came like a flash of lightning and caused my stomach to lurch and my mouth to run dry. Not a single thought of him; how was that even possible?

One dinner and I put him out of my mind? I was ashamed, and there was a numbness spreading through my limbs. The only thing I could focus on was the fogginess in my brain from the three too many glasses of wine.

My trance was snapped by Theo’s voice. “Did you drive yourself here?” I didn’t remember getting up to leave, but we were somehow standing in the parking lot. My phone was in my hand ready to call Abby to come pick me up.

“Don’t worry, Abby will come get me.”

"Let me take you home," he said as he walked towards his car. I wanted to protest the offer, but what would I tell him? That I couldn't be around him because when I was, I lost all sense of who I had been these past two years. That my world didn't implode on itself when he was near. That a few hours with him and I forgot all about my husband.

None of this came out, of course, as I slid into the passenger side of his car as he held the door open for me. The leather was cool on my burning skin and I realized that I was way more tipsy than I should've been. Fingers crossed the drive was quick, and I could get out of here without embarrassing myself. I gave the address as I didn't trust myself to give correct directions while he drove, and he pulled out of the parking lot onto the street.

The music was faint as it played on the radio, and I kept the window down and let the wind rush into the car. My hair was whipping around my face as I breathed in the nighttime air. I loved this time of night when it was just after dusk and the stars started to shine. My head rested against the edge of the window as I looked up at the sky, searching for the first stars to make their appearance.

"Why didn't you tell me you were moving back when we were in Scotland, Theo?" Yeah, I was definitely drunk. In my head he came back for me, but I knew that wouldn't be the answer. It would be too much to hope for and it was only my wishful thinking.

He was quiet for a long time after I asked, and I was silently kicking myself for letting the words slip out at all. I glanced sideways and observed him behind the steering wheel. There was a steady rise and fall of his chest under his shirt that caught my eye. We were only a few streets from my house, and I was starting to think he either didn't hear me or he was going to ignore me altogether.

After what felt like forever, he forced out a husky laugh before taking a deep breath in. "I didn't know I was coming back. I had no plans to come back at all, actually. Then I spent two weeks with you." His words had me on the edge of my seat as my hands gripped the door handle for support. "I knew I couldn't go another day without seeing you. So, after you left, I asked for work to bring me back home." He exuded confidence with his statement.

He knew what he wanted, and it was me. Or to be around me, either way his answer sent shockwaves of fear and excitement through my system.

My whole body shifted in my seat to look at him as his car turned into my driveway. My knee knocked against the center console, and a faint laugh fell from his lips and into the darkness that surrounded us. I was well aware that I was gaping at him. I was sure my mouth was hanging open and everything before I remembered to shut it.

He came back for me. The words bounced around in my head.

He came back for me, and I didn't even have words for him. I was wracking my brain for something to say, anything would work at this point. But what would I say? 'Thank you' didn't seem like it would be the right sentiment for this situation. Before I could find the right words, he leaned forward and brushed my cheek with the back of his hand. His thumb dragged down the side of my face and along my jawline slowly. If the electricity that coursed through me could've been seen, sparks would've been exploding around us. He returned his hand to the steering wheel, leaving every molecule in my body in a state of want.

"I'm not here because I expect anything, Lenny. But I couldn't live with myself if another seventeen years went by only for you to be a part of my past. So, if it's not too much to ask, I'd just like to spend time with you, in whatever capacity you'll have me," he confessed, and there was a part of me that wanted to give him anything he asked for, but my fear of the unknown would always win.

"Okay," I said with a voice that trembled. Every thought I ever had left my brain and the ringing in my ears grew so loud I was sure he could hear it as well. My tongue ran along my bottom lip absentmindedly and his eyes tracked the movement before they flicked up to meet my gaze again. We sat there a minute longer before I could get my legs to start working enough to carry me inside.

Before I climbed out of the car, I turned back to him, compelled to let him in on the war that raged inside my brain most days since Camden died. He needed the whole truth. He needed to know being around me wasn't all sunshine and happy days. That some days, it was like I was being dragged out unwillingly into an unforgiving ocean and I was constantly working against the current to get back to shore. Sometimes the fight to get back to me again took its toll on my mind, leaving me drained of all my energy. I didn't know if telling him for his sake or mine.

"Theo, I haven't been the same since Camden died. Most days, I can fake my way through and pretend everything is okay. But I'm a mess. I already feel like I am too much of a burden to the people around me. I wouldn't want to put that on you. I could definitely use another friend, but I don't know if I can be anything other than that." I braced myself for the blow back, where he would tell me it was nice seeing me, but had suddenly decided going back to Europe would be best for him. I was surprised when a smile broke out on his face.

"If a friend is all you have room for, then I would like to fill that spot."

A fluttering in my chest erupted as I bit back a smile. I told him goodnight and noticed the way he waited for me to unlock the door and go inside before he started pulling out of the driveway. Anakin meowed at my feet as I made my way through the house. I scooped him up and carried him back to the bedroom and deposited him on the bed.

I could do this, another friend would be good for me. It was just that normally your friends didn't give you butterflies and make you wish that you didn't have to go to bed with only your cat for company.

FIFTEEN

Lennon

THE SHARP RING OF my phone pulled me out of my sleep. There was a soft pounding in my head that reminded me why two glasses of wine were my limit. The phone rang again. I cracked one eye open in time to see Charlotte's name flashing across my screen and to see that it was nine o'clock.

Shit.

I forgot that we had plans. I picked up before she thought I was ignoring her. "Good morning, dear," she said, sounding as chipper as ever.

"Hi Charlotte, are we still on for today?" I was slowly rousing myself out of the warmth of my bed. She was going to say yes, I already knew this, but for as long as I could remember, she always called to confirm any plans that had been made. I still hadn't been able to get her to switch over to texting; her reasoning being you never knew when the last time you would hear someone's voice was, so she would take every opportunity she could find. The phone call was over in less time than it took me to answer as I rolled out of bed to start getting ready. It had taken me longer to get back to her about getting together than it should have, even though she had been so excited to hear about my trip. It was my problem; she was so happy all the time and it was exhausting. I wished for once I could act as miserable as I felt with someone.

Regret brewed in the pit of my stomach as I pulled up to the tasting room at Off the Vine winery, for more reasons than one. My head was still pounding from last night, and I had no interest in explaining to her that my solo trip had turned into two weeks with a former boyfriend. She'd be on the phone with Hallmark to sell the rights to the story faster than I could blink.

We took a seat at one of the outside tables. The patio had a view that went on for miles and allowed the warm breeze to flow around us. I sipped my wine and admired the mountains in the distance, with their fading snow-capped peaks and the vibrant green vines of the grape bushes that cascaded downhill and out of view.

I loved June, it was the perfect temperature. Warm enough for me to wear one of my most loved sundresses without issue, a deep green color with tiny white flowers that were splattered across the fabric. It fluttered in the slight breeze as I smoothed my hands down the front of my dress. Charlotte sat across from me, visibly holding back her excitement. She was dying to ask how my trip went the same way I was reluctant to tell her the truth.

Her eyes wandered until they fell back on me. There was no use dragging out the inevitable. "Do you want to see some photos of my trip?" I asked, while opening the photo app on my phone.

She clasped her hands together as she squealed out a laugh and said, "yes." Her finger swiped back and forth on my phone as she commented on the different sites. Every little detail I came across was on my phone and she was more than content looking through the vast amount of photos I took.

"These are so beautiful, and it looks like you had a wonderful time. And how was it just being by yourself?" Her eyes flit up to me and then back down to the screen. I'm pretty sure there were none of Theo, but why did it feel like she already knew?

I scrunched the skirt of my dress between my fingers. The silky texture helps ground me to the present but doesn't stop me from wearing a hole in the fabric. "Actually, I wasn't alone. I ran into a friend from high school who was working there as a photographer, so I kind of tagged along with him. It was a lot of fun." I didn't meet her eye.

I told her about the accidental run in and time we spent going from site to site, even about the cottage that I had booked. To my surprise, she didn't have much to say about the man I had been with, but seemed genuinely interested in the experience I had when I was there.

"So tell me about him—Theo. What's he like? Is he kind or funny? Will you get to see him again?" Ahh, there it was. I had too much hope.

"Theo and I dated in high school, and before my trip, I hadn't seen him in about seventeen years. It's funny how it worked out. He is very kind and sweet and probably understands me more than I give him credit for." The amount of honesty that spilled out of me caught me off guard. Maybe if I said it out loud more often, I could convince myself that Theo wasn't just some random man. That he could be someone worth my time.

The way she was looking at me had me bouncing in my seat. A small smile ghosted her lips, but her eyes were lost somewhere in the past. There was a click of her tongue and she shook the look from her eyes. "I'll be able to see him more, as well. He took on some new work that brought him back to California, to Fairvale, actually. It could be nice," I went on to add.

Camden's father died when he was young, and Charlotte never remarried. I always assumed she loved him too much to move on, a sentiment I resonated with. Or at least it was, but I'm beginning to think there could be more for me and I wanted her to tell me it was okay.

"I think that's wonderful, Lennon. You have endured a hard few years and deserve something for yourself, something that will make you happy."

Tears pricked my eyes as she patted the back of my hand. She answered my unspoken question, and I held my breath as she told me everything I had been waiting to hear.

"You never met John, but after Camden's father died, I lost myself completely. I wanted nothing to do with the world or this life without him in it. It was selfish, but it's the truth. So I threw myself into the person who was still here—Camden. He was the light of my life, and I made sure that boy never knew of my sadness or the hole that seemed to be growing in my chest." Charlotte never brought John up willingly, so my knowledge of how they were as a couple was severely limited, but as she spoke, it was like she had taken the words straight from my heart.

"There were men after my husband, some a little more involved than the others, but no one could ever compete with my John." The wistful sound of her voice carried years of heartache. "I never loved anyone else after him." She looked down into her lap where her fingers were laced together and stared at the dull gold band on her left hand.

"Charlotte, I—"

Before I could finish, she cut me off. "I don't want that for you, Lennon. It's the one regret I have in this life. I was too lost in my sorrow to find my way out of the grief, and I lost out on a part of life that everyone should have. Love is too important to not be a part of your life."

She was right. I knew she was, but missing him was not something I could turn off and then move on. A tear escaped and ran down my cheek. "I'm afraid that if I move on, I'll forget him. That the only thing keeping him close is my grief, and I'm not ready to let it go yet."

"Honey, you could never forget him. I can promise you that. Whether you heal from this hurt on your own or you have the love and support of someone new, Camden will always be a part of you."

We finished the rest of our tasting with fewer tears and a new-found lightness in my chest. On the drive back home, I made a promise to myself to allow myself the space to grieve Camden but to remain open to the possibility of a future. The sun was setting over the river as I pulled into my neighborhood, and I thought of Theo.

The universe brings people together every day for a million different reasons. Maybe he was brought back to prove that I was ready to fully heal. Lord knows I could use the help.

SIXTEEN

Lennon

MY FOOT TAPPED ON the hardwood floor as I waited to be called back. It had been a while since I'd gone to an in-person therapy session. I noted the new plants in the corner trying to give the office space a more homey feel. I didn't think it was doing quite what it was supposed to do; there was still a sterileness to the space.

The door creaked open, and Dr. Audrina Williams poked her head out, her glasses pushed back in her gray hair, her face kind and welcoming. "Hi, Lennon. Come on back." I picked up my phone and followed her into her office.

I took my place on the soft beige couch, where the sunlight was trailing through the windows. My eyes tracked specks of dust that were floating around. I'd been seeing Dr. Williams for years. Just before Camden and I got married, I sought out counseling after spending more time agonizing over masking my anxiety than working through it. After Camden died, I spent more time in her office than I did in all the prior years combined, and with her help, I put in the work and made it to the other side.

"How have you been Lennon? It's been a while since I've seen you." I blinked and switched my gaze over to her. She sat back in her chair with a notebook balanced on her knee. I'd always been curious about what she scribbled down in these sessions.

I slid my hands down the front of my jeans and onto my knees, my shoulders lifting up. "I've been good. I, uh, went on a trip a few months ago. That was great."

She smiled kindly back at me. "Where did you go?"

"Scotland."

Her glasses were back in place, and she peered at me over them. "Is this the trip you had planned with Camden for your anniversary?" I nodded.

"And how was it for you to do this on your own?"

We were getting right into this today, I guess. I rubbed my lips together as she stared back at me. What I liked most about her was she didn't push. She just waited.

"It was nerve-wracking at first. I hadn't been so far from home before, let alone on my own, but once I got there, I knew I was exactly where I needed to be. It was beautiful and everything I hoped it would be."

"And I wasn't alone, exactly. I met someone while I was there." Her face didn't move, but looked down to write something in the notebook.

"Tell me about this new person."

"He's not new, exactly." My fingers twisted around each other as I avoided her gaze. She cocked her head to the side.

"How so?"

I told her about Theo, about us as teenagers, and that at one point we were in love. Not simple puppy love, but the type of love that bent the fabric of time and existence. Our age didn't make a difference to our feelings. They were large, but they were also real.

Then I explained to her how it didn't last because even though he swore he would love me forever; it felt like he woke up one morning and left. She listened intently and chimed in occasionally or nodded along to my story.

"I physically ran in to him the second day I was there out of nowhere. He called it fate, and if this had happened to someone else, I would never believe the story."

"Why is that?" she questioned me, and I had to pause and search for my answer. It seemed too good to be true, which would be my honest answer. What are the odds I would stumble into a person who just happened to fit so seamlessly into my life? Someone who was caring and kind. Someone who could trail behind me to pick up the discarded pieces of my soul for safekeeping and still look at me like I was whole. Good things like this didn't happen to people like me. But I didn't say any of this as I gazed down into my lap to pick at my nails. She was very aware that I was using my silence as my answer as she set her notebook to the side and leaned her arm onto her knees.

"It sounds like you had a really great time, Lennon, but now you're looking for a way to diminish what you experienced. You have a habit of bringing yourself or your experiences down when they are what you deem to be too positive or too good to be true." She leaned back in her seat. That was the thing about therapy—they really knew how to call you out on your shit. "We have worked on this in the past, but I think it would be good to remind you that you are not your past experiences. Yes, they happened to you, but they do not get to define you. You are allowed to have good things happen to you and for you."

"He moved back to town about two months ago after our trip, which has been good." A smile inched its way across my face. "Great, actually. It's been great. We have dinner together and watch movies. He will stop by to see how I'm doing. Just normal things, but it's been really nice to share that part of life with someone again."

"Is this a relationship you are pursuing romantically?" My smile dropped immediately, and the nail picking picked up. Why was everyone so interested in me getting back out into the dating world? Couldn't I have someone and not have to define what it was? Defining it would mean it would change, and change opened the door for complications. There had been no one since Camden. I wouldn't even begin to know how to act if I went on a real date with someone. And the last thing I wanted to do was start that experiment on Theo.

Theo had been back for a month, and already, he wove himself into my life. I blinked, and somehow we'd established a routine. Lunch on Tuesdays, dinner and a movie on Thursdays. We talked and texted daily. It was exciting and there were moments when it made me rethink telling him I only had room for another friend. When I was near him, I felt better than I had in years. I almost felt whole again.

"Lennon." Her voice pulled me out of my thoughts.

"I don't know what I want. What if we take it further and I can't handle it? It would ruin everything." I avoided her gaze and looked out the window. "Two years have passed me by, and I am just as broken as the day I put Camden in the ground. What if I'm never ready for more?" I questioned her, anger and fear weaving themselves through my words.

"That will be a decision you have to make for yourself. But you can't make it without trying first." Her face softened a bit. "Are you still gardening?" she inquired, and I snorted in response.

"No, the boxes have been empty for a while."

About a year ago, when I was still in the thick of therapy, she suggested a hobby to help with my anxiety and the sleepless nights that were plaguing me. Something, anything, she stated that would get my hands moving with the hope that it would get my mind off the pain and onto a task. I tried everything from crochet, scrapbooking, painting—I even tried learning the trumpet. That was a week my eardrums would never recover from. Nothing seemed to work. Carina was the one to suggest gardening, and from the moment I sunk my hands into the dirt, something inside me changed.

Various herbs spilled out of pots that I had set up on my front patio until I ran out of the room. Then I moved to the backyard and made an attempt with vegetables; they were not quite as successful. Every morning was spent tending to the garden, checking over the leaves, or tending to the soil. Each time a new flower or bud appeared, it would be like this big accomplishment, and for a little while, the tight coils that formed in my head would lessen, allowing me to breathe easier.

I didn't mean to stop, but at some point, everything began to die around me, and I couldn't find it in me to try to bring them back. The empty pots taunted me every time I passed them. "How about some unconventional homework?" My eyes panned back to her as I crossed my arms, preparing for whatever nonsense she was about to ask of me.

"Re-start your garden, plant something for this new season of life. And try going on a date," she said nonchalantly, like the words weren't meant to knock me off my rocker. My eyes flashed as I clenched my jaw so tight there was an instant headache exploding in my temples. She could see the frustration blooming in my eyes as she further explained .

"You said what if you can't handle it and there's no way to know for sure unless you put it to the test? It doesn't have to be Theo. Talk to your friends, maybe they can help with setting you up with somebody. If it's too much, then you don't have to go through with it, but at least you will have a better idea of what you can handle." My body melted a bit into the furniture, and I let out a breath before I reluctantly nodded my head yes.

Abby and Carina would have a field day with this assignment. I could already hear their squealing. The session finished, and like every time before, I was both lighter and a bit worse for wear, if I was honest.

Fairvale passed by me as I drove through town, and there was a sinking feeling that started to worm its way through my system. Theo and I weren't a couple, so I didn't have to tell him anything about the possibility of me going out with someone. The thought ping ponged in my head about what would be worse—to tell him or not to tell him.

Seventeen

Lennon

It was too far into the season to plant vegetables, I thought to myself as I pushed a cart up and down the gardening aisles. I didn't have any plans to start my homework yet, but today had been one of those days where everything seemed to have a fire that needed to be put out. It dragged on forever. By the time I logged off, my head was reeling, and I desperately needed an outlet for the pent-up frustration.

My feet splashed through the puddles of water from the employee's duties as I stopped in front of a row of potted daffodils. I rolled my lips in between my teeth, mulling over the options. I could stick to easy gardening with the plants I've had before, but these flowers were so pretty that I couldn't help but add them to my cart. With a final lap around the store's garden center, I had everything I needed to get the massive number of flowers I piled into my cart planted before the sun set.

An hour later, I was lugging a soil bag up to dump into the only garden bed I had in my backyard. My nails were stained brown, and sweat was pouring down my back by the time I placed the flowers into the dirt and dragged the last pile across the base of the stems. I drew in a deep breath as I admired my work and stretched my aching arms above my head. Of course, my therapist was right; my mind felt lighter after turning my focus onto the plants versus letting it wander onto the unknown.

I switched my gaze over to my pool, and a half second before I decided to jump in, my phone buzzed in my back pocket. Looking at the message from my sister, I wondered if she had a sixth sense about when I needed her.

Dinner at Carina's at 9 tonight

The opportunity to ask them to set me up with someone fell into my lap. I huffed out a dry laugh just thinking about the look on both of their faces when I told them. There were still a few hours before I had to leave to meet up with them, and my mouth was already watering at the thought of food from Carina's.

Her parents opened a trattoria style restaurant in town about five years ago, and of course, named it after their only daughter. Her mother's recipes made up the small menu, and I didn't know a single person who'd had a less than stellar meal there. My stomach growled in protest that I hadn't eaten, but it could wait. A dinner at nine meant they were testing a new menu item, and the place would be closed just for us.

My impulse control gave out. I tossed my phone aside and I took a running start and dove into the pool. The water doused the heat that was building on my skin from working in the setting sun, and the day finally started to look up as I broke the surface. I drifted around in the water, staring at the sky for a few minutes longer, and I was not surprised my mind drifted to Theo. It had been a few days since I'd seen him last, and I could already feel the need to be close to him again moving through me.

I was slow to drag myself out of the pool, but the need for food outweighed my desire to stay in longer. By the time I made it to the restaurant, I'd changed my mind a dozen times over if I really wanted to be set up on a blind date. I rapped on the door window while I bounced slightly on the balls of my feet, and just as Carina swung the door open, I made my final decision.

"Good, you're here," she greeted me as she flashed me a warm smile. Her blonde hair was piled up on top of her head with pieces falling out, and the red apron she had cinched around her small waist was dusted with flour. Abby was already seated at a table in the middle of the room, the red and white checkered tablecloth topped with plates of food. I collapsed into the chair across from Abby, who barely gave me a glance as she devoured the food in front of her.

"Are you even tasting it?" I questioned her as I poured myself a glass of water from the table carafe. She flipped me off before turning back to her food and scrolling on her phone. "I've missed you, little sister," I said as I looked over the options on the table. Everything was like a home cooked meal, making it hard to choose.

Carina backed out of the doors that led to the kitchen, carrying three plates. "Okay, ladies, we have Penne alla Amatriciana. I have been begging Mamma to add this to the menu forever. It's been my favorite since I was little." She set the plates down in front of us and saliva pooled in my mouth. Without a second thought, I dug in. The first bite hit my mouth, and I practically moaned in relief.

"This is so good," I mumbled out with a full mouth. Carina looked relieved and started on her plate.

After a while, our plates were empty, but we remained at the table, Carina's face animated as she recounted an argument she was in with her co-worker today. "He does it on purpose, I swear. He is just so infuriating," she growled out before her head fell forward onto the table.

"You know, Carina, the line between hate and love is often very thin," Abby laughed out while patting her on the back. Carina mumbled something that sounded awfully like "I could only hope", and I placed that little fact in my back pocket for another day.

My fingers fiddled with my napkin, and the skin on the inside of my mouth was chewed raw at this point. I needed to get the words out there. If I didn't ask them tonight, I was liable to never ask them. That, and there was a tiny voice in the back of my mind pushing me to figure out if I could actually handle dating because there was a certain man that would benefit from it. I sucked in a long breath, and on the exhale, my request came flying out.

"Ineedyouguystosetmeuponadate."

Carina's head popped up from the table as Abby's eyes widened as she stared back at me. They glanced at each other and then back at me, and the waiting started to eat at my self consciousness. "What did you say?" Carina said in a slightly more demanding tone than usual.

"I said I would like it if you guys could set me up with someone." My voice was as calm as someone who was asking to set up their next eye appointment. "You know, like on a date." I clarified, although it clearly wasn't needed.

They turned back to each other, and one said, "I thought that's what she said," while the other said, "It's about time." I rolled my eyes at both of them, waiting for them to turn their attention back to me. Abby was the first to respond back to me by asking about Theo.

"I'm sitting right here, you know. And what about Theo?" I snapped back. "We're not together."

"I know, but... you know what? No, I don't know. You two kinda act like you're together, so why are you asking to be set up with someone?" she interrogates. I cursed the amount of time I spent around her because, of course, she'd ended up in the same room as Theo and I. And apparently, she saw something I didn't.

"We do not act like we're together," I said with enough conviction that I almost convinced myself. Only to be met with a snort of laughter from Carina.

"Whatever you say, *amore*."

Maybe this was a mistake. I thought I would be met with enthusiasm. That I could handle, but this push back they were giving was not what I had in mind, and I was growing more uncomfortable by the second.

"We're not together, and I want to see what it would be like to try to actually date. That's all."

That wasn't all, but they didn't need to know all the details.

The girls shared a look, and when they did that, it meant nothing but trouble. If years of being around them had taught me any-thing, it was that when they worked together, only chaos ensued. I was getting ready to call off the whole thing when Carina spoke up. She leaned forward on the table and a glint of mischief flashed in her eye. This was a mistake.

"Okay, *sorella*." My demeanor shifted at her use of the word sister. Carina was as hardheaded as they come. She didn't give her affection out to just anybody. You had to earn it. There were very few people who could say that they had it, and I counted myself lucky to be among them, along with Abby.

She called me sister, and it was a privilege that I would covet forever.

"We'll set you up with someone, no worries." Her voice was so sweet I could taste the ulterior motive. I had worries, lots and lots of worries, but I pushed them down. I could do this. It was one date. The worst that could happen was they were so boring that I never wanted to date again,

This shouldn't be so bad, I hoped.

EIGHTEEN

Theo

Friends, that was what she said she needed, I could do that. When it came down to it, I would be anything she needed. What I didn't anticipate was it being the hardest thing I'd ever do, but she was worth having in my life.

I was beginning to realize people didn't run into the one person they've loved for most of their life out of coincidence and go on to ignore it. Fate, the universe, God, it doesn't matter who was orchestrating it. I knew that I was meant to be close to her.

We've been tip-toeing around each other, staying in the clear boundaries she had drawn for us. We texted frequently throughout the week and spent most weekends together. There were dinners on Saturdays and strolls through the farmer's market on Sunday mornings. Every day I spent with her had me inching closer and closer to the line between us.

My camera was fixed on the front entrance of Lobo Castle in Agoura Hills, CA. The stone masonry that was taken from the surrounding canyon was remarkable. I was surprised by the number of "castles" that were in California. I used the term a bit loosely, as none of them could even compare with the sites Europe had to offer and the history that went along with them, but still, impressive.

Twelve hours until my flight, twenty-fourish until I could see her again, but who was counting, right?

Lennon and I had started a tradition, for lack of a better word. It was silly, but it kept her smiling when we were together, and that was what mattered. Every week, we decided on a movie, and we paired a home cooked dinner with it. Sometimes, we did drinks to match or a dessert, but the time we took to work together had been the highlight of my return home. Lennon was always full of laughter and quick remarks on my less than stellar cooking. It was so easy being around her.

I was living out of a too small Airbnb while I was in California, so every dinner was at her house, which was immaculate. There was not a frame or pillow out of place; it seemed as if nothing ever moved or changed. She gave me a quick tour the first time I came over. I saw every room except hers. That door always remained firmly shut when I was over, and I swear it was on purpose. It seemed as though she kept that side of her, the more intimate side, hidden from me. A quick chime came from my phone.

How do you feel about magic...?

I smiled down at my phone like an idiot. It doesn't take a genius to know where this was going. I shot back a quick reply.

> Hate it, definitely the worst movie option to choose.

There was an angry face emoji on my screen now, along with a slough of GIFs of people giving me the thumbs down.

Too bad. It's my week, and I'm choosing.

She was as predictable as she was at eighteen, but it's what I loved most about her.

I cringed at my internal thoughts, but I really couldn't help it. When I left her seventeen years ago, it wasn't because I had fallen out of love with her. Very much the opposite. I needed to leave for her, and now it was like I was picking back up in the same spot I left her.

Years ago, she buried herself into my soul, into the very fiber of my being, and I was content with letting her consume me. Then, by some grace, she loved me back, and I knew I would spend the rest of my life being the best person I could possibly be for her. Everything about the love we shared burned bright.

She was all I wanted to be around, but she couldn't always be around me. She had Abby to think about and often chose to stay home to help shield her from the chaos that ensued their house. Without trying, I found myself falling into a crowd that was everything Lennon wasn't.

It was slow at first, a few drinks at a kickback or a party someone in our class was throwing. Lennon would rarely want to come.

I knew she was a bit guarded when it came to drinking. Her mother was terrible, drunk every night and every morning, blaming Lennon and her sister for her problems. The cycle was never ending, and most nights I would sneak out to be with her and hold her as she cried.

I never imagined that I would end up on the same path, but partying once on the weekend turned into every weekend night to a few times during the week as well. I fell into a crowd where it all seemed normal, but then I realized I was biding my time with her until I could get away and find the next party.

It didn't take long for me to start failing out of school or missing shifts at work. Everything began breaking into pieces around me, and it was all my fault. Instead of working on myself or asking for help, I would seek out the next party, my next drink, anything to mask the issue I had been causing. I didn't want to admit that I might have had a problem.

I was young, I told myself, I was like every other high school kid. They partied, they didn't have a problem with alcohol.

Then I caught myself lying to her.

We had plans to go to the movies one night, but there was a party a few towns over that I found out about at the last minute. Without a second thought, I told her I was suddenly sick, and I had to stay home. She was so understanding. Offered to bring me food or medicine, but I fell into the lie so easily, and she never had any reason to second guess me. So I turned off my phone and spent the night drinking with people whose names I didn't even remember.

The next day I had a hangover that lasted days. My parents had their suspicions, but stumbling home that night was their last straw. The next morning, they sat me down and told me they had plans to move to the East Coast. I could either stay here and continue on the path I was on, or I could come with them and I could get the help that I needed. It didn't take me long to hear about the couple from the party that drove home drunk, either. They lost control of the car and wrapped it around a tree. The girl died and her boyfriend spent the next ten years in jail. All I could think of was Lennon and it made my decision easier.

I had been sending everything down the drain—my life, my relationship—and I didn't know how to fix it. And what's worse, the guilt from lying to the one person who always saw the best in me started to gnaw away at my heart. I didn't want to live like that any longer and my urge to drink wasn't going away on its own, so I decided to leave with my parents.

The right thing would have been to tell her what I was going through, but I didn't know how to explain what I barely understood. So I took the coward's way out and didn't. I thought a few months would be enough, and I could come back to her, beg for forgiveness. A few months away turned into a few years and then she was married, and I was too late.

There were a thousand different ways I could have asked for her to wait for me, and parts of me wished I would have. It wasn't the path that was written out for us, but I was here now, and I would do whatever it took to stay.

One of the better things about the work on the West Coast was the shorter commutes. Every flight within California was a few hours tops for me. I wasn't stuck in customs every time I crossed a border, and there were no translation apps or books needed. It had been a breeze, so by the time I stepped off my flight from LA the next morning, I didn't feel like I needed a day's rest from the amount of travel. Which was great for me, but I needed to find something to occupy the rest of my day until I could get back to her.

By the time five o'clock rolled around, I'd edited most of the photos from Lobo Castle, and my eyes were straining to see straight. I was walking up the pathway to Lennon's house, rubbing the heel of my hand into my eyes, while the smell of lavender wafted up from the plants that lined her walkway. She lived in an achingly charming house that was painted a uniquely Lennon green color. White flowers lined the front windows and were spilling out over the boxes. It was a house that you see in movies, the kind you live happily ever after in. My heart seized at the thought that it was not how she ended up.

She appeared in the open kitchen windows, and there was some song playing but it was being drowned out by the sound of her voice singing over it. She was swaying back and forth, using a pair of tongs as a makeshift microphone. Her long hair was swept up off her bare shoulders and was in a bun on top of her head with curls falling out around her face; she was absolutely breathtaking like this.

Carefree.

Happy.

I knocked a few times, but she couldn't hear over the music, so I opened the door and walked inside. I propped myself up against the doorframe of the kitchen with one shoulder, crossing my arms across my chest, waiting for her to notice me. She still hadn't seen me, but the song was winding down and she hit some note she had no business trying to sing. I began to slow clap for her performance as she jumped about a foot in the air, shrieking at my sudden appearance.

"Theo!" she half growled at me. "You scared the bejesus out of me." There was a towel soaring past my head that I dodged.

She looked beautiful, and I was feeling a little bold tonight.

Moving farther into the kitchen, I walked toward her, stopping behind her while her body still faced the counter and window. I leaned down slightly so my head was by hers. "My apologies, love." My voice was low and filled with more emotions than a "friend" should have right now. A shiver moved through her body and I was pleasantly surprised she made no move to get out from in front of me.

Wanting to drag out the moment, I waited a hair's breadth away from her. The desire to touch her was overwhelming, and my hands flexed by my side. My body moved on its own as my hand drifted up to trail one finger down the bare curvature of her neck and across her shoulder blade. She was as soft as I remembered, maybe even more so. I ached to press my lips against the skin that I once called home.

She sucked in a quick breath but remained a statue in front of me. All the life we lived between who we were and who we are seemed to hang in the delicate balance we've created. She clearly drew the line of friendship out in front of us, but that didn't mean that I didn't enjoy toeing the line from time to time.

Making sure I didn't push my luck, I moved from my spot and asked for her to give me a task to help finish dinner. My hands needed to be occupied, otherwise I'd have to fight to keep them to myself again.

Her house was on the smaller side, and there was only one couch, not much bigger than a loveseat. We had settled on opposite ends like normal, and watched a movie with a foot of space in between us that might as well have been the Grand Canyon.

I think I paid more attention to her than to the TV tonight, but if she noticed, she didn't let me know. Instead, her eyes would bounce from the screen over to me from time to time. She was fidgety, her mouth would open before she would snap it shut without saying a word.

When the movie ended, I didn't want to leave. I wanted to stay wrapped up in the comfort of her home, where I could be close to her even if she kept me at arm's length. I contemplated coaxing her into starting the next movie in the series. Until she hit me with a statement I didn't see coming.

"So, I'm going on a date," she said, while fiddling with the frayed edge of the blanket and avoiding eye contact with me.

"A date?"

What. The. Fuck.

She made a noncommittal noise in her throat, still with no eye contact. She shrugged her shoulders at me while I kept staring. "Abby and Carina set me up with a guy they work with." She finally looked up from her lap at me, her brows pinched together. She was nervous about it, my answer or the date, I couldn't tell which.

Fucking Abby.

She was the first person to know that I came back for Lennon, she knew my feelings. But what did she do? Went and set her up with some pretentious ass from the law firm she worked at.

My blood was boiling beneath my skin as I scrubbed my hand down the length of my face. "That's great, Lennon. If it's what you want, then I'm happy for you." I decided against the second movie. We cleaned up the kitchen in silence and plates were put back with a bit more roughness than I was going for.

It wasn't anger that was coursing through my blood; it was blatant jealousy.

That should be me taking her on a date, not some random man she knows nothing about. Would he know not to take her to sushi because she hates the smell of fish? That she prefers quiet booths over tables in the middle of a restaurant? Would he know that even the slightest change in plans causes her mind to reel?

These are little pieces of her I've discovered over the new time we have spent together. I know I could make her happy. I just needed a chance.

Lennon trailed behind me as I made my way to the front door, her sock cladded feet shuffled against the wood floor. Before I made my way out of the door, a quick decision passed through my mind.

I turned back to meet her gaze. Her eyes were wide and full of concern as she looked back at me. Scanning her face for any sign that I should stop, I took a step closer, and then another. Until I could see the faint marbling of silver in her blue eyes.

For the second time, I reached out to her. My hand cupped her cheek briefly before sliding it back so that my fingers were tangled in her hair. My thumb stroked the soft part of the underside of her ear and her eyes drifted close slowly.

"Lenny." My voice was dangerously low and laced with a hundred different versions of I want you.

"Yeah." The word came out as a breath that skirted across my neck as she looked up at me. I cracked a smile—not just any smile, but a full teeth and dimple inducing smile—as I leaned in a fraction of an inch closer towards her full pink lips, her tongue darted out to wet her full bottom lip. I needed a Nobel Peace Prize for the amount of restraint I was exhibiting right now.

"Have a good night." And before she had a chance to move or speak, I was out the door, grinning the entire walk to my car.

If she was opening up to dating, then I was throwing my hat in the ring. I needed to figure out how to tell her that I could fill that spot, too, if she'd let me.

Nineteen

Lennon

Why was I doing this? I asked myself as I slipped my feet into my favorite black leather mules and turned to the oversized mirror in my bedroom. I tilted my head from side to side and pursed my lips. I didn't hate what I was wearing, but I didn't feel like I'd hoped I would. The green silk of my thin strapped top gleamed against my tanned skin from the summer sun, but I would admit, it did look good.

Abby was supposed to be here by now.

I was hoping to exude confidence, enough to make it through the date without a full breakdown. The front door swung open and Abby's voice carried back to my room. She appeared a few seconds later in the doorway and let out a low whistle.

"Damn, Lennon, you still got it." This remark earned her an eye roll so hard I think I saw my brain for a second. Her reflection appeared in the mirror as she flopped onto my bed. She landed so her head hung over the side closest to me and stared a bit before rolling back over.

Her tongue clicked. "So, how did Theo take it when you told him about your date?" There was a gleeful sort of smirk spreading across her face.

"Fine. He didn't say much but—" I whipped around to face her; the smile was only bigger. "How do you know that I told him?"

"We talk," she stated simply.

"You talk?"

"Yeah."

She offered nothing more to the conversation, but there were about a thousand questions running through my mind at that statement.

Why did they still talk? What did they talk about? My mind was spiraling.

Did they talk about me?

Then I realized if they talked, then she knew he was coming back. She knew and she let me spiral for longer than I'd admit. What was I supposed to do with this information? I didn't enjoy being kept in the dark. Surprises, on any type of level, and I do not mix.

However, before I completely derailed, she answered.

"You forget that I was close to him, too. Yeah, you were his girlfriend, and you guys were in love—blah, blah, blah. But Theo was like a brother to me during that time. Every time you'd call him over after mom would disappear in the middle of the night to go drinking, God knows where, he didn't check up on just you.

Every time, he made a point to make sure I was doing okay, too," she admitted to me. The bed squeaked as she rolled off and walked towards me. "He's a good man, Lennon, so yeah, we still talk."

My gaze softened as I looked back at my sister. At the same time there was a clenching inside of my chest. A tightness that came with the pain of growing up with a parent who never really cared about us.

Without realizing what I had been doing throughout the years, I had blocked out most of the pain our mother had put us through. As much as I'd like to forget everything, it was impossible to forget the way she made us out to be the problem. No matter how hard I tried, I couldn't forget her sneaking out of the house and leaving us alone to go drinking, the bottles of liquor she would attempt to hide around the house, or the way she would beg me to tell her I loved her when she was drunk. As if my words would erase all her wrongdoings.

I drew in a ragged breath as the memories I'd stamped down bubbled their way up out of the recesses of my mind. If I were a better person, I would have something to say back to Abby, but expressing myself had never been easy. I wondered what Theo would say to her in a moment like this or any of the nights I would call him over for my own comfort.

It had only been a few days since I last saw Theo. I was surprised by how much I missed him in my home, although I really shouldn't be. He noted the details of my life and committed them to memory, the little things that I only had to mention once in passing. Like how I preferred my plates stacked with the bowls resting on top instead of off to the side. Or how he would load and start the dishwasher before he left because he knew I slept better, knowing everything would be clean when I woke up.

My mind lingered on the last night we were together and how his hand slid into my hair and that smile that lit the room on fire. What I wouldn't give to have him pull me in a little closer, and finally have his lips on mine once more.

"What are you thinking about?" Abby's voice pulled me back suddenly.

Shit.

"Nothing."

"Sure, nothing." She laughed out as she left my room and made her way to the living room. My shoes clicked against the hardwood as I followed her and shook my head to rid myself of my thoughts.

"You going to hang out here while I'm gone?" It wasn't really a question. I knew she would want to know how it went as soon as I got home. And since I was not reliable enough to text her as fast as she would like, she made herself comfortable on my couch, set on waiting me out.

"I'll be here," she shouted at me while I walked out the door.

There was a bundle of nerves wrapping themselves around my stomach as I backed my car out of the driveway. The odds of this night derailing are pretty good and there was a nervous breakdown tugging at the back of my conscience like a warning.

What did you even talk about on a first date? If I had to sit through dinner and talk about mundane things like 'what do you do for work' or 'what's your favorite color', I might actually scream. Hopefully, my overthinking was getting the best of me and this night went smoothly. I wasn't looking for anything long term, or really anything past dinner, but if I could do this, then maybe I'd be more willing to let Theo in.

If he wanted that too, that is.

God, I hoped he wanted to.

It was so easy with him—too easy.

There were no awkward lulls in conversation that threw me into a panic, thinking I was talking too much or not enough. He kept me laughing and calm, and when I was with him, life didn't seem so hard.

And I couldn't forget the way I would catch him looking at me from time to time. His eyes would search my face as if he was mapping every freckle and imperfection for his own record. Or the way he would brush fallen curls out of my face without a second thought. It might be an excuse to get his hands closer to me, but the sensations it would leave behind were indescribable. What I wouldn't give to have his hands run through my curls nightly.

I shook all thoughts of Theo from my mind as I pulled up to the restaurant. "Be in the moment. You can do uncomfortable things." I whispered to myself before getting out of the car, crossing my fingers for not having to play twenty questions with a stranger.

The door slammed against the wall as I charged back into the house. My keys and purse were tossed haphazardly onto the nearest counter. My entire body was in flight mode, but with no way to escape myself. Everything was boiling over.

"Stupid, stupid, stupid." The tears had been burning the back of my eyes since I all but ran out of the restaurant. Abby came flying off the couch and raced down the hall to follow me.

I kicked my shoes off, and they went flying to the opposite side of the room as I ripped my hair from the tie that had been holding it up. There was going to be a hole in the floor where I was pacing in short circles in front of my bed. Abby stood in the doorway, eyes wild as she experienced my breakdown in real time.

Torment was tearing through my veins like thick sludge. "I thought I could do it. I really did," I said, speaking to no one and her simultaneously. It didn't bother me that she didn't answer. I charged forward in my one-sided conversation.

"It started out okay. He seemed nice, you know, but at some point I was telling a story and he reached across the table to touch my hand, and I froze." The pacing stopped as I squeezed my eyes shut, willing the tears to not fall.

He really was nice and my reaction surprised us both. The second his hand brushed against mine, it was like ice was poured down my back. I yanked my hand back so fast I knocked over my water glass. Apologies spilled out of my mouth like the water that was dripping onto the floor. I asked for the check as soon as possible, then ran.

Not literally, but it was so abrupt, I barely had time to return his goodbyes.

My pacing resumed as I rubbed my hands up and down the tops of my thighs. My chest was tight and there was a lump forming in my throat, making it difficult to keep speaking. Abby creeped farther into the room to sit on the bed, her moves cautious and slow. In a second, it was like someone switched on the faucet and the tears came pouring out.

"I thought I was ready. I want to be ready," I said as I pressed the palms of my hands into my eyes, as if I could physically stop the tears from falling.

"What is wrong with me, Abby?" The words escaped against my will.

Why couldn't I just be normal?

Why did I always act like the world was ending when all I wanted was to live?

Abby stood to hug me, but I shook her off before she could get her arms around me fully. "It's okay, Lennon." She gently offered her affection, but I barely picked it up over the roar of my blood rushing in my ears.

"It's not. I shouldn't have reacted like that. I don't know why I did. I have never responded like that any of the times Theo has touched me," I shouted. Yelling wouldn't do me any favors, but it felt good to get out the frustration, and I didn't miss the way her eyes widened at my revelation about Theo.

I sat on the edge of my bed, clutching the frame until it creaked under my grip. I wanted to scream or cry; anything would be better than letting this disappointment fester inside of me.

"I am dead inside. I am dead inside this house, Abby. I am a corpse living inside a fucking time capsule. He is everywhere I look, and it's like I'm just biding my time until I can get back to him." Everything was pouring out of me, and there was no way to stop it. Uncontrollable sobs were bubbling up out of my throat.

"And I do not want to feel like this anymore." My voice broke as my epiphany poured into the room. I twirled my wedding ring around my finger, too ashamed to look to Abby for the comfort I was so desperate for.

Missing Camden had been all that I was for the past two years. Every waking moment had been dedicated to the void he left in our home, in my life, in my very soul. There would never be a second that passed where a piece of me did not long for him.

But there were more pieces that yearned for life again. For happiness that would breathe life back into me and I wanted it so badly that I was willing to do almost anything for it.

I loved Camden with every fiber of my being, but I needed more. I needed something bigger than what I was now.

I sucked in a shaky breath as Abby came to take her place next to me. With a low voice barely above a whisper, I continued, "I want to be excited about life again. I want to laugh with someone, I want to be loved again. I want someone to touch me and to be able to touch them without feeling guilty."

She snaked her hand into mine and gave it a squeeze. "You can have whatever you want in life, Lennon. Do you know what you want?" My eyes panned around the room. Everything was a reminder, and it continued to open wounds that never seemed to scar. I didn't want to forget, but why did it have to be so hard to be reminded that he's not here?

"No... I don't know, maybe."

She raised her eyebrows at my statement, her expression saying, 'I know you're lying, want to try again?' "Don't think I didn't notice that little Theo comment." My lip pulled up a fraction in an attempt to smile.

"I can be myself around him. I can be happy with him. *He* makes me happy, and when we're together, it just feels..." With my head turned towards the ceiling, I searched for the words. There were so many ways to describe what it was like when I was around him.

"Easy." I settled on.

Theo had this way about him that set me at ease. He'd been a safe space no matter what version of me he'd get. I didn't have to put on a facade that everything was all sunshine and clear skies, but not everyone was meant to dance in the rain and there was a possibility he would run at the first sign of trouble. Regardless of that fear, he brought more peace to my life than I even thought possible. "It could be more, we could be more," I finally admitted.

Her shoulder knocked into mine. "Well, maybe you should tell him that." A simple 'hmm' was all I could muster as an answer at this point.

Tonight was supposed to be a chance to put myself out there and allow myself the space to grow. All I wanted was a simple evening where I could talk to someone new, to laugh and be able to prove to myself that I was ready to move on—romantically. Now I didn't know what I was ready for. If I couldn't get through a simple dinner, how could I expect to actually be with anyone?

I can't, was what I was beginning to realize. Maybe I wasn't meant to be anything other than what I was now. A thirty-five-year-old widow, destined to be alone forever.

Even if my gut was telling me, it wasn't what I wanted.

My face was taut once the tears dried and I was drained. Abby knew that I didn't want to be alone, so together we crawled under the safety of my blankets. For a moment, I was transported back in time, and we were ten and seven again, seeking refuge from our mom in my bed.

Before I drifted off to sleep, Abby whispered into the dark that as long as she was here, I'd never be alone. But tonight, as I slept, it was only dreams of Theo and a life that we could have together that were waiting for me.

TWENTY

Theo

SOULMATES WERE A FUNNY thing. Whether you believe there was only one person for everyone, or you have soulmates that are there for different parts of your life, it's all such a strange concept to me. Either way you spin it, I knew in my bones that Lennon was the one for me. I knew it when I was fifteen and pining after her while stuck in the friend zone. I knew it at eighteen when I was breaking her heart in order to get my life on track.

And I knew it now.

Out of all the souls that have existed and would exist, mine would forever belong to hers.

But her date was unexpected and sent me into a spiral the moment she told me. That was until Abby reached out last night to let me know it apparently didn't go well. There was a side of me that was dying to race over to her and offer whatever comfort she was willing to take from me. Then there was the other side, that had been walking around with a smug look on my face. One less person I would have to potentially compete with.

He must have done something so out of pocket for it not to have been a good night. Or... what if he did something that scared her? What if he pushed her too far into doing something that she wasn't ready for?

There was also a third side that was fuming. All it would take was a quick call to Abby to find out who he was, and I may not be a top investigator, but for Lennon, I would find him in a second. But that was not what I wanted right now.

What I wanted was to see her. It was currently eight in the morning, and on a Sunday, no less. Being the king of impulse, I was walking up toward her house an hour later with grocery bags filled with everything to make brunch, but the closer I got to the door, the more doubt started to kick up.

What if I was overstepping? Maybe she'd answer the door and want nothing to do with me after whatever she went through last night. It was too late. My hand was raised to knock at the door. A beat passed before the door swung open and there she was.

For the rest of time, the sight before me would be ingrained in my mind.

Lennon stood in the doorway, like an angel with a halo made of hair. It was everywhere. I mean, everywhere. The strands fell down around her face in unruly curls. It was standing up in the front and somehow in the back, as well. There was so much of her skin exposed in the small sleep set she was wearing. The blue stood out against her skin, showing off the sprinkling of soft brown freckles on her chest. The shorts were barely grazing the tops of her thighs. I involuntarily swallowed the lump that had formed in my throat.

I was staring, but my God, she was beautiful.

She shifted back and forth on bare feet as she stared back at me. Her arms folded tightly across her chest, the thin strap of her top slipped off her shoulder and pulled my focus from her face. I shook my head slightly to bring myself back to what I was here for. Plastering a smile on my face, I greeted her.

"Good morning," I said, my voice took on an annoying sounding pitch.

"What are you doing here?" her voice was thick and cracked as she spoke. After taking a step forward, I noticed her eyes were rimmed red. I settled on half honesty when I answered.

"I missed you. And I thought I'd bring over everything to make breakfast." Not *I missed you and I hated that you sat across from a man who wasn't me for a date. Please let me love you.*

She tilted her head to the side. I braced myself for the rejection, a door in my face or her telling me flat out to leave. I wondered which would be worse, but she was full of surprises. She moved out of the doorway and walked toward the back of the house. I took my chance and followed her inside, but turned toward the kitchen. That was when another voice spoke up to say good morning.

Abby was sitting at the island in the middle of the kitchen, clutching a coffee mug beneath her chin. A coy smile took up the space on her face as she arched her brow at me. I groaned internally, but I was sure she could see the way my shoulders sagged slightly.

"What a pleasant surprise, Theo. What are you doing here?" Her voice dripped with sarcasm and amusement. I placed the bags in front of her on the counter and with daggers in my eyes. It only made her throw her head back and laugh out.

Abby had been a saving grace for me since I'd been back. She might be the only one who realized I never stopped loving Lennon, and it had been great to actually talk to someone about it. Lennon walked back out in time to watch the end of my stare off with Abby. My eyes skated over her new outfit choice just in time for Abby to continue laughing. I took a deep breath and shook my head of the thoughts that were beginning to cloud my brain.

Her smile was back, if only slightly ,and it felt like the sun's warmth was filling this room as she climbed up onto a stool and relaxed back into the seat. "So, you brought breakfast," she stated as she crossed her arms.

"Yes," I answered as I held her gaze. Showing up unannounced wasn't something I did, we had fairly clear boundaries of our friendship. I might toe them here and there, but I knew my place, even if it was one I would like to break free from.

She shook her head. "Well, what did you bring?"

Oh, good. She wasn't going to kick me out for showing up like a creep.

The morning sun was shining through the front window as I shuffled around the kitchen. The coffee pot bubbled in the corner as its aroma filled the space around the three of us. I listened as Lennon talked to her sister about her plans for the upcoming week, and it was in this moment I realized what I wanted was to be doing this every weekend. Every day. Any chance she'd allow, I wanted to be by her side.

It was easy and comforting, in a way. It was what all my deep-seated dreams were made of and I would give anything to prove to her that this, us, could work. I liked moving about her house, taking care of her. I liked hearing her laugh with her sister and the way she devoured the pancakes I placed in front of them. By the end of breakfast, I felt lighter than I ever had. This was what I wanted. I wanted a life with her.

I cleaned up the mess in the kitchen after I shooed Lennon away from the kitchen. She reluctantly left, leaving me alone with Abby.

"You should tell her," Abby commanded, and my hands stilled in the soapy water. "You have real feelings for her, Theo. You wouldn't have come back if you didn't. You might think she knows or that maybe she'll figure it out, but she needs to hear it. You know this about her."

My jaw tenses, grinding my molars together. "She's not ready, Abby."

"Says who?" she said firmly. Her eyes narrowed while redness bloomed on the tops of cheeks. "Let her decide for herself." She didn't wait for me to respond before she stood from the island top and stalked to the entryway. Her hand hovered over the door handle before turning back to me.

"She's not as fragile as you might think, and I promise it will be worth it." She yanked the door open and disappeared out of the house.

Once the last of the dishes had been put away, I went to find Lennon. The living room was empty as I moved toward the backyard, until I caught a glimpse of her. She was sitting on the edge of the pool, dipping her legs into the water. I pulled the sliding glass door open, and her head snapped up as the sound caught her attention. She gave me a small smile as I kicked off my shoes and sat down beside her. The water was cool against my skin, but it did nothing to quench the fire that started up every time I was close to her.

A soft sigh escaped from her chest. "It didn't go well last night. The date," she said as she lazily kicked her feet back and forth in the pool. We watched the ripples expand across the water's surface for a few moments.

"Do you want to talk about it?"

"No, not really."

"Okay, Lenny." I loved the way she smiled at the sound of her name on my lips.

The summer sun was beating down on my back, sweat began building under my shirt and dripped down my back. My head tilted backward to meet the sun's rays as I closed my eyes. Abby said she needed to hear the words, and even though my stomach twisted in knots at the thought, I knew she was right.

"You know, I used to think of you like a sunny day."

She scoffed at me. "Used to?"

"Yeah, used to. I always only saw what you wanted me to see, the happiness in you, even when you were sad. But now... you are so much more than just one thing, Lenny. You are captivating and moody and passionate and so perfectly you. I have seen more sides of you since Scotland than I ever let myself imagine, and now that I have the whole picture, I only seem to want more of you."

I didn't look at her, I couldn't, but there was a sharp inhale from her.

"We all have cloudy days, Lenny, and just because you can't always see the Sun doesn't mean that it's not there."

It was quiet except for the cars honking in the distance and the children playing in the summer sun around her neighborhood. I started thinking that maybe it was too much or too real of a sentiment for her. I could be entirely on my own in my feelings, and this was the tipping point where she would tell me and would send me away.

"What if there's more rain and clouds than sun? What if it gets to be too much for you and you drown in my downpour?" she whispered in a shaky voice. "What if I ruin you?" The quiet words tortured parts of my heart, the parts that always belonged to her.

There was no end to the amount of time I would spend waiting for Lennon. Even if it meant waiting for another lifetime entirely. She was worth every second of the constant state of longing I was in. I took her hand in between mine and held it for a moment. My thumb skimmed across the soft flesh before I replied.

"I'm not a fair weather type of man. Whatever comes, I will be right here with you. With an umbrella or a life vest, it doesn't matter because no amount of rain could ever keep me from you," I said, and there would never be words more true than those.

"How do you do that, Theodore?"

"Do what?"

"Make me feel like..." she trailed off, but her eyes searched my face, looking for something.

This should be the moment I told her. Told her everything about why I left or the fact I never stopped caring for her. At the very least, I should have asked her out on an actual date. Before I could form the words, she'd turned back toward the pool. A second passed and her head came to rest on my shoulder. The heat of the sun felt cool in comparison to her body pressed into mine. It seemed unimaginable that there would ever be a time where she didn't set my world on fire, but I welcomed the inferno, even if it meant I'd burn. Nothing else mattered because this moment—here with her—was enough.

TWENTY-ONE

Theo

MY CHAIR TILTED BACK from my desk as I stretched my arms out in front of me. The glow of my computer screen was the only thing illuminating the dark room. I took a day trip to Preston Castle earlier, since the site was only a just under an hour from Fairvale and had returned home well after dinner.

My eyes were bleary, and they burned as I dug my palms into the sockets. The pictures started to morph into shapeless blobs about an hour ago, but I'd been pushing through in order to submit them to Archie for the upcoming deadline. Glancing at the clock, my stomach growled, reminding me I also hadn't eaten in hours.

Pushing away from the desk, I set out to find my keys. It was only eight o'clock, and there was bound to be a taco truck set up in some parking lot close by. It took me about ten minutes to find a spot, and I silently thanked America's need for food at any time of day. The line was about five people deep as I waited to give my order.

My thumb swiped up on my phone as I scrolled through my emails when someone shouted my name. My head popped up, and I scanned the parking lot, looking for the source of the call, when my eyes landed on Abby and a blonde woman walking toward me as she lifted her hand up in a wave.

"What are you doing here, Abby?" I asked as they joined me in line. I gave Abby a quick side hug, while the blonde scanned me from head to toe as a smirk played across her face.

"We just needed to pick up some drinks. It was a long week at work." As she lifted the black bag and pointed to the convenience store.

"It's Wednesday," I said pointedly.

I laughed as she replied, "Exactly." I shook my head, and we moved forward in the line. The blonde cleared her throat and nudged Abby.

"Oh shit, my bad. Theo, this is Carina. Carina, Theo." We shook hands, and a wicked smile stretched across her face.

"Well, good to know what's been getting Lennon all worked up," she stated. Again, her eyes skated across me and twinkled with some unknown secret. I shifted my weight back and forth, waiting for a follow up comment that never came. Abby bumped her with her hip and the two burst out in laughter.

My lips lifted up in a confused smile. "Are you a friend of Lennon's, too?"

She rolled her eyes like it was something I should have known about this complete stranger. Abby answered for her. "Don't mind her attitude. She's like this with everyone. Carina is basically our other sister." Carina's smile softened at Abby's declaration of sisterhood, and a small part of me was happy there were more people in Lennon's life than she led on.

I expected them to head out as I stepped up to the window to give my order, but they lingered to the side, huddled together. My foil wrapped burrito appeared, but before I could tell them goodnight and head to my car, they approached me again. If they were twins, it would be a lot creepier, as they moved in unison as they walked toward me.

Carina spoke first and asked me if I was busy this weekend. Besides my parents and Lennon, there was really no one here I spent time with. The only other people I knew that stayed in this town were the same ones who would make it easy to lapse back into a lifestyle I had no business being a part of. I shook my head no and skeptically let her know I was free. My eyes bounced from Abby's shining face to Carina's mischievous one, waiting for them to let me in on their secret.

"Perfect. The three of us are going out on Friday for my birthday, and I think you should join us." Carina's eyebrows lifted in a way that said this was a demand, not really an invitation. She was about a second away from becoming a movie villain and tapping her fingers together like there was a master plan behind her statement.

"Why does it feel like I can't say 'no'?"

"You can, but you shouldn't," Abby replied and Carina's head bobbed in agreement next to her. If Lennon was the softer side of Abby, then Carina was the wild side. In this small amount of time, they'd worked up some plan, and I'd be lying if I said I wasn't curious. My tongue dragged across the inside of my bottom lip. I didn't have a reason to say no, and it would mean more time with Lennon.

At this point, I'd take any excuse to be close to her.

When I agreed to meet them on Friday, they cracked twin grins. It was super creepy.

Abby said she'd text me the details, but more than likely, they'd be at Liquid Alchemy. Since I moved out of Fairvale at eighteen, I'd never been on the bar scene here, but I knew the name. It was an average town bar—live music, overpriced drinks, and probably dancing. Not my scene, but it was not my birthday. I made my move to start heading back to my car when Carina stopped me. She placed a single finger on my shoulder before I turned away, stopping me from leaving and said "Oh, and Theo? Let's keep this a secret from Lennon, yeah? Think of it as a birthday present of sorts to me." They left me standing in the parking lot as they laughed their way back to their car. I was dumbfounded about what had actually happened.

But I would keep the secret as I was curious about what their motive behind all this was.

By Friday night, I was twitchy. I had seen Lennon for lunch, and she went on about the bar Carina picked, exclaiming they were in their thirties and couldn't party like they used to. "I'm thirty-five, Theo. Which means I'm tired by eight and will have heartburn by nine. I have no business being out in a bar," she rattled off to me, causing me to choke on the water while laughing. None the less, I kept quiet and didn't tell her I had met Carina, let alone that she invited me out to her birthday.

My phone pinged from where I threw it on the bed and Abby's messages flashed on the home screen.

We're heading out now.

Meet us in about forty-five?

It was after eight, so I hopped in the shower to kill time before I needed to head out. The warm water pelted at my back, and I used the time to let my mind wander. As always, all roads led to Lennon. It was summer, and I let my mind conjure what type of outfit she might decide to wear. Bare legs were the only thing I could think of. Would she have her hair pulled up off her shoulders, exposing the long lines of her neck or down in erratic curls, which was a personal fan favorite of mine? Before my mind went too far, I finished up and stepped back into my room. I slipped a pair of black slacks over my legs and a white polo shirt and sneakers. I toweled off the remaining water droplets in my hair and raked through some product to keep my curls in place.

Small towns had their perks, one being it took me only ten minutes to get to the bar. Ten minutes to get anywhere, really. I spent longer looking for a spot to park. The street was alive with people walking in and out of restaurants and a few other drinking spots on this end of Main Street. The other end was usually deserted since it was mainly office buildings. The music blared from each building as I walked by and made my way to Liquid Alchemy.

Standing out front was perhaps the largest man I had ever seen. He blocked the door, checking the ID of every patron before allowing entry. He nodded at me like we were old friends and stepped to the side to let me pass after I presented him with mine. Even though it was dark outside, it was darker in the bar somehow, as my eyes still needed time to adjust when I stepped inside.

The cement flooring stuck to my shoes while the air was already thick with the smell of spilled drinks, sweat, and desperation. Everything was tinged in a red glow as the large dingy chandeliers hung from the ceiling. There was a stage in a corner with the band blaring through the speakers and the bar scaled the length of the other side of the room. The place was packed with people as they leaned on tables or against the walls, talking and laughing, and the dance floor was full of couples who were glued to each other.

Maybe Lennon was onto something. I was feeling very old in the midst of this crowd.

My eyes scanned the room, and like a magnet, my sight landed on her. They were gathered at the far end of the bar, pressed against the wall. The bartender set three small glasses in front of them. Lennon's face pulled into a grimace as the two other girls coaxed her into taking the shot. By the time I reached their spot, their heads all tilted back in unison. Abby and Carina spotted me first as I slid up to the bar next to them.

"Can I get one more round for them, please?" I requested from the bartender. Lennon's eyes flew open at the sound of my voice with a lime still wedged in between her teeth.

Abby slung an arm around my shoulder, or at least tried, but I stood about a foot taller than her, so she'd stretched up on her toes and pulled me down to her height. "Theo, what a coincidence running into you here. Don't you think so, Carina?" These two were trouble as they fell over each other, laughing.

Lennon blinked from where she'd pressed herself further into the wall as her forehead creased. "What are you doing here?" she questioned, eyeing her sister and Carina, who were still gasping for air over their master plan. Her hand drifted up to pull on her necklace, sliding the charm back and forth, waiting for one of us to reply. I'd leave it up to them. Better she knew I was invited, not that I just showed up after she had told me where she was going to be. I had done enough showing up out of nowhere.

Carina decided to speak up first as the bartender slid the next round in front of them. "I invited him, *sorella*. Abby and I ran into him a few days ago." Her voice was tender as she moved to her side. Carina leaned forward and whispered into her ear, leaving me out of the rest of their conversation.

Abby nudged me with her elbow, drawing my attention away from the two women, who had moved on to laughing. She lifted one of the shot glasses for me to take, but I waved her off. "I don't drink hard liquor," I explained and ordered a beer, even though I knew I would take maybe a sip and nurse the bottle for the rest of the night.

"Really, why?"

"Long story, Abby." Just because we kept in semi-contact after I left doesn't mean she had the full truth. That was still a secret that I had been wrestling with. I needed to tell Lennon, but what would she think of me once she knew. But that was for another time.

Lennon's stare was heavy on me as I grabbed the bottle from the counter and turned back around. I leaned in closer to Abby. "You sure it's okay that I'm here? She doesn't look too happy."

She rolled her eyes at me in a way that was clear to anyone that her older sister was her favorite person to imitate. "Lennon likes to think she knows what's best for her and never likes to ask for help. It's time for me to start repaying her for all the times she took care of me." She winked as she threw back the next shot before dragging Carina off to the dance floor. The music moved through my chest as it blared through the bar, my blood seemed to pump along with the beat as we stared at each other for a second longer.

There was a wall around Lennon; she'd been carefully laying brick after brick in front of her in order to keep herself safe. First from her mother, and then from the pain left behind after losing her husband. But when I was with her, the light she was made of would shine through all the layers she had built. It exposed her weak spots and allowed me to peer through the cracks to see her for who she was. It made me want to break down her walls and show her she didn't have to hide.

Her hair was down, a personal favorite of mine, and the neon from the bar signs bounced off her auburn strands in a halo-like fashion. I drank in her appearance like a man dying of thirst. Her red dress was a striking color against her skin and it hugged her curves. It stopped mid thigh, the soft flesh tempting and inviting. I stood there, merely staring at her while tongue-tied and her chest stuttered on her next breath as my eyes burned into her exposed skin.

I stepped forward, pushing the drink forward along the counter. "For you, love." She plucked the glass from the table and brought it to her lips with eyes that bored into mine and beckoned me to come closer. One more step placed me a breath away from her. I placed my free hand on the wall beside her head and leaned in even closer. With the bottle in my hand, I pressed it against the bottom of her shot glass. I tilted it against her lips and let the liquor pool into her mouth. Her throat worked to swallow while her eyes pinched closed to try to stave off the burn before popping back open. Her lips parted, and she used her thumb to wipe away the excess liquid before sliding it in her mouth to get every last drop.

There was no way she didn't know exactly what she was doing to me.

I took a step back to defog my senses. "You look good tonight, Theo." Her breathy voice full of surprise. There was a sudden rush of blood into her cheeks at her boldness, turning them into the most perfect shade of rose. I set my beer on the counter and reached to grab her hand. She pulled back for a fraction of a second before her hand relaxed into mine.

"And you are utterly breathtaking."

I wanted to kiss her, devour her, spill every ounce of my affection into her until she was drowning in me, and only me, for the rest of time. If I could only help her heal her past, I could ruin her for a future man. She tugged me in closer and pressed into me ever so slightly, urging me to follow through with that thought, but her eyes were glassy. When I actually got the courage to act on my desires, I wanted her to be completely present. I wanted there to be no doubt that she wanted it, too.

The moment broke when Abby and Carina returned to drag Lennon out with them. I excused myself to the bathroom for a minute. As I passed by them on the edge of the dance floor, my steps faltered as Lennon swayed her hips and body back and forth to the beat. The movements caused her dress to ride up on her thighs, and I couldn't help but imagine what they would feel like in my hands.

Focus. Bathroom first, then maybe I could get her to dance with me.

By the time I made it back to the main room, there were twice as many people. I scanned the crowd in the middle of the dance floor but didn't see Lennon. The only person I could find was Carina, who was speaking to a man with hair pulled back into a bun at the base of his neck. "Carina," I said, interrupting what looked like a conversation that would either end up with them kissing or fighting—I couldn't quite tell. "Have you seen Lennon? I can't find her."

Her eyebrows lifted as the man she was with introduced himself. "What's up, man, I'm Levi." I shook his hand briefly and Carina scoffed.

"A nuisance is what you are, Decker." She chastised, as she swatted at our hands. "She was still dancing a minute ago. She's around here somewhere." She turned back to her conversation.

One more scan of the room revealed Lennon in the middle of the dance floor. I started to make my way through the crowd of people when I noticed a man come up behind to a spot that should be mine. Lennon froze and shook her head at the guy. He leaned into her ear and whispered something that caused her to jerk backwards. Her head snapped side to side as her eyes danced around wildly until they landed on mine. They softened slightly the second she found me and attempted to walk away before the guy snatched her upper arm to stop her from leaving.

All I saw was red. Pulsing, radiating, blood red. It clouded my vision at the sight of his fingers digging into her.

I shouldered my way through the last remaining people, placing myself between her and the idiot, knocking his hand from her arm. I drew myself to my full height, which alone was usually intimidating. My arm wrapped behind me to keep her close, but out of the way. "You touch her, or any other woman for that matter, like that again, and you'll be leaving here with a broken arm," I barked out, my voice low and dangerous. I had never even been in a fight before, but I was convinced I could snap him like a twig. The guy stalked away without another word.

Lennon's hands scraped down my back as the guy walked away. "Thank you," she breathed out in relief. I took her face in my hands and searched for any sign that we needed to leave.

"Are you okay?" I'd never felt so panicked. Just the thought that she might be hurt, or that someone had their hands on her when she clearly did not ask for it had my blood boiling.

A laugh escaped her that softened the heat in my veins. "I'm fine. He was an ass." She pulled at my shirt to bring me in closer and started moving to the music again. I had completely forgotten we were on the dance floor for a second. She spun, pressing her backside into me, and I had to stifle a groan. My hands found her hips, and I let go of my restraint just a fraction. My head dipped, and placed a brief kiss on her exposed shoulder, and it felt like I had come home.

TWENTY-TWO

Lennon

IT COULD HAVE BEEN two or twenty songs that passed before we stumbled off the dance floor. I couldn't remember the last time I felt this carefree, unafraid of what the people around me were thinking. My brain was in a haze from the liquor and the way Theo's hands found their permanent residence on my body. Abby and Carina were chatting at a table when I collapsed onto the top with my hands, not entirely drunk, but definitely not sober. A slow fire ignited in my lower belly, threatening to engulf my entire body in flames as he drew small figures on the fabric along my hip.

"Having a good time?" Carina crooned at me. I flashed her a dark look and played her game.

"Who was the man you were cozied up with earlier, Carina?" I questioned, then cackled as she tongued her cheek and drew in a quick breath.

My feet started to ache and my dress was getting tighter and tighter with every passing minute, but Carina showed no signs of stopping. "Hey, are you okay if I head out early?" I asked the birthday girl, who was all too willing to send me home.

"As long as Theo drives you home," Carina replied. His hands trailed up from my hips and came down to rest on my shoulders, and I leaned back into him absentmindedly.

"No problem, Carina. I can do that." He grinned at her as he rested his chin on the top of my head. They watched as Theo and I made our way out of the crowded bar and into the night.

The wind whipped around my hair as we pulled into my driveway. I half expected him to watch me disappear into my empty home and half wished he would follow me inside. My hand hovered on the door handle. It wasn't unreasonably late, I bargained with myself and I wanted him to follow me inside.

He didn't give me a chance to open my mouth before he got out of the car and was opening my door. With my hand laced in his, I trailed behind him along the pathway to my front door. I fumbled with my keys, trying to get the lock to work with me. The house was covered in darkness as I crossed the threshold. Only the light of the porch illuminated the area where Theo waited. The light bounced off his skin, painting him in the most beautiful glow.

"Do you want to come inside?" I fumbled over the words as the air caught in my throat. He nodded and brushed past me as he stepped inside. The door clicked shut behind him, sending us back into the dark. We stood there, just shadows, hovering around the mountain of feelings we have been too scared to admit.

His breath skirted across my face, and I ached to reach out for him, to pull him close and make it so this house didn't feel as barren as it was. All it would take was a one simple touch and I could have it. My arm lifted from my side, but before I could get any further, I stumbled in my step. He caught me by the shoulders and the simple touch of his hands sent sparks throughout my body.

He chuckled softly. "Okay, let's get you to bed." Before leading me down the hall. The hazy part of my brain wanted to reply with a suggestive remark, but when his hand reached for my bedroom, I froze.

It was just a room, I wanted to tell myself. No different from every other place in my house, but I had kept this part of me closed off every time he'd visited. It was the only room Camden was still alive in; to bring another man in would be a betrayal.

It was just a room and even when he saw what was behind the door didn't mean it would change anything.

Then the door swung open and I had no more time to dwell on the thought. He pulled me inside and I squinted as the switch was flipped, and the room flooded with light. Gently, he nudged me to the edge of the bed, and I plopped down on my unmade bed. Kneeling in front of me, he slipped my aching feet from the sandals. The haze began to take over, pushing the overwhelming sense of disloyalty to the back of my mind, and I decided to unpack it later.

"What a sight you are on your knees, Theo," I said, pushing his fallen curls back into place. He looked up at me and for a second I remembered what it was like being eighteen and so in love with someone you couldn't stand the thought of ever being without them.

I wondered if it was something you could get back once it was lost.

"Yeah, it's definitely past your bedtime," he retorted as he stood. "Where do you keep your pajamas, love?" He asked, as he started pulling open dresser drawers.

"I told you I was too old to be out," I said through a yawn as my back pressed into my mattress. My blankets were soft, and it took a lot not to curl into them and let sleep take over. Just before I let my eyes close, pajamas landed next to my head. "You're not going to ask me to strip for you, are you?" said my sleep filled brain. He appeared above me, laughing, a smile plastered across his face that caused my heart to stir. The longer he looked at me like that, the more I began to think I might do anything he asked.

"Are you tired?" He questioned me, and while my feet hurt from the amount of time I spent on the dance floor and my body ached, my mind was racing.

"No," I said, with only the tiniest bit of wariness in my voice. He took my hand and hauled my body upright.

"Good. Get changed. We can watch a movie." He left me alone, and I scrambled into the clothes he picked out. I was drowning in my sweats and oversized tee when I entered the living room. Theo reclined on the couch, scanning through the channels for something to watch as I shuffled over. Dragging the blanket off the back, I arranged myself close to his side. There was no point in fighting my attraction, so for the rest of the night, I gave into my urges.

Nothing crazy. I only wanted to be held by him, if only for a little while.

His arm slipped around my shoulders, pulling me deeper into his side. Right before sleep took me, I felt the brief press of his lips on the top of my head. And for the first time, I didn't want to escape to the space that held Camden. I wanted to stay in the moment. I wanted to stay with him.

TWENTY-THREE

Lennon

THE HANGOVER WAS REAL. My feet dragged underneath me as I carried myself into a booth at Wake Up Café. Abby and Carina seemed to be in worse shape than me on the other side of the table. They were both supporting their heads in their hands, dark circles encompassing their eyes with last night's curls barely hanging on in their hair.

"Alright, I'm calling it. We're officially too old for bars," I groaned as the waitress poured much needed coffee for all of us and they nodded in agreement.

We sat in silence and let the grease of our food soak up the remaining alcohol in our systems. Carina seemed to perk up first. She leaned back in the booth, eyeing me from across the table. "How was the rest of your night, Lennon?" She arched a thin eyebrow at me as Abby snickered next to her.

"Yeah, did you have a good night?" The two of them together was like wrangling cats, you get one under control in time to see the other swinging from the ceiling fan.

I tore off another bite of my toast, chewing longer than needed in order to digest it. "It was good." My shoulder lifted to my ear and came back down. It wasn't that I was a private person, these two knew everything about me. I'd trust either one of them with my life, but I couldn't even make sense of the relationship or lack thereof that Theo and I had, and their opinions mattered. I was protective of what Theo and I could be, and letting someone else into the little world we were creating could collapse it before it had time to flourish.

"Did you sleep with him?" Carina questioned as I choked on my food, sputtering as bits of bread flew out of my mouth and onto the table.

"Ew," was all Abby said as I gasped for air and they were both back to laughing.

"I'm not answering that." I could see the follow-up questions in their eyes. They brightened like I gave them a new toy. "That doesn't mean yes," I shot down their hopeful eyes, omission was not an admission, and they both deflated. Carina muttered in Italian. All these years as her friend, and I still had no clue what she said. But I was pretty sure that's why she did it.

"Fine." She said the word, but the three of us knew this was not the end of the conversation.

By the time we were done eating, my headache had subsided, and the only reminder I had of the night before was sore muscles.

We went our separate ways in the parking lot, and I could almost hear my couch calling my name. I needed to do nothing for exactly twenty-four hours in order to fully recover. My phone buzzed, I dug through my purse for my keys, and Theo's name popped up in the notifications and my heart fluttered.

How's your head, love

Better now that there are eggs and bacon in my system

Ahh, the world's best hangover cure… grease. What are you up to today, I was going to see if you wanted to go to the river later?

Come by around 5?

I'll be there

Fairvale was vastly unappreciated by me. I'd spent my life in this town and forgot that I was surrounded by landscapes that people paid to have paintings of. There were trees of all kinds that went on for as far as you could see as the river cut through the edge of town.

As a kid, I would ride my bike along the trail that followed Orange Grove River to escape my home, even if it was only for a few hours. I'd pedal as fast as I could, letting the wind blow away the tears that usually sparked my ride.

Thinking about it caused a burn in the back of my throat. It didn't matter the amount of therapy I'd gone through, nothing would erase the sting of rejection from your own parent, and I was certain that I would carry it forever.

Adult me understood that we were all just people, regardless of the titles we held—mother, father, sister, friend. We are all human, and for some of us, when life isn't kind, we take it out on those closest to us.

I understood it, I'd felt it. I could see that my mother had endured some unknown pain and could understand why she was the way she was. But underneath my grown-up exterior, there was still the little girl version of me that struggled with forgiveness, and carried resentment for the life I had to claw my way out of. The older sister in me would never understand how she could look at Abby and not want to be the best version of herself for her, for us.

Losing Abby and I should have been her rock bottom, but she continued to spiral until even the smallest interactions with her became too much of a burden. Abby and I went full no contact with her not long after Theo left. I couldn't bear to watch her slowly kill herself, and I needed to put myself first.

There were some days where I wished it were different, days where I longed for a mother that loved and cared for me, but I know that would never be possible. Not while she stayed on the path that she was on. She still lives in town and every once in a while we cross paths, but it was like walking by a stranger. She let her addiction rule her life, and I was forced to live a life that didn't include her.

My knees shook as I waited on my porch steps as the sun was began its descent into the horizon. The flutters returned to my stomach as Theo's car pulled up to my house, and I was beginning to think that they were going to make my stomach their permanent home. I bounced off the steps to meet him on the sidewalk, and we started our walk down the block to access the Orange Grove River trail.

We wound our way through the pathway as it cut through the grass, my hand trailing along the tips of the dry, overgrown weeds. We didn't speak until we reached the river's edge. A wave of nostalgia struck me as the water gently lapped over the rocky shore.

"Thank you for coming to get me." My breath came out as a smoke puff above us as we laid in the bed of his truck. "I couldn't breathe in that house any longer." Abby was at a friend's house when our mom stumbled into the house, drunk before the sun had even gone down.

I tried to make it to my room without her seeing me, but I wasn't fast enough before she started shouting about how I ruined her life. I lasted a few hours before calling Theo to come get me and take me anywhere.

Anywhere that wasn't home, which is how we ended up down by the river in the middle of the night.

The plastic of the truck bed dug into my back as we gazed at the stars above us. We didn't speak. We laid side by side under the stars with our hands clasped together so tight that my fingertips started to go numb. He didn't ask what was wrong, he didn't try to offer comforting words. He held my hand, and it was exactly what I needed.

"You know I'd do anything for you, right?" He whispered without looking at me, causing my next breath to stay in my chest. "I love

you and whenever you need somebody, I'll be there for you." His voice trembled over the words, but he spoke with such conviction it left no room for me to doubt him. "I will always be here." He finished with and squeezed my hand.

Our heads turned to meet each other's gaze. The only thing that illuminated the night was a sliver of the autumn moon and the dusting of equinox constellations. None of that mattered though, because even in total darkness, he would be the only thing I would need. I thought I was out of tears to cry tonight, but the way they slipped from the corners of my eyes and ran down my cheeks proved me wrong.

"You love me," I said it as more of a statement than a question.

"I love you," he repeated. I reached up to push the fallen curls out of his eyes and scanned his face for anything that told me he might have been lying, but there was nothing but pure adoration.

"And you would do anything for me?" I don't know why I was asking. I think I just wanted to hear him say it again. He reached up and cupped my cheek. "Anything for you."

This was the first time anyone had told me they loved me, and the weight of the words settled deep into my soul. It no longer mattered that I was screamed at for simply existing in a world I had no choice but to be in because he loved me.

"I love you, too."

Theo never wavered in his love for me back then, which was why it never made sense for him to just up and leave. I was hesitant to ask him, fearing that his answer would be as simple as him losing interest in whatever he loved about me.

"Do you remember the time you brought me here to look at the stars?"

"I do," he answered.

He sensed that I had more to say because he didn't speak, didn't push. He waited and listened.

Somehow, he always knew what I needed.

"When Camden and I began looking for a house to buy, I knew I wanted to stay in Fairvale, and I wanted to get as close to the water as possible. Our house came up for sale out of nowhere. It was perfect. The second they placed the keys in my hand, I saw it, our whole lives played like a movie in my head. We'd build a life together in that house, and every night we'd walk by the river as we grew old together."

My head tilted back to soak up the last of the sun's rays and I let out a shaky breath. "I don't get to see him gray and old, and that will haunt me for the rest of my life. But I still have the river, and now that you're back, I have you again." I turned to Theo, and for once, it felt like I finally got to talk about Camden and not have someone's eyes fill with sorrow when they looked at me. Finally, my heart wasn't being ripped apart at even the feel of his name on my tongue.

The hurt was still there, but it wasn't exposing itself to me in a fit of rage, demanding I feel every ounce of pain it held. It was softer somehow, like a dull constant ache in the base of my heart. I had a sense of security from being close to Theo, and I knew I could pour my heart's secrets out to him because, with him, they would always be safe. I would never have to worry about being judged or that I'd be treated like my pain isn't still raw.

Our eyes held, and my pulse quickened because he looked at me like Camden did. He looked at me like I was the answer to all of life's questions and he would spend the rest of his life asking them. I'd been saying that it was the universe or fate that brought us together, but maybe it wasn't either one of those at all. Maybe heaven was real, and Theo was sent to me by the only other man that ever held my heart.

I didn't know what this was between us, or what to call it, but I could be okay with it.

TWENTY-FOUR

Lennon

THERE WAS A HEAVY weight settling inside of me, causing my chest to cave in on me. My heart hurt, plain and simple.

I missed Camden.

Even worse, I had been missing him less and less the more time I had been spending with Theo. And I didn't know what to do with this new revelation. If there was a way to see the future and know how this all ends up, I would gladly accept whatever the consequence would be.

Could I be with Theo and still be able to keep space for Camden, and was that even fair to ask?

Theo made me feel again, and I couldn't imagine going back to how I was before he reappeared in my life. Every day, Theo showed up and was present in my life, and it was his consistency that had me falling for him all over again.

For two years, I'd shut myself away, afraid to be a part of anything because there was always a chance it would fail. Or that there would be some unexpected event that would turn me on my head again, and I wasn't willing to risk my time or my heart. But slowly I had been able to come out of the shell I closed myself in, and I have him to thank.

Even with no one around, there was a heavy sigh that left me. Yes, I missed Camden, but today, I was missing Theo, too. The only difference was I had the chance to see Theo. It hurt to acknowledge this new reality, but I was hoping that, for once, I could have what I wanted without getting hurt in the end.

A knock echoed through my house. I wasn't expecting anyone today and if it was Abby, she would have already been halfway through the house by now. Reluctantly, I moved from my couch. When I pulled open the door Theo was standing on my porch, as if I'd conjured him from my thoughts alone. The heaviness I was carrying in my chest moments before lessened. The heat here had been in full swing, and even though it was only eleven in the morning, it was about ninety degrees and dry as a bone outside.

His skin glistened where there was already a thin layer of sweat forming from the brief moments he had been outside. It shouldn't have been attractive, but my brain had gone a bit fuzzy at the sight of him. His hair was slicked back slightly, like he just stepped out of the shower and he had the top few buttons of his shirt open. It was his smile that held my gaze, though. It was brighter than the sun and directed straight at me. It took me a moment to come back to the present.

"I brought you something," he began, and I was finding it hard to form a thought. I let him inside, so maybe he'd stop sweating and I could start thinking. He pulled me briefly into a hug, and I breathed in his scent deeply; it'd been so many years, and yet it'd never changed.

I hoped it never would.

He set a bag down onto the counter and fished out whatever it was he said he brought, but I was so distracted. I took a moment to let my eyes roam over him. Everything about him seemed to do something to me. The way his skin looked in the sun or how he wore his shirts a touch too tight, so it strained around his biceps and chest when he moved. My mind started drifting to another place as I thought about what was hidden underneath all his clothes.

I shouldn't be standing here ogling him, but yet it seemed to be my new favorite pastime. Then I saw the stack of books he was pulling out. My eyes skimmed across the titles, and then it clicked.

"Hey, I had these on hold at Nevermore." He placed them in my hands, and I started rifling through them. I didn't remember telling him I had an order or that I sometimes have books on hold there.

His laugh filled the room, and I shut my eyes, for a second, to let the sound sink into my skin. It was like a tiny piece of heaven moving through me. I must have had them shut for a touch too long because I didn't notice him move closer or that he'd reached out until his hand trailed across my cheek. "I was at Nevermore just looking around when Mrs. Andrews mentioned you had an order, so I thought I would save you the trip."

It was a normal sentence, but it had goosebumps pricking up along my skin despite the rising heat outside. Cared for—that was the part I had been missing since Camden died. That there was not only someone thinking of me and my simple needs, but that they were also willing to take the time to help me.

My bottom lip tucked inwards and I chewed on the soft skin as my brain chanted, 'don't cry, don't cry, don't cry.' The ache that formed in my throat was overwhelming, and I struggled to clear it. "Camden used to pick my books up for me." My eyes lifted to meet his gaze, and his face held a soft look. "Mrs. Andrews told me," he said as he reached out again, but this time tucked a piece of hair behind my ear. He let his hand trail down the lock. He fiddled with the ends, rolling them into between his fingers.

"It's silly, but I didn't realize how much I missed having someone help with my errands." I gave him a soft smile as he dropped the strands from his fingers.

"Is it okay? I don't ever want to overstep or anything." Even though he was doing something nice for me, he was worried about my perception of his actions. I was finding there were more and more reasons to fall, and his thoughtfulness had me gone for him. He was still close, much too close, but I couldn't find it in me to move away. I tilted my head back slightly, so his face was in my full line of view.

"Yeah, Theo. It's more than okay."

Over time, you forget the little details of a person you once thought you'd never live without. Like the way his green eyes held specks of gold that reminded me of emeralds in the sun. Or how his pillowy bottom lip beckoned me in with whispers of unspoken secrets waiting to be told. But my favorite was the small smattering of freckles along his nose that matched mine. So light that unless you were as close as I was now, you'd never know they existed.

But I knew, and I didn't ever want to forget again.

Bravery was not a trait I would normally assign myself, but right now, I could take on the world single-handedly. I reached my hand up and trailed it down his arm and laced my fingers into his. His breathing picked up slightly, and I could see the rise and fall of his chest with how close I was as I swiped my thumb along the inside of his wrist.

It would take one simple muscle movement, a quick press up onto my toes and I could kiss him. The want was there. It coursed through every fiber of my body and set off a ringing in my ears. I could do it, and I wanted to, but I didn't. I let that fantasy remain in my head.

"Thank you," I said, and my hand gave a gentle squeeze. I inhaled deeply as he pulled my hand up towards his mouth, and so lightly, that if my full attention wasn't on him, I wouldn't have noticed and placed a quick kiss to my knuckles.

"Anything for you, Lenny," he replied before my hand fell back down by my side.

Every part of me was alive. There was electricity surging through me, and I couldn't seem to figure out what to do with it, but my brain seemed to be working again because, without deciding, I took a step back and broke the moment.

I took the books and placed them on my shelf in the living room. Theo trailed behind me, and over to the couch, where he plopped down into the soft cushions. There was a chiming of bells and Anakin jumped up onto Theo's lap, purring loud enough for me to hear. He stroked his fur as he sprawled out, and it hit me like a truck in traffic—I liked seeing him here, in my home. Not only that, I liked how relaxed he was when he was here.

He looked up from his spot and caught me staring. "Are you free two Saturdays from now?" he said without breaking eye contact, but there was a small smile on his lips. He was well aware that I did nothing on the weekends, that I filled my days with endless amounts of junk TV that I'd also been able to sucker him into.

Regardless that I already knew I didn't have plans, I pulled out my phone to check my blank calendar. I didn't know what he was about to ask, but I was trying not to seem too eager. I waited in anticipation after confirming that I had nothing scheduled.

He seemed nervous as he shifted back and forth on the couch. It was projecting back onto me, and my head was swirling with worst-case scenarios about what he was about to tell me. Was he leaving and wanted a ride to the airport in two weeks? Was there some deadline he'd given himself on the time he spent with me, and in two weeks was the last we would see each other?

My brain never granted me a moment of peace. There were more days than I could count where I spent my time in crippling doubt and anxiety over simple phrases. The thoughts started small in the back of my mind until they were the loudest ones I had and impossible to ignore.

In the months after Camden's death, they were the only thing I could hear; they burrowed in and snaked around my mind, cutting off any glimmer of positivity I was able to muster at the time. I was grateful they never won, therapy helped immensely and over the years, I'd been able to cut short the spiraling, but it didn't mean I still didn't have a lapse in progress.

I reeled myself back in and listened to Theo explain the gallery his employer was putting together for the special edition of the magazine and the photos he shot while on our trip. "I was hoping that you would like to be my date to the event, Lenny." My heart leapt into my throat.

Did I hear him right? Did he ask me on a date or to be his date? I wasn't even sure there was a difference, but either way, yes, the answer was yes. With the number of butterflies currently stirring in my stomach, I was surprised I hadn't taken flight.

My face must not have been expressing an answer he was hoping for, because he was quickly backpedaling. "Only if you want to, of course. I thought since you were there with me, it would be fun for you to see it to the end—party included." His brows were pulling together, leaving a deep line in between them, and it was taking every bit of strength in me to not reach out and smooth it away. Then he went and pulled his bottom lip in between his teeth briefly and suddenly my knees were jelly.

A date.

He'd asked me to be his date, and he was nervous about my answer. It was so endearing and comforting that I didn't notice that I was probably taking too long to answer. "Yes. I'd love to," I said, as I thumbed the edge of the book that was still in my hands, but the way he was smiling at me was enough to cause my body to break out in a sweat.

He didn't stay long, and suddenly, I was alone. Normally, this was the part where dread started to set in, when there was no one to distract me from the emptiness that was my home.

However, the air was lighter around me, there were no dark clouds, and the intrusive thoughts that tended to linger in the back of my mind seemed to have vanished completely.

TWENTY-FIVE

Lennon

Late Summer would always be my favorite time of year. Days would bleed into slow nights, and the heat would wrap around your body long after the sun sunk below the horizon. I loved being able to stay outside until the stars were dancing and with only the soundtrack of leaves rustling in the slight breeze.

Tonight was no different, as I stretched my body out on a deck chair and looked up at the sky. The pink and orange sunset was finally starting to fade into the deep blue of early night. The moon was full in the sky, with more stars appearing every time I blinked.

For hours, Camden and I would lie out here during the warm months. Some days we'd sit in silence, and I would listen to his soft snores that would inevitably come. Other nights, we would share a lounger and I would wind myself around him as we talked about what we wanted, from each other or from life in general. It was in these chairs we decided to elope rather than a large wedding, that we loved kids, but they weren't for us. We planned vacations and birthdays in these chairs. We fought and loved each other in these chairs.

The first night I was alone after he died, I laid in bed for hours while silent tears streamed out the corners of my eyes until I couldn't stand the sight of the empty spot next to me. At some point, my feet carried me out to the backyard and into one of these chairs. Frozen in the harsh November night, I sat for hours and stayed until the sun began to peek up above the top of our house. Out of all the places in the world, this was where I felt closest to him, in these thrifted pool side loungers.

My head tilted back onto the chair when the wind picked up and blew warm air around me. If signs from heaven were a real thing, the warmth that was surrounding me would be from Camden. My hands itched to feel him again, to have his arms wrapped around me, and to be reminded that he loved me and that I loved him. But when my eyes drift closed, the image of Camden was only a flash, and my vision was filled with the sight of Theo. Guilt set in quickly.

I've been holding myself together for so long that when my knees pulled up towards my chest, I wrapped my arms around them without a second thought. I used to talk to Camden after he died, but I grew restless with the one-sided conversation, and in a fit of rage over his death, I stopped altogether.

The wind beckoned me to rethink my ban. My head tipped back towards the sky and, with a voice so quiet, I begged for forgiveness. "If loving you was enough to bring you back, you would be here now, but it's not, and I need more." The tears were hot on my face as they spilled over my waterline.

I was a second away from feeling silly when the wind picked up and rushed around me. The leaves shook on their limbs while a few flurried to the ground. A slow smile spread across my face. I whispered, "I love you too," and went inside.

The next morning, I called Abby in a panic. She barely answered my call and said hello before I was word vomiting all over the place.

"Theo asked me out on a date, and it's to a gallery opening, and I have no idea what people wear to a gallery opening and help me, please." I sucked in a large breath at the end of my very jumbled sentence and waited for her response.

"Wait, what?"

"There is a gallery party for the photos Theo took in Scotland and for the magazine. He asked me to go with him as his date, and I am freaking out." This was an understatement, as I was one bad outfit away from burning my whole house down in frustration.

"He's asked you on a date. Like a real date?"

"Really, Abby? That's what you're choosing to focus on? I don't know what to wear. That is the emergency here." My room was so destroyed that FEMA would need to set up camp in order to help me find anything. She let out a loud sigh before agreeing to go shopping with me.

Within hours, we'd been to about a dozen stores, but I was hopeful about the choices I made. I still had no idea what people wore to a photo gallery party, but in reality, I was dressing for one person and one person only.

Abby was lounging on my bed again as I tried on the options that I came home with. I turned to Abby and flapped my arms out to my side after checking my reflection in the mirror. "Well, I think this is the one." The satin dress fell below my knee on one side, while the other side's hem hit my mid-thigh. It hugged my hips and stomach in a way that made me feel desirable instead of my normal, insecure state. The delicate straps tied at my shoulders, and the fabric dipped in the back, exposing my skin in a show-stopping display.

"So, are you guys staying in the same hotel room while you're there?" I stopped adjusting the dress and turned towards her with wide eyes. She looked back at me, waiting for an answer that wasn't coming. "It's in the Bay Area and it's a party. You're not going to drive three hours back home that late. I assumed you would get a hotel," she continued.

"That never crossed my mind. I have no idea." Why couldn't I think of what Theo was telling me about the party? Did he say we're staying? If we were staying, was he assuming we'd stay together? If we did, was that something I was even ready for? The amount of questions I had made my head spin.

"I can tell by the look on your face you two haven't discussed it yet," she snickered.

My body heat began to rise, and I was suddenly feeling like a sack of lumpy potatoes in this dress compared to the goddess I was two minutes ago. "I haven't been with anyone since Camden died," I blurted out.

She eyed me from the bed. "Well, duh, I think I'd know if you were dating someone, Lennon."

"No, Abby. I haven't even *been* with anyone since he died." I bobbed my head along with the cadence of my voice, trying to get her to catch my drift. Once her eyes widened, I knew she understood.

"Lennon!"

"Abigail!"

"It's been over two years and you haven't had sex! How are you functioning?"

I nearly toppled over with how fast I turned to look at her, my eyes widening as I shot her an exasperated, "What?!" She had to be kidding me. "Oh, of course, how could I forget, my bright and shiny personality has me drawing in the prospects. Where would I have found the time to meet someone for that, Abby? Be serious."

She snickered from her place on the bed. I whipped around to face her. "Oh no. Abby, what if I'm bad? Like, what if I've forgotten how to do it?" This only caused her to laugh harder. She fell to the side and into my thick comforter, clutching her chest as her feet kicked back and forth.

"It's not funny," I whined. "Oh god, I'm going to scare him off before we even start." My stomach turned. Abby might find this funny, but I had actual fears floating through my mind.

My throat bobbed as I tried to swallow around my dry throat. "Are you nervous?" she asked me. I threw my hands up and moved towards my bathroom. I needed to get out of the dress.

"I wasn't until now, Abby." I shut the door harder than needed. I ripped the dress off over my head and slid into the comfiest pair of sweats and oversized t-shirt I had.

I re-entered my room and joined Abby on my bed. We laid side by side, staring up at the ceiling. I blew air out in a huff and turned my head towards her. "What if this is a mistake? I like what I have with Theo right now. It's easy and comfortable. I don't want to mess it up." There was a part of me that was aching to self-sabotage in order to keep things the way they were.

If nothing changed, I couldn't get hurt, right?

"I can't answer that for you, but what's the worst that can happen? Take the risk, Lennon. I promise it will be worth it."

What was the worst that could happen? *He could die*, I wanted to scream out. He could die, and I would be left alone... again. My heart could not take another crack in its foundation, any more than the one it already supported would cause it to crumble away completely, leaving a gaping hole that I would never recover from.

What I wouldn't give to be a risk taker, to be the type of person to jump in headfirst, with no regard for how far the bottom was or if it was a safe place to land. The fear of the unknown would always hold me back in some way, but maybe Theo would be the one to jump first and encourage me to follow.

When Abby decided to leave, I was still facing the ceiling, contemplating the weight of my decisions. I could choose to stand still and let life pass me by while I only grasped at tiny moments of happiness. But what good would that do me when what started this all was my desire to move forward?

With a deep inhale, I rose from bed and headed to my dresser; with shaking hands, I removed his wedding ring. There was an indent in my finger where the ring sat, and I missed the weight of the gold immediately. With tears in my eyes, I slipped it into the far corner of my jewelry box, where my wedding band sat and closed the lid.

Twenty-Six

Theo

I MIGHT HAVE A bad habit of speaking before I think things through—although, the last time I did it, it worked out great. This time might be a bit different, though. When Lennon agreed to be my date for the gallery party, my brain went blank besides the sounds of crowds cheering in my head. What I didn't put any thought into was the logistics of the party, its hours outside Fairvale, and Archie had already set me up with a hotel for the night. I'd been kicking myself over my lack of attention to detail and was anxious about what to tell her.

My only problem was the hotel was booked full for that night, and there were no other rooms for me to book for her, and we left tomorrow.

If she wasn't comfortable staying, I'd drive home that night, no problem. All I wanted was for us to go at whatever pace she was comfortable with, and something told me staying in the same room on our official first date might not be her ideal plan. Scotland was different. We might have spent every day together, but we always had our own hotel rooms. Even in the cottage, we might have shared the house, but we were always separated at night. But all my worrying seemed to be for nothing after I explained to Lennon the issue.

"You understand that there's just one room, right? For both of us to share." Good, Theo, be as clear as possible, limit any possibility of confusion.

"Umm, yeah. That's fine, it's just one night. Unless you have an issue with it," she replied. Me have an issue with not only being able to have her on my arm for the party but that I get an entire night to be close to her? I didn't think I could find it in me to refuse the situation, even if it was the right thing to do.

I cleared my throat. "As long as you're okay with it," I said.

"Theo, it's fine, I promise." With that, a grin spread across my face that I had no desire to change. Since the party was for my work exclusively, I came down the day before to oversee the setup and Lennon would arrive the next day on her own. Not how I hoped it would be, but I was still grateful she was choosing to come at all.

We were about two hours away from the exhibition starting, and Lennon texted that she was walking into the hotel. I raced to the elevator and tapped my feet impatiently while I waited for the cart to hit the ground floor. The doors opened with a ding, and I stepped out, scanning the room for any sign of her. She was passing through the revolving doors when I saw her. She had her dress slung over her arm and was tugging up a bag strap up over her shoulder. Before she saw me coming, I was by her side, taking the bag from her before it got caught in the merry-go-round doors, and it pulled her in for another spin. She looked up as she stumbled to confirm I was not a thief and offered a bright greeting and slung her dress into my other open hand with a thanks.

She looked me up and down as her brows creased together. "You're already... ready. I'm not late, right?" Her eyes gave me another once over that had me pulling at the bottom of my suit jacket and looking down at my loafer clad feet. I wore my normal attire to these types of parties, black on black on black, so I blended into the background of wherever I was with the hope of slipping out early.

"I have a few more things to do before it starts, so I got ready early." We walked toward the elevator and stood in comfortable silence on the ride up. Taking the lead as we walked down the hall, we stopped in front of the room. I twisted my body towards her and offered my hip. "My hands are full. Can you grab the room key?" She hummed out a response, and her hand snake into my pocket, while she let her fingers trail firmly along my leg until she reached the plastic card.

I felt like a fucking fifteen-year-old schoolboy whose girlfriend just touched him for the first time. I cleared my throat and awkwardly shifted my body away from her, but I saw a smirk cross her face before she walked into the room. There was a laugh that escaped Lennon as I followed her inside. My head whipped over to her, and I immediately scrambled over my words. "We don't have to stay here. We can drive back home tonight if you're not up to this."

I was an idiot. What was I thinking? I knew what I was thinking, actually, and I was an idiot for it.

She rolled her eyes at me and walked over to the bed closest to the window and climbed onto it to sit in a crisscross fashion; the sun had begun to set and was splashing rose colored light into the room. It draped her in a soft glow that I couldn't take my eyes off of. I'd rather skip the party altogether and stay here with her. It didn't matter if we sat in silence for the rest of the night, it would still end up being one of the best night of my life.

"I'm serious, Len. If this is too much, we can go." She barked out another laugh. She was fresh faced and barefoot. I could die right now and I would have no issue with this being my last sight.

"It's fine. Honestly, I was half expecting to walk into a room with one bed is all." She said it so nonchalantly, but my blood had suddenly caught on fire.

She thought there was going to be one bed in a room that we were sharing and came, anyway. I pocketed this information for now. If I thought about it any longer, I would lose all sense of decorum. "So, I'll leave you to..." I cleared my throat again as I started to back out of the room, "get ready, and I'll meet you in the lobby at seven." The last thing I saw before closing the door was a shit-eating grin plastered across Lennon's face.

The two hours flew by, apparently the crew that was hired to install the photos was short a few people, so just before seven, I found myself on the top step of a ladder stringing wire from a ceiling and into a poster-sized photo. There was sweat gathering around my hairline, being this close to the photo lights, and I was slowly losing my cool trying to get these pictures to hang the way I wanted.

Finally, the last wire was threaded, and I jumped off the ladder for someone to take away. I shook my head as Archie approached me from across the room. His shorter stature was clothed in a vibrant explosion of color and patterns, with a crisp white shirt peeking out from beneath his jacket. "Ah, Theo, just like the old days. You do all the work, and I get to walk around looking like I didn't just run a marathon," he said as he stopped in front of me. He looked around the wide space, nodding in appreciation of the work that had been put into the space.

The gallery we rented was situated next to the hotel we were all staying at. It had a large brick-covered front with glass bay windows that caught the morning light and was still as charming in the dark night. Light hardwood floors covered the space through the multiple rooms, and like most galleries, the walls were stark white. The first room through the front doors was lined with photos from our first week, castles of all varieties sat on the wall, waiting for the people to come and see the secrets I attempted to capture.

My favorite was the back room where the installation pieces were. I was able to talk Archie into it, and I didn't know if it was because he thought it was a good idea or that he had a soft spot for me. It was the last room you could walk through, and as soon as you went to the threshold, there were photos hanging from every height throughout the room that had been blown up in assorted sizes.

The deep greens and grays of the landscapes filled your eyes, making the room seem less like a sterile hospital and more like you could walk right into the photograph. Normally, the magazine was strictly the architecture and landscapes of the estates, but I was given the freedom to stage this room.

What better way to fill a space than to fill it with my favorite view?

Pictures of Lennon from different aspects while on our trip hung from the ceiling like my thoughts being plastered across the room for everyone to see. In one, she was only a speck of a person lost in a sea of rolling green grass while Kilchurn Castle looked out over Loch Awe. In another, her profile was the main focus as the mist and the fog surrounded and enveloped her on the steps of Midhope Castle. Each photo was like a glimpse inside of my head. I only hoped she could see the version of her I saw.

A woman who was resilient, captivating, and worth all the love I was desperate to give her.

I left the room and went to wait by the elevator doors; I paced the length and waited for her to come down. At exactly seven, the doors dinged and slid open, and everything went into a standstill as Lennon stepped out and moved towards me.

The clicking of her heels echoed around us as I dragged my gaze from her face down her body. The black dress she was in was some type of shiny material that looked like water as it moved with her, with thin straps that showed off her shoulders and chest.

She gathered her hair at the nape of her neck, with curls threatening to spill out of the pins. I swallowed thickly as my hands itched to let them free, to rake my hands through her hair and pull her into me.

She stopped in front of me, a sheepish smile slowly stretched across her painted lips. I blinked once, then again.

Think, Theo, think.

"You are beautiful, Lennon." She was radiant, and in her presence, I was left utterly defenseless and speechless.

When I offered her my hand, she slid hers into mine without a second thought and interlocked our fingers. "You ready?" I asked, and she nodded for me to lead her towards the party. There was a warmth spreading throughout my body from where we were joined, and suddenly, the world started spinning again.

Being with Lennon was a feeling that I would never get past. It was like slipping into my favorite sweater that had been misplaced for so long. That initial excitement you have once you've found it and relief that washes over you when you realize it's exactly how you remember.

I took a leap of faith and ducked my head down to place a gentle kiss where her ear and jaw met. Her lashes fluttered briefly.

We walked next door and her hand stayed clasped in mine as I absentmindedly rubbed my thumb along the back of her hand. Two or three passes over her hand and my brain registered that where I should have felt the cool metal of her wedding ring, there was nothing. A quick look down confirmed her finger was bare, and I didn't quite know what to make of it, but she offered me another small smile as an answer.

I opened the door to the gallery and moved my hand to her low back and guided her in. Her mouth parted slightly as an "oh," escaped her. "Theo, look at this. This is beautiful." We were barely in the building when she let go of my hand to go to the photo in the middle of the room. She examined the photos, her head cocked to the side in thought, and I knew I could watch her like this forever.

I led her around the front room. We stopped at each photo and made small talk with the guests that were mingling around. Archie appeared from one of the back rooms, and I pulled Lennon to meet him.

"Lennon, this is Archie, my boss for all paperwork appearances. Archie, this is Lennon."

He took her hand in his. "The famous Lennon? Well, it makes sense why you'd cross the ocean to be near her. You'd be stupid not to." My eyes pinched close at his confession of mine. Lennon bit back a grin, and when he dropped her hand, it found mine again. I was back in a haze from the closeness of us. For months, this was all I had been thinking about, and now, I couldn't even focus long enough to enjoy it.

I couldn't tell you what Archie was saying to her, but she threw her head back in laughter and clutched me tighter while leaning into my arm, and everything was in slow motion... again. I really should get this checked out. Whatever he was saying, I would pay an exorbitant fee to have him do it again and again. Anything to keep her like this, because having her on my arm felt like home.

We finally left Archie and slowly walked through the front rooms. She studied each one as if she wasn't at the exact place with me in real life. A couple of hours passed, and I led her in the direction of the last room. "One more to go," I leaned down and said by her ear, and a shiver moved through her body as my breath hit her neck.

Stepping into the last room, Lennon didn't speak, and I was suddenly watching everything go down in flames. A minute passed and still nothing, and I was beginning to think I had definitely fucked this up, but then I moved around to her front and looked at her. There were tears brimming along her waterline as she looked back at me with wide eyes. "They're all of me." It was my turn for silence.

We were walking a ship's plank and we could either both jump or one of us was going down alone.

"Don't you know?" I moved a piece of her hair off her forehead and let my finger trail down the side of her face and under her jaw. With my finger, I tilted her head up slightly, so her eyes were back on me. "You have been and will always be everything to me. So yes, they are all of you. I would spend forever behind the lens as long as you were on the other side." My truth had me jumping off a cliff into the vast unknown. I wanted her to jump with me so we could fall into the next chapter of our lives together. She sucked in a breath but said nothing, and suddenly I was on my own. But as long as she knew, the jump didn't seem as daunting.

Then she joined me in a free fall.

She lifted up onto her toes and crashed her lips into mine. It wasn't a kiss filled with trepidation. It was passion in its purest form, almost frantic. My hand moved through her hair to the back of her neck, and I pulled her closer, my mouth parting when her tongue traced the seam of my lips as she molded her body against mine.

It didn't matter that we were in the middle of an open room or that there were still people mingling around. I kissed her with seventeen years' worth of unspoken words. Every moment I had of longing and remembrance was poured into her in this one moment. It all melted away, every doubt and worry I had that she might not return my affections, and was replaced with unyielding devotion. Her hands dragged across the front of my stomach and around to my back as she clutched on to me. A groaned stuck in the back of my throat when she broke the connection. We were left intoxicated by the intensity of the moment.

Her chest was heaving, and I was no better off. Her cheeks were flushed a dark pink and her lips reddened by my mouth. Even her hair was falling from her pins like I had imagined earlier. "Do you want to go back to the room?" she asked, barely above a whisper, as she tucked her bottom lip in between her teeth.

"Okay," was the only word I managed to get out before she led the way out the front door.

TWENTY-SEVEN

Lennon

THERE WAS COMPLETE SILENCE in my brain the moment his lips touched mine, and it was overwhelming. The only thought that forced its way through was how familiar this was and that I didn't want to stop. The elevator dinged shut, and gravity pulled us together again. We were all hands and tongues, pulling and grasping. My body flushed with heat and electricity surged through my veins, causing a whimper to escape me, but Theo's mouth was on me again and swallowed the sound with a groan of his own.

We broke apart briefly to dash down the hallway. I trailed behind him into the room with my hand still clasped in his. He turned back around and pulled me against him. The air in my chest came out as a small gasp with his name attached to it as I hit the hard planes of his body.

He planted hungry kisses along my jaw and down my neck until he reached the base of my throat, where he placed another kiss and then slowly dragged his nose back up my skin. His breathing was labored, and I was feeling everything and nothing at the same time. My senses have gone into overload and I never wanted it to stop.

Then my knees hit the bed as he walked me backwards, causing my eyes to fly open.

What was I doing? Did I want this? *Yes*, my brain screamed at me while my heart wept. Camden flashed through my mind, and my stomach lurched.

"Theo, I umm..." I stuttered. He pulled back and roamed over my face. Whatever he saw, it was enough to douse the fire that was in his eyes mere seconds ago. He cupped both sides of my face, his thumbs rubbing small circles in the hallows of my cheeks.

"What is it?"

"I don't know if I'm ready." I gulped down my embarrassment. "For that," I said as I nodded my head back towards the bed. He pulled me in for a final lingering kiss and added a peck in for good measure.

"Let's get ready for bed," he said as he released me from his arms, and I was suddenly rethinking my decision, even if I knew it was for the best.

The coolness of the water from my shower did nothing to quench the heat that was coursing through me. I took my time drying off, dragging the towel down each limb, acutely aware that the only thing separating Theo and me was a door. Pulling my pajamas from my bag, I realized how unprepared I was, as I only brought sweats and an oversized shirt to sleep in.

Barefoot, I padded out of the bathroom and saw Theo was already under the covers of his own bed. A tight black t-shirt stretched across his chest and I found it hard for me to skip past him to my own bed.

But I did it.

The sheets were cool and buttery soft as my legs slid under the covers. I wrestled with the sheets as I searched for comfort, but with Theo mere feet away, it proved hard to find. I wanted to give in, but the moment Camden appeared like an apparition, a thought cropped up in the back of my mind.

He left you once, it said. If you could do something once, it only made it easier to do again.

We remained silent until I couldn't hold back any longer.

"Can I ask you something?"

His eyebrows rose up. "Ahh, every man's favorite sentence." I snorted at his attempt at humor. "Go for it, Lenny."

I contemplated telling him nevermind but there was a nagging voice in my head that was demanding an answer to the one question that kept me up at night for what seemed like years.

"Why did you leave?" Panic wormed its way through my chest. But I needed to know why he left and for him to tell me history wouldn't repeat itself.

"You were eighteen. You could have stayed when your parents left, and we had all these plans for our life. But then, I don't know, you just left. You left me, even though I *know* you didn't want to." He rolled onto his back and stared up at the ceiling, his chest moving with each breath he took.

There was a secret on the tip of his tongue waiting to spill over.

"I had an issue," he started before he took a long pause. "With drinking. Not really a problem at the time, but it would have easily turned into one if I had stayed."

I shot up to a sitting position and gaped at him.

"What are you talking about? You didn't have a drinking problem. I would have noticed that, don't you think?"

My mind raced as I tried to bring up any memory I could conjure of Theo from back then for a sign that I missed, but I came up blank. He was struggling back then, and I didn't notice. I thought I knew everything about him, but instead I'm finding out that he had to hide a part of himself from me, to the point where he couldn't stay with me and get the help he wanted. He had to choose.

How often did I blow off plans in order to stay home with Abby or the amount of times I ranted about my issues with my mother without ever thinking about asking how he was?

My eyes fluttered while I attempted to contain my composure, but it was of little use. He was struggling, hurting, and I did nothing.

"Did you leave because I didn't notice enough to help?" I asked as my voice trembled. He was on his feet faster than I could blink and was at my side.

"No. No, I left because I needed to be better. I wanted to be better. For me and for you. I told myself that I would come back and tell you everything as soon as I could." He grabbed onto my hands. "I thought I'd be gone for a few months, but then it turned into a few years, and by the time I was ready, you were with Camden. You were happy, and I wouldn't risk coming back and possibly ruining that."

My head swam with this newfound knowledge. What else had I been missing? Was I so blind that I couldn't see what was right in front of me?

"Why didn't you tell me? I could have helped, I would have waited—"

He cut me off with a sharp, "No." He leaned over and rested his forehead on mine. "I'm sorry I never told you, Lennon. I wanted to, believe me, I did, but I didn't know how, so instead I ran. Yeah, I could have asked you to wait for me and you would have because you are an inherently good person, but I only would have hurt you." He sounded like he was in pain, while telling me all of this. That having to finally speak the words out loud to me brought him back to the tormented feelings he had been carrying for all these years.

He pulled back and peered into my soul. "And I would have rather lived a life without you than one where I caused you any amount of pain."

He's right, I would have waited. I would have done anything for him and that included putting my life on hold while he got his together. It wouldn't have mattered how much it would have hurt to do it, I would have followed him through any amount of darkness.

How different things would have been if I had known.

I pulled our joined hands up to my mouth and placed a kiss on his hand. "Idiot." He chuckled at my statement. "And the drinking..."

"Under control. I still drink on rare occasions, but I'm very mindful of where and when and how much." He stood to move back towards his own bed, but I couldn't seem to let him go. Even if it was just across the room.

"Stay with me."

We moved under the sheets as one, and I clicked the remote and plunged the room into darkness. He molded his body along my backside while his arms snaked around my waist to pull me in closer. There was a sigh of contentment that heaved out of my chest as Theo buried his nose into the curls on the back of my head. "I've missed you," he spoke gently into my hair.

When Camden died, little holes started to appear in my heart. The longer I went without him, the larger they got, but it felt as if all the holes started to close themselves up ever so slightly. Everything was right.

"Theo," I whispered in the darkness. "Don't ever leave me again."

"Anything for you, Lennon."

The next morning, I didn't wake up with the sun, in fact, I had no idea what time it was because the hotel blackout curtains were working overtime. What I did know was I woke up in a tangle of limbs and sheets. Theo was on his stomach with one of his arms thrown over my waist where my shirt had ridden up during the night. His leg pinned down my own, and there was a buzzing beginning in my toes from the lack of circulation. But I didn't want to move and break this moment.

I had forgotten what it was like waking up in someone's arms and being wrapped in the warmth that they would lend you through the night. This was what I had been missing, and it was like I'd gotten a little piece of it back.

He stirred slightly, his legs stretching out as his hand cinched tighter around my waist. I was dragged in closer to him, and he turned to meet me in the middle. His head nuzzled into the crook of my neck when I told him good morning.

"This might be my favorite morning," he replied, his voice muffled by my hair that was undoubtedly in his mouth by now.

I inevitably tore myself away from him and went to the bed to start packing. Within the hour, Theo walked me to where my car was parked; he was staying a bit longer to help pack up the photos and for a meeting.

He pulled open the passenger door and set my bags inside before coming over to my window. He rested his forearms on the window and leaned in so he was closer to me.

"Can I take you to dinner tomorrow?"

"Another date already?" I feigned an exasperated look, but inside, my heart was soaring.

"A date or just a dinner; doesn't matter the word, as long as I can see you." He leaned through the window and kissed me. It was slow and sweet. He kissed me and I wanted to say yes to any question he asked.

With a foggy mind, I ruined all his plans. "Sorry, I can't. Abby and Carina are coming over for dinner." Crestfallen, he told me he'd let me know once he was back, and I, in turn, promised him dinner the following night.

If my favorite sight was Theo in the morning, then watching him in a rearview mirror as I left had to be the worst.

TWENTY-EIGHT

Lennon

DUSK WAS BARELY SETTLING over Fairvale the next night when Abby and Carina blew through my front doors like a pair of twin twisters. Bags of groceries and drinks were littered on my kitchen counter before they pounced on me in the living room, firing questions one after another.

Abby met Carina when she started at ALA Law about seven years ago. Carina was everything I wasn't, but wished I was—outgoing, alluring, and headstrong. The two became fast friends, and soon after, the three of us were always together. Carina said what was on her mind, no matter if someone might think it was offensive or crass, but I liked that most about her. When she found me on the couch, the first thing she said was, "So, did you sleep with him now?" I didn't even bat an eye. Instead, I produced the most dramatic eye roll in existence.

"Is that a yes? I can't tell," she said while Abby nodded fervently behind her in agreement.

"You two are the worst." They both groaned in disappointment, but they left the matter alone, for a while at least.

We were three bottles of wine deep, and had polished off some of the best Italian food, courtesy of Carina and her mother's recipes, and I couldn't dream up a better night to spend with them. My sides were pinched and my cheeks were aching in laughter from listening to Carina rehash an argument she had with a co-worker this morning. "He's infuriating. I just want to..." She made a strangling hand gesture as Abby doubled over on the couch.

"Tell us about the photo exhibition, Lennon."

"Mmm," I hummed out as I placed my glass down and stood. "It was beautiful. I know I was there with him, but the photos he took are impossible to describe. He's so talented, and kind, and you wouldn't believe the final room he had set up even if I told you." My heart practically skipped a beat, and my stomach flipped back and forth, thinking about last night.

I'd never been one for grand gestures, but seeing that room filled with photos was a moment I would cherish forever, not because they were of me, but because they were how I looked through Theo's eyes.

"Aww, look at her, Carina. She likes him," Abby teased. I let out a heavy sigh as I flopped back down on the couch.

"I do, I really do." A weight lifted off my shoulders by saying it out loud with somebody other than my reflection to hear. They both squealed in excitement, and the rest of the night I was hounded by questions from each of them.

Carina never knew me before Camden, so she mainly asked for every detail about Theo and about our teenage years together. At some point, my phone went off and a message from Theo flashed across the screen and caused my heart to flip.

I'm home. The final meeting went on way longer than I thought and I'm ready to crash.

It's so late. I'm glad you're back. Sweet dreams, and I'll see you tomorrow!

My dreams are of you, so no matter what, they always are, love.

There was a darkness I found myself in after Camden died, a place that was so void of light I eventually forgot what the world looked like. All the things that had once brought me joy in life seemed to vanish. The sun lost its warmth and the stars their sparkle. I had forgotten what it was like to feel at all, or how it felt to have someone douse me with affection. Camden had lived his life for me and my happiness. There was not a moment that went by where I was not reminded of his unwavering devotion. I was wrapped in constant warmth and light when I was with him, but it all vanished the moment he did.

Within a few short months of being close to Theo, there were moments where I would catch glimpses of what I had lost, brief flashes of light. Now, though—now, they're all I see. A blazing inferno that had me desperate for more. More light, more warmth, more love—more Theo.

Both girls helped with the cleanup of the kitchen, and Carina left soon after. Abby approached me from behind before we left the kitchen. "I love seeing you like this," she said, resting her chin on my shoulder. It was simple enough to appear a certain way to the public, but to have Abby notice the change in me was entirely different.

Abby saw me in a way that could not be replicated. It was as if she could look through me, see my very soul and the color it took on. From the pale colors of innocence in our youth, to the dark blacks and blues that swirled in the depths of me being after Camden died. I wondered what color she would see now. If I had to guess, it would be the color of his emerald eyes.

No matter the color, she stood by me; she lifted me up when my world crashed down around me and rejoiced in my happiness as if it were her own. My sister was my soulmate. I knew this from the moment I laid eyes on her. She was a champion for my happiness, just as I was the protector of hers. I was certain no greater bond existed.

She was plucking about the kitchen like she was working up the courage to ask something, and I already knew she was staying the night, so I waited for her to find it. She finally turned to me. "So, Camden's birthday is soon." I stilled. His birthday, how could I forget? "I was just wondering if you want me here this year."

We had a tradition for our birthdays—Camden and I would write a letter to each other about the year we had together, what we loved and cherished about our time, and the hopes we had for the year to come. First thing in the morning of our birthday, we would get to read it, and it was always my favorite gift to give him.

I hadn't written a letter in two years, and that realization rained down on me, soaking me in instant misery and sorrow. It clung to every pore of my body, weighing me down, and that happiness I was just feeling seemed so far out of reach.

"Oh, umm no, that's okay. I'll be fine." A weak smile played across my face. I wasn't entirely sure she bought it, but she said nothing further.

I wouldn't be fine, but she didn't need to worry about this. I could handle it.

TWENTY-NINE

Theo

IF I COULD LIVE off the sound of Lennon laughing, I would. I would keep her laughing until her cheeks were permanently stained pink and I would live forever. She threw her head back, and the red glow of Vince's Pizza sign bathed her in its light. The summer night breeze picked up and the warm air rustled through her curls, blowing them back off her shoulders. It was tiny moments like this that had me thankful for whatever it was that brought us back together.

Pizza and Lennon go together, like cheese and pepperoni. It'd been her favorite as long as I had known her, a fact that I was happy to know never changed. I had been waiting to take her back to the one spot that's been on my mind. For two teenagers with little to no money, you couldn't do any better than Vince's Pizza. We would sit outside under the tall oak trees and make up stories for the people we saw to pass the time. Those plastic chairs that lined the outside of the building carried some of my favorite memories of Lennon.

The night was dripping in nostalgia as we sat in the outdoor seating. The table was draped in predictable red and white checkered fabric, with only our drinks remaining. Lennon dragged her finger through the condensation that had gathered on the side of her glass in a way that had chills flooding my body. She looked up and caught me staring, and there were zero parts of me that were ashamed.

"What?" she said as she arched one of her full eyebrows at me and leaned forward to rest her chin on her hand.

I didn't answer. Instead, I grabbed the seat of her plastic chair and dragged her over to my side of the table. The way her breath hitched and the coy smile that crept across her face only encouraged me further as I wrapped my hand around the back of her neck and pulled her in close. Her eyes fluttered the moment my lips touched hers. My tongue traced the seam of her lips lightly, causing her to sigh and allowed me to deepen the kiss. She pressed her chest into mine, and it felt as if time had stopped.

I wondered if it would be like this every time we kissed. Would the world stop turning every time my lips were on her? If so, I was in trouble.

She pulled back, her mouth hovered millimeters from mine for a moment longer. "Thank you for bringing me here. It's always been my favorite," she whispered before placing another slow kiss against my lips. She was my favorite type of drug at this point, and I was on a constant high.

"I remember," I said as I dragged my thumb across her jaw and down the column of her neck. She snorted out a laugh before plying me with another quick kiss. She was still pressed against me when I sensed someone freeze while walking by our table.

I looked over to see an older woman staring back at us. Her face was aged with lines and her dark brown hair fell in limp curls around her face. My eyebrows pinched inwards, my brain working in overdrive to figure out why I knew her face when Lennon tensed up under my arm. My head moved back and forth between the two women when it dawned on me.

Shit.

"Lennon," the woman questioned. Her voice lacked any warmth. Lennon moved slightly from under my arm to turn and face her.

"Mom." Her voice was like ice as she greeted her. Their relationship had been strained since the beginning. That was never a secret, and if I was being honest, it was a miracle both girls were as productive as they were. If I had a mother like Susan Faulkner, I might have gone off the deep end myself and never look for a way back. While I strived to not hate much of anything or anyone, this woman made all of that go out the window. Lennon never talks about her mom, for good reason, but I had no idea she still lived in the area.

One of my favorite things about Fairvale was that you get a small town feeling without being too far from all the city's best necessities. It wasn't a small in an everyone knew everyone type of way, but in a you're likely to run into someone you know once you're out of the house type of way.

Susan's eyes roamed over me, then widened slightly as she realized who I was. Her eyes pinged between us, noting the closeness of our bodies and the way my arm was draped across the back of Lennon's chair. She jutted out her chin and squared her shoulders. I didn't know what she was about to do or say, but the way the hair on the back of my neck was standing up, I know it couldn't be good.

"Well, don't you two look cozy?" She then looked pointedly at her daughter. "Really, Lennon, your husband dies, and you find your way back to this boy?" She sneered, and at the same time, my body lit on fire with rage as my blood began to boil. I moved to stand, but Lennon pressed her hand onto my thigh to keep me seated. I glanced over, and she remained unfazed from years of practice, if I could guess.

"What I do with my life is none of your concern anymore, remember?" There was close to no emotion in her sentence; it was chilling. All traces of the Lennon I loved and admired were locked away to avoid the venom this woman spewed over everything.

I'd never given much thought to my upbringing, but never did I have any doubts that my parents loved me or that they wouldn't flip the world on its axis to help me. It was easy for me to assume it was like that for every kid. I was rudely awakened to different ways as I grew closer to Lennon as a teenager. There were endless nights where I would hold Lennon while she cried over her mother, watched as she begged to be loved by her, and now, it was clear that it was all for nothing.

My head was reeling, trying to wrap itself around the interaction happening in front of me. Having to witness Lennon fight for every scrap of affection from this woman, and the hoops she jumped through for Abby, broke my heart, and I was only a bystander. A person could only imagine what the years of exposure had done to her heart.

Susan scoffed at her statement. "If I remember correctly, he left you once before. I doubt whatever game of house you're playing now is enough to keep him this time."

You've got to be fucking kidding me.

"You need to leave. Now," I barked out. My voice was completely unrecognizable to even myself.

I was grateful that at eighteen I had the strength to ask for help when I thought I needed it, and long before I ever hit rock bottom. There are countless stories of people who never find what they need and spend their life searching for the bottom of the bottle. Seeing Susan only illuminated the path that would be so easy for me to slip into. Learning to live with the tendencies that could lead to addiction was an everyday battle, but one that would always be worth the struggle.

She hesitated for a second, and I braced myself for another snarky comment. Instead, she stormed off down the sidewalk. I waited until her entire frame was gone from view before I turned back to Lennon. She'd brought her glass up and was draining every ounce that was left from her drink. "Lennon, what she said, it was…" She held her hand up to stop me and shot me a look that would have most men cowering.

"Don't even think about apologizing, Theodore. You know better than most people than to apologize for anything that woman says," she snapped out.

I'll admit I loved it when she used my full name, just not necessarily when she was irritated at me. The wind had picked up again. For a restaurant on Main Street, it was eerily quiet, so all I heard was the rustling of the trees overhead. She pulled her bottom lip in and as she worked something over in her mind. It didn't take long for her to start talking again.

"I stopped talking to my mom shortly after you left. I moved out of her house, brought Abby with me after she graduated so she wouldn't have to face her alone, and never looked back. Of course, with Fairvale being Fairvale, we see each other every once in a while."

She paused and looked past me, down the street where her mother had been. "I can't fix her, as much as I wish I could, and the issues that she has are not my responsibility. It took me a long time to come to terms with that, because no matter how much she hurts me, she's still my mother." Her chest heaved. "There's always room for forgiveness. She just needs to ask for it. Until then, I can't have her in my life." There were no words of comfort I could offer her. Instead, I did what I used to do. I pulled her into me, wrapped my arms around her, and held her.

One of the first times she called me to keep her company after going at it with Susan, I tried to talk her through it. I didn't know what else to do. There was nothing I could say would remove the sting of rejection. Until it dawned on me to ask what she needed. "Can you just hold me?" she would ask through the tears, rage, or any other emotion that was coursing through her. My answer was always the same—anything for you.

Seventeen years later, we sat in one of our favorite spots, doing the same thing we would do as teenagers. I kissed the top of her head and breathed in her familiar scent before she pulled away. There were no signs of tears, and I didn't know if that made me proud or sad. I made a mental note to call my mom after this.

There was only a lingering look of defeat in her sapphire eyes when. For as long as I'd known her, she's had to be strong for herself and for her sister, in order to get through life. She would pile the weight of the world on her back until Atlas himself would have nothing left to carry. Not once did she think that maybe it was too heavy for one person or that she should ask for help. My guess was that since Camden died, it had only gotten worse, but she would never have to carry the burden of being strong by herself again.

"Do you want to go on an assignment with me?" Maybe not the smoothest segue, but I'd do anything to get her to smile at me again. "It's not for another month, but I'd really like for you to come with me."

"You have a thing for getting me to crash your work trips, don't you?" She flashed me a smile, and all was right again. Without thinking, I leaned in for another kiss, and it was quite possibly my favorite thing to not have to think about anymore. "Anywhere I am is where I want you." My hand trailed down her arm, goosebumps erupted over her skin in my hands wake, and landed on her hip.

Lennon was clear that she wasn't ready for anything more physical at this time, but it didn't stop my thoughts from jumping to visions of her lying beneath me or thoughts of how her hair would be splayed out over a pillow next to me. I reluctantly pulled away so that I could get an answer.

"I will if you will do something for me?" she asked me while pulling at her fingers. I wanted to tell her I would do anything; all she had to do was ask. "Will you come to dinner with Charlotte and me?" Hope and fear swirled together in her eyes as she waited for an answer. "She is the closest thing I have to a real mother, and it would mean a lot to me if you two could meet." I struggled to clear the desert that was suddenly occupying my throat.

Camden was like a figment of my imagination at this point. Obviously, he existed, but all that I knew of him was what he meant to Lennon. Meeting his mother would make him real, and this woman could make or break everything we had been working towards. She could take one look at me and decide I was no good for Lennon, and I would be left powerless to convince her otherwise.

Lennon continued to watch me as I wrestled with my answer, but it was no use. "Just tell me when, and I'll be there." She smiled, and I swallowed all my worries.

"Where are we going?" she asked as she shifted her chair back to the opposite side of the table. "Not far, Castello Di Amorosa. It's about two hours from here. They built the winery to be a replica of a 14th century Tuscan castle—it's incredible. We can do a tasting tour while we're there. I think you'll love it." Her face lit up as I gave her a brief description of the winery.

"How have I lived this close to that place and never heard of it?" she exclaimed while looking at her phone. The details I was giving were clearly not enough, as she started pulling up photos for a better look. "It's beautiful, the castle and the grounds, all of it. I can't wait."

Score one for me.

She was still scrolling through their website when she looked up suddenly. "Do you want to stay down there for the night?" It was suddenly very hard to swallow as I choked on the swig of water I was taking when she asked.

"I um... I... I didn't have plans since it's so close, but we can if you'd like?" Stammering out this sentence wasn't exactly exuding the amount of confidence I wished it was. I was also feeling a tiny bit self-conscious, like she could see the prior thoughts that were just flashing through my head.

"I think we should stay. I can make the reservation if that works for you?"

"Yeah." I cleared my throat. "Yeah, that's good."

"And is one room, one bed okay with you, too, Theo?" My eyebrows shot to my hairline as I gawked at her before I reeled it back in. "Really?"

"Really, Theodore." This was when I liked hearing her say my full name. We sat for a beat longer, staring at each other, before she arched an eyebrow at me. The slow movement caused a thousand more images of Lennon and me in more compromising positions than just her under me that were going to be burned into my conscious thoughts.

This was going to be a long month.

THIRTY

Theo

THE LAST TIME I was this nervous was when I had to tell my parents I thought I had a drinking problem at the age of eighteen. The fear of rejection swam through my veins and was hard to shake. Lennon and I were meeting Charlotte at her house for dinner. I would rather be in a restaurant and on neutral ground, but she insisted.

"Stop fidgeting, you look fine." Lennon laughed at me as I adjusted my jacket for the tenth time. She reached up and placed a chaste kiss on my cheek, but that only did so much to calm me. We approached the large oak door, and, for a brief moment, I thought about running. I'd built Charlotte up in my head to be a person who had already decided I was not good enough for Lennon. That no one could ever take her son's place and she would spend the entire night talking only about Camden. Then, by the end of it,

Lennon would realize that I was not the man for her. My stomach turned just thinking about it.

The door swung open, and I was greeted by a woman with short straw-colored hair and a smile that touched her eyes. She pulled Lennon in for a hug before turning towards me. "Charlotte, I'd like you to meet my..." She trailed off for a second—was going to say boyfriend? It seemed like she was, so what was stopping her? I'd be anything she wanted. "My... Theo," she finished her thought, and I was fine being just hers.

I extended my hand forward, but she swatted it away, and I was pulled into my own hug that caught me off guard. "Theo, it is so good to meet you." She pulled back to look up at me with kind, dark brown eyes. "Anyone that has been making my girl this happy is good in my book." The words slammed into my heart and dissolved all of my previous notions about Charlotte. She towed us into the warmth of her house, leaving all of my fear out on the porch.

Her home was full of warmth that seemed to leech into the room directly from Charlotte herself. Conversation flowed easily between the three of us, and by the end of the night, my stomach only hurt from the amount of laughter. Charlotte busied herself in the kitchen packing us both food to take back with us when Lennon excused herself to the restroom before we left. She scanned the hall before coming to sit next to me. I was alone with the mother of my maybe girlfriend's dead husband and I thought this may be the oddest pairing of people someone could come up with.

She leaned in, placing her hands on top of mine. "Theo, I cannot thank you enough for what you have done for Lennon," she said in a voice just above a whisper and glanced up if someone would overhear her words. She wasn't telling me anything that she wouldn't say to Lennon, I was sure of it, but she wanted these words to be for me only.

"I haven't done anything." I tried to fend off her compliment, unworthy of her praise. I loved Lennon, and sometimes I think it's so clear that even strangers on the street could see it. But it wasn't so other people could witness it, or to be thanked.

I loved her because she made me feel like I had a place in the world. I loved her because when I was with her I didn't feel like I had to run, that I could finally rest.

Lennon once told me that loving Camden was the easiest thing she's ever done, and I finally understood what she meant.

"Oh, but my dear, yes, you have. After my son passed, Lennon was lost for a long time. Everything he loved about her—her smile, her spark—died along with him, I'm afraid." This wasn't new information, but for some reason, hearing it from another perspective made it more real. "And then came her trip, and it was like a switch was flipped. Slowly, the Lennon we all knew, the Lennon we longed for, started to return, and we have you to thank." Her eyes shone with the tears that gathered in her waterline.

I shifted in my seat, trying to shake off the insecurity that her words doused me in. I never thought to look at what I had with Lennon from an outside perspective. I knew I would do anything to help her, but I never realized that the people around her would notice or even care. "I don't know what you believe in, Theo, but I know that you were sent to her by my son. Even in death, he would want to take care of her, and you are exactly the person she needs. I just ask that you keep her happy. She deserves the very best."

"I would do anything for her," I said, letting my honest desperation slip its way through the words.

"I can tell, dear." She patted my cheek in response as Lennon appeared back in the kitchen. We left just as the moon took its place in the sky. Her hand stayed clasped in mine during the drive back to her house, and my mind wandered back to Charlotte's last words to me. In case she was right, I sent a silent promise to the man who loved her before me that I would do whatever it took to keep her safe and to keep her happy.

My parents' new house was on the outskirts of Fairvale, tucked away in the trees on about an acre of property. Vastly different from the small home I grew up in, a large two story that was smack dab in the middle of a cookie cutter neighborhood. The automatic gate swung open and I crept along the driveway up to the house.

It was a quaint house, with a full wrap-around porch that allowed my mom to watch the sun rise and set. With it being only the two of them, I wasn't sure what they would do with anything bigger. My mom appeared in the front door and waved from the porch while I parked and got out of my car.

I turned in a circle to survey the plot of land, the trees towering around the perimeter of the area, and it seemed to be an endless amount of space. It was exactly perfect for them. It was also the type of place I imagined myself buying, if given the chance. My mother waited for me to make my way over, her hand firmly planted on her hips, and a towel thrown over her shoulder and her apron covered in flour.

"Oh my boy, I'm so happy to see you," she said, while pulling me in for a hug. I would normally slink out of her arms quickly, but today I took the time to hug her back. It'd been two weeks since my dinner with Lennon when we saw her mom. I called my own mother almost immediately after, just to remind her that I loved her when she invited me for dinner.

As much as I wanted to be here, my stomach had been in knots for hours. For two weeks, I had been with Lennon more than I had not been with her. Then suddenly today, it was like a ghost town. I heard from her yesterday briefly; she mentioned she was busy today but didn't say with what. No problem, it was just that she hadn't replied back to any of my messages. Calling her to check in seemed a little over the top. We were both entitled to our own lives, but something about this was off.

I pushed down the panic that was slowly setting in for the next couple of hours as I took the time to spend with both my parents. By the end of the night, I was stuffed so full of food I could barely move. I leaned back in my chair and honestly contemplated unbuttoning my pants when my dad asked how my work was going. "It's good. I've gone to a few places out here already. I'll be at Castello Di Amorosa in a couple of weeks. Oh, and I'll be in the Tacoma area in about another month or so." He nodded his head to let me know he was listening, but I was pretty sure he was close to falling asleep.

The sun had started to set, and I'd been glancing at my phone every minute. Still nothing from Lennon. "So, Theo, have you been spending time with anyone in particular since you've been back?" Generally, my mom was not the type to beat around the bush. She'd come out and say whatever was on her mind. So, when I looked at her and saw her eyes shining back at me in amusement, there was no point in lying and omitting any part of the truth—she already knew.

"Who have you been talking to, Mother?" I shot back at her playfully.

"You know this town and how it works. I was informed that you have been spending quite a lot of time with Lennon Faulkner again."

"It's Arden. She was married, Mom."

"Oh, yes, poor girl. Terrible what happened. I can't imagine what it would be like to lose your husband. And at such a young age." She made a tsk sound with her mouth and shook her head as her hand unconsciously reached out for my father's. "But it's nice that you two have reconnected." I nodded my head in agreement and dodged dany further questions she tried to pin me with.

She walked me to the porch and, as always, she pulled me in for a hug before telling me she loved me. I held her a little tighter once more. "I love you, too, Mom, and thank you for everything." She let me go and looked up at me a little misty eyed.

You forget while you're growing up that your parents are growing older alongside you. I looked down at this woman that brought me life, and for the first time, noticed how much she'd aged and my heart seemed to constrict.

"Next time, I'll bring Lennon with me. How does that sound, Ma?"

"Wonderful," she replied. I placed one last kiss on her cheek and jogged back to my car.

The second I was alone, the knots continued to tie themselves tighter. My phone was still blank.

No call.

No texts.

Something wasn't right. I could feel it.

I debated for a few seconds before I called Abby, who answered quickly. "Hey Abby. I haven't heard from Lennon all day. I've tried checking in with her, but I get nothing back. Is she alright, have you heard from her?"

The air was dead between us for a moment before she let out a long sigh. "Figures she wouldn't tell you." It could be anything, but my whole body froze at her statement. Before I could ask, she answered my question. "Today is Camden's birthday. Lennon's fine, I'm sure, she's just at home. Hiding if you ask me, but fine, none the less."

I exhaled loudly into the receiver, grateful that she was okay, but I felt useless. I didn't know what to do in this situation, but the pull to go to her was overwhelming.

There were nights that Lennon would call me to come over after her mother would disappear, leaving her and Abby alone with no warning. I would stay for as long as possible doing whatever I could to make sure she was okay and that included checking in on Abby. She was fifteen and would mainly hole herself up in her room during these nights. Before leaving, I would duck my head in to see how she was doing, a short conversation, but one I always made sure to have.

"Are you okay Abby?" It was second nature for me to ask.

The line was quiet for a second before she replied. "I miss him. I really do, but I think that what I miss most is my sister and who she was before all of this heartbreak. I don't know if that makes me a shitty person, but it's the truth," she confessed.

"You're good for her, Theo. You've brought her back and I can't thank you enough." She sounded so sure of herself. As if she knew for certain that my presence in her sister's life was the exact thing that was bringing her back to life. I didn't have words for her confession.

Loving Lennon was as easy as breathing, and the people in her life keep thanking me for it. There was a steady feeling of embarrassment that coursed through me each time it happened.

I pushed my car past the speed limit recommendations throughout town. It might have been overstepping, but there was something telling me she shouldn't be alone. My car pulled up outside of Lennon's house as the last of the sun fell below the horizon. The house was dark, but her car was here, so Abby was correct.

My knuckles hit her door, and I waited and listened for the sound of footsteps, but nothing came. This might go wrong, but I reached for the doorknob and turned.

As I stepped inside, I called out her name, but still silence. The kitchen and living room were empty. There was still no sign of Lennon until I turned down the hallway. Her bedroom door was closed, but there was soft light coming out from underneath.

I tapped on her door gently. "Lennon, love. Are you alright?" The knob turned without any resistance, and I stepped into her room.

She was the first thing I saw when the door opened, sitting in the middle of the bed with her legs tucked underneath her. Her head hung between her shoulders as she looked into her lap where her fingers twirled a pair of rings around in circles, and there were papers strewn around her.

I took a few steps closer when she lifted her head to meet my gaze. Her eyes were bloodshot, red splotches adorned her cheeks, and by the looks of it all, she hadn't left this room all day.

She looked right through me, as if she couldn't decide if I was really here or not. I crouched down in front of the bed and into her line of sight. Her brows pulled together in confusion. "Theo, what are you doing here?" she asked, her voice deep and raspy as it cracked over the words.

"I got worried when I didn't hear from you. I know it's Camden's birthday. I didn't want you to be alone."

Her chin trembled and tears gathered in her waterline as she looked down at me. "I didn't write him a letter, Theo. Two birthdays he's been gone, and I don't get to write him letters anymore." The tears were spilling down her face, and I was helpless.

From the way the papers were crinkled, I could tell she had been reading them over and over throughout the day. I didn't understand what they meant. I just knew that they meant something. The way agony was splashed across her face, it was clear that they were important to her, important to them.

I gathered her in my arms and moved to lie with her on the bed. Curling behind her, I pulled her in close as the sobs wracked through her body. The room filled with the deafening sounds of heartbreak as she clung onto my arms.

Coming back for Lennon might have been a decision that was based on emotion more than logic, but it was one I would make over and over again for her. For me, this was reason enough. To be here for her when life got hard and when she wouldn't ask for the help, I knew she craved.

I held her tightly as she fell apart in my arms, trying to keep the pieces in place while my heart broke with hers. There was no instruction manual for how to help with this situation, but if there were a *helping the woman I love grieve her husband* book, I'd buy every copy. Anything to help her, because if this was killing me, my mind could not fathom the pain coursing through her.

In the dead of night, after her tears had dried and her cries were silent, I gently, with so much love and affection, promised to put her pieces back together.

THIRTY-ONE

Lennon

THE FIRST THING I noticed when I woke up was the way my comforter was tucked in around me. It was tightly wound around my body, like a swaddled newborn. I didn't exactly hate it. Next was the throbbing headache behind my eyes. The steady pounding was like someone was playing the drums in my head.

My feet thrashed their way out of my blanket confinement and my chest vibrated with a low groan when I sat up. It was like a house was dropped on top of me or like I had spent the night hysterically crying in the arms of a man about my dead husband.

Embarrassment was only the beginning. The lingering feeling of defeat engulfed the room, smothering any chance I had of redeeming myself. I made sure to seclude myself yesterday. I hated being around people when I was vulnerable, but I'd be lying if I said having Theo show up wasn't comforting, but obviously too much for him.

The bed was empty beside me, and I didn't blame him for leaving. If there was a way to escape myself when emotions took over, I would take it, too. I flopped backwards to wallow in my self pity for a few more moments while I battled the need to find the largest cup of coffee.

Then the door swung open.

He's still here, was the first thought that popped up, followed by, *thank God he had coffee for me*, when I noticed the steam rolling out of the top of the mug that was clutched in his hand. Last, but certainly not least, he was shirtless, with a pair of gym shorts slung so low on his hips that saliva pooled in my mouth.

I should call Dr. Williams for another session and talk this through because there was no way this one-eighty in emotions was healthy. Crying over one man at night to be turned on in the morning by another.

"Good morning, Lenny," he said while smiling brightly at me. He walked over to my side of the bed and plopped the cup down on my cluttered nightstand. I would have tidied up, but of course, there were clothes strewn about the room, and my nightstand was littered with empty water bottles and overall junk.

My head snapped from side to side, looking for the letters. The letters I refused to pull out for the past two years, but thought last night would be the best time to see them again. Then I saw them, they were folded neatly and sitting on the twin nightstand on the other side of the bed. My throat started to dry up seeing them again. It's funny the thing we give stock to, and how words on a page could spark an entire melt down.

He leaned down and placed a kiss on the top of my head like it was what he did every morning without fail. The smell of coffee filled the room, its aroma called out to my exhaustion. The bed creaked beneath his weight as he sat on the edge. I took my first sip and sighed. Why was coffee always better when it's made for you by someone else?

"I slept in the guest room. I couldn't bring myself to leave. I hope that's okay with you," he said as he reached out and stroked the high part of my cheek.

It was simple phrases like that. The ones that fell from his lips so effortlessly and made me think falling in love again could be possible. Phrases that calmed me down and sent me into panic within mere seconds of each other.

I set my cup back down and shifted around in bed so that I was fully upright. He probably showed up last night thinking I needed company, or someone to talk to or sit with, instead he witnessed a full breakdown. "Listen, about last night, I feel like I should apologize." My hands twisted themselves into the blanket to match the bundle of nerves that knotted in my stomach.

If there was ever a chance to run from a relationship, or whatever it was that we were, this would be the time to do it.

There was a nagging voice in the back of my head saying he was going to take the opening.

"Normally, I spend the big days alone. Birthdays, our anniversary, and whatnot. No matter how many times I tell myself I can get through the day without breaking down, that it's okay to be sad, but don't let it overwhelm you, I still haven't mastered it. As you witnessed." I tried to look at him, but my throat began to constrict, and there were tears threatening to gather again. Instead, I focused on the French doors that led out to the backyard. From here I could see the pool; the sun reflected off the water, causing flecks of light to bounce off of the top. It was one of my favorite spots in the house, but now, it wasn't doing much for my nerves the way I'd hoped it would.

He didn't run. Theo's hand reached out to hold on to mine. "There is nothing you have to say sorry for. The love you have for Camden was life changing, the grief that followed his death was bound to be just as large."

Was it that simple? I had been trying to stuff Camden into a box that I could slide under the floorboards and would only pull it out when I thought I could face him. But the issue was I never should have tried to hide away and or fight the pain that still lived inside me.

My husband was dead. I was still completely wrecked, and that was okay.

The hurt that I was holding onto was a part of me; there was no shame in letting people in to see. Having Theo here last night made me realize I could use the company on the days when it was too much for me to hold on to.

Morning breath be damned, I leaned forward and kissed him. Every part of me wanted to reach for him and pull him closer. Instead, I pressed my lips harder into him, in an attempt to put everything I have been too afraid to tell him into this one kiss. I broke down every ounce of affection I had, every moment where he made me feel like I was finally whole again, and poured it into him.

One, two, three more kisses, he pressed against my lips before pulling away. His eyes roamed across my face, and then I saw it. It came like the flash of green you see in a sunset over the ocean. If you blinked at the right time, you'd miss it.

It stopped me in my place and caused my heart's rhythm to unbalance. He looked at me like I was the last thing he wanted to see at night and the first thing in the morning.

He looked at me like he could love me forever and it wouldn't be enough time.

The heaviness that followed a breakdown and that blinding green flash from Theo hung in the air. I needed to do something before I became antsy with an emotional hangover.

I looked around the room, then threw the covers off to drag myself out of bed. Theo stood with me, waiting to see what came next. There was no booklet on how to handle someone else's trauma. But he did it beautifully, regardless.

My hands ran through my tangled strands of hair, and I drew the confidence to ask him to stay. "Do you need to be anywhere, or can you stay a while?"

His eyes softened at my words. "I'm all yours, Lennon," he replied, and the statement resonated down into my bones—he didn't just mean for today.

I reluctantly told him to go put on a shirt while I changed out of my pajamas, then dragged him down the hall and out to the backyard, to the lonely garden box in the corner. The flowers had been flourishing since I'd planted them, the bright white could be seen from any part of the yard, and it brought me comfort to see them do so well.

"This is my garden. My therapist likes to give unconventional homework." I bumped his shoulder with my own. "This is what helps me," I said, as I knelt down beside the box and began to pull at the weeds that had formed. The dirt was cool under my hands and I finally began to relax.

"There's something about putting my hands into the dirt and tending to the plants that calms the storm that usually takes up space in my head," I admitted. He joined me on the ground and mimicked my movements as I worked.

"These are daffodils, right?" he asked as he sat back on his feet.

"Uh, yeah, they are."

"Did you know that daffodils are a symbol of new beginnings?" I turned to look at him. *Such a strange fact*, I thought, as I pulled the last of the unwanted weeds from the dirt.

"How do you know that?" I shook my head in amusement and looked back at the flowers.

"I had a girlfriend who was really into flower language. She came with me on an assignment somewhere in England, and one of the castles talked about it on a tour. They used it a lot in Victorian times. She loved it. Sometimes, I would bring her flowers based on what they meant because I knew it made her happy." He smiled down into the dirt in remembrance, or embarrassment, I couldn't tell.

I wasn't surprised in the slightest that he treated everyone he'd been with, with the same care and tenderness that I get from him. It might've been one of the best parts of him. He was truly an amazing human to be around.

"Did you ever think about getting married?" There was a craving to know everything about him, every detail he was willing to spare, I'd gladly take. Anything that would allow me to get closer to him.

"Not really. I've dated, obviously, but nothing ever lasted. We'd get a few months in, and I'd begin to think it could last or that I could love them. Then it would fizzle out or something would happen, and we'd break up."

He stood, pulling me with him. "Nothing has *ever* felt like this," he said, keeping my hand laced with his while he bared his truth to me. How did you respond to a statement like that? A statement that had me flushed with panic over all the complications that came with falling in love.

Sometimes, life had a way of revealing that I was on the right path when I least expected it. My eyes drifted towards the daffodils. All I had to do was stop and smell the flowers.

He left me for the day after I promised I was better, and soon I was alone with only my thoughts. I would never grow out of who I was if I didn't take the risk, and the broken pieces of my heart fit so well in his hands.

Thirty-Two

Lennon

Castello Di Amorosa was beautiful, and I couldn't, for the life of me, figure out why I hadn't heard about it before now. Theo drove the car through the winding driveway until the castle came into view.

It was exactly what your mind conjures up when someone says castle. The stone walls and towers were all I saw once we were past the towering cypress trees. I'd never been to Italy, but we seemed to have stepped into a little piece of Tuscany's countryside.

We were in the grapevines for the last part of the day, that way the sun was setting behind the winery. Theo was setting up his equipment while I laid back onto my hands on a blanket I had spread out. He was pulling out tripods, lenses, and a whole host of other devices I couldn't name and began to assemble it all for use. I'd been referring to myself as his assistant throughout the day, but really, I'd done nothing except walk slowly behind him as I took in the craftsmanship of the castle site.

"Taking a well-earned break, I see." He teased. Reason number I-couldn't-remember that I liked being around him: the playfulness.

"Union fifteen," I answered, as I relaxed back onto my hands, with my sandals crossed in front of me. Thankfully, I had put some effort into my outfit this morning. The simple black sundress hit mid calf but had been riding up the longer I lounged on the ground. His gaze tracked up and down my body slowly before he blinked and turned back to his work. The movement sent a heat wave through my core.

The sky was painted in soft pinks and oranges as the sun cast the last of its shining rays over the castle. Theo snapped away, and for the next hour, only silence surrounded us. I was content in watching him work in comfortable silence. Nothing but the sound of the wind and the soft clicks of his camera were in the air.

He began to pack his equipment away, and I took that as my cue to gather my stuff so we could head to dinner. That was when I saw him reach into his bag and pull out his Pentax 67. I still had a hard time wrapping my mind around the fact that he still had that old thing. He walked toward me with a sly smile on his face as I reached down and picked up the blanket I had been lounging on.

"Smile," he said as he pointed the lens in my direction.

"Oh no, don't waste your film on me." I turned my back on him as I swatted him away.

"Just one picture. I'll eventually get a place of my own and I'll need something to go on my nightstand," he said to plead his case.

How could I say no?

I turned back around and threw my arms out to the side in compliance. The castle and most of the vineyard were behind me, offering the perfect background. I'm awkward, and I had no idea what to do with my hands, so I waited for his direction. "You look beautiful," he announced, and my insides melted. He snapped the photo as the words hit my ears and a grin spread across my face. I stood there watching him watch me through his lens and I couldn't imagine a better place to be.

"Is there a way to take one of both of us? My nightstand could use a photo, too, you know." He set down his camera and rifled through his bag.

I didn't want to think about the fact that our nightstands might never be in the same room. These past few months have been like a fever dream and it's been easy to forget that he's here on assignment. This was not his home. I'm not his home. But if he's going to leave, then I'm going to soak up every ounce of happiness I could get.

"Unfortunately, not with this one. You need someone to move the shutter. But…" he trails off as he pulls out his standard camera, "this one is connected to my phone so we can both be in the frame, and I can still get the shot."

He set up the tripod and placed the camera on top. He spent a minute behind the lens toying with the settings before joining me. His arm warmed my lower back as he tugged me into his side, and his breath skated across the curve of my neck before he planted a kiss there.

"When do we say cheese?" I asked, as he smiled against my skin. He pulled back and rested his forehead on mine.

"Ready?" he said as I looked into his impossibly green eyes that seemed to transport me back to the Scottish Highlands. There was a faint click of his camera, but I couldn't tear my eyes from him.

"Perfect." His voice was low as he dragged his hand slowly up the expanse of my back.

"You haven't even seen the photo yet," I replied. We hadn't moved, and we were so close that our lips were practically touching as we talked. There was no up or down, right or wrong, broken heart or broken soul. In this moment–it was just us.

Everything came to me at once as he brought his lips to meet mine. He had a way of making me whole again, and it was a feeling I wanted to drown in.

"Do you want to go back to the hotel and order room service for dinner?" I asked, looking anywhere but into his eyes as I acted on the lust that was fogging my brain. I was entirely aware of the insinuation my sentence held, and I had every intention of fully embracing it. By the way his pupils dilated, and his hooded eyes stared into mine, I could tell he was on the exact same page as I was. It didn't take him long to agree and for us to gather the rest of our things and hightail it back to the car.

We didn't check in before we came to the winery, so we were entering the room for the first time now; the bed seemed to be a daunting focal point as it loomed in the center of the room. My hands were shaking as I set my suitcase in the corner and kicked off my sandals and sat on the edge of the bed. Theo was doing the same on the opposite side of the room, and I was almost positive he was looking for things to fidget with so that he didn't join me.

"This is weird," I said out loud, only halfway on accident. He barked out a laugh.

"So weird." He dragged his hand down his face and scratched at the stubble on his jaw. I wondered if he was nervous. It would've been nice to know that I was not the only one in that boat.

"Do you remember our first time?" I wondered out loud. Nothing calmed your nerves more than bringing up a past encounter where we fumbled our way through two minutes of awkwardness.

"Vividly," he said as he winced and slunk down in the chair that sat next to the desk in the farthest corner of the room.

"This feels kind of like that. I'm nervous and excited, but also terrified of what will happen after," I said.

The stories ran rampant at school of boys dating a girl, telling them how much they love them, only for them to leave once they got what they wanted out of the relationship. While I never consciously lumped Theo into that category, as an eighteen-year-old girl, it was still in the back of my mind. Nearly two decades later, my self-consciousness was still lingering in the back of my brain. I was terrified of this next step and that it would ruin what we had re-established and the closer relationship we had cultivated in the past few weeks. I wanted to stay in this bubble we had created, where the tension was so thick, I could taste it.

But when he looked at me the way he was now, with eyes that burned with desire, I was the fastest to shred what thin barrier we had left.

In a flash, he was off the chair and kneeling in front of me. His head tilted up, and he looked at me with pupils blown so wide they dripped with desire. His tongue popped out to wet his bottom lip as he kept his hand on my bare knee to steady himself. "Lennon," he exhaled as his hand trailed up my thigh, so slow that I squirmed under the anticipation, but the heat that it left in its wake was an excruciating bliss. My legs parted of their own volition at his touch. "All you have to do is tell me to stop, and I will." His voice was low and commanding, with just a hint of desperation.

"I don't want to stop." My confession spurred him forward, and that was all it took before his mouth was on me. He pressed wet open mouth kisses to the inside of my thigh, causing my head to fall back and my eyelids to drop closed.

"Eyes open, Lenny, I don't want you missing out on any of the fun." His voice taunted me into submission and my eyes opened.

He pushed my dress up past my hips, exposing the black lace underwear I thankfully chose to wear today. He groaned at the sight as he pressed his cheek against the inside of my knee, causing my legs to spread wider. I watched him through heavy eyes as he dragged his tongue closer to my center, causing me to squirm in my spot. I couldn't tell if it was because it had been so long since I'd been intimate with someone, or just the sight of Theo on his knees in front of me that had me soaked.

It didn't take long for him to realize it, either, as he dragged his thumb along my covered slit, causing a shiver to rake through my body from his touch. There was a dark chuckle from him as he hooked his fingers onto both sides of my underwear and dragged them down my legs at an unbearably slow pace. The second they were off, they disappeared as he tossed them to the side, and his hand returned to my thighs, pulling me to the edge of the bed. I squeaked at the sudden movement, and my eyes flashed open when he licked the full length of me.

"Heaven," I heard him say before he dove back in, latching his lips onto me.

"Oh God," I panted out. My brain had actually stopped working; there were no other words in my head.

Please. The word echoed through my head.

I couldn't help it as I fell back onto the bed, unable to support my weight and focus on the pure bliss that was consuming me. I was being devoured, and I loved every fucking second of it. The room was filled with the sounds of my heavy breathing and I wasn't making any sense as I chanted the word *please* over and over. The tightening in my lower abdomen wound with every stroke of his finger.

"Please, what, my love?" he said as he placed a soft kiss on the inside of my thigh.

I didn't realize I had said that out loud

"More, I need more," I panted out. He pulled his hand from me when he stood, taking my dress with him and it joined my underwear somewhere else in the room. I sat up and pulled his shirt from where it was tucked into his pants and slid it up over him, letting my hand trail back down his chest and stomach as I sat back down on the bed. His abs tightened where my nails skimmed across his skin and followed the trail of hair down his stomach to the top of his pants. I held his gaze as I slipped open his belt, and popped open the button of his pants. His breath hitched when I dragged the zipper down and shimmied him out of his pants.

Gone was the boy with the hands that would shake and fumble when he would unclasp my bra. Standing in front of me was a man that looked as if he had been sculpted for a museum; my head hurt with how beautiful he was.

Turning my body, I crawled towards the middle of the bed and beckoned him to follow me, which he did eagerly. The sheets were cool to the touch of my blazing skin as Theo fell between my knees. His tan arms bracketed my head as he looked down at me with lust clouded eyes. He searched my face for something.

Please was still the only thing I could think of in this moment.

"Hold on, let me grab a…" I didn't let him finish before I tugged him down to me into a searing kiss.

"You don't have to. I… I have an IUD and I trust you," I stammered as I scrambled to get his boxers off his hips and down his legs. He met my fervor with a kiss of his own. My body melted underneath him, and I knew I didn't want a single thing coming between us.

Before I could draw my next breath, he entered me, capturing my moan with his mouth, and my back arched off the bed.

"I was wrong before—this is heaven. You are my heaven." He was rambling, but his words added to the euphoria I was currently swimming in. Every stroke, every kiss, every touch caused my heart to race and sunbursts to erupt behind my closed eyes. Theo spewed nonsense in my ear, but I could only catch words like perfect and mine. He was relentless as he continued to slide in and out of me until the tightness in me finally snapped and I fell over into bliss with Theo not far behind.

My name was the last thing out of his mouth.

We laid there for minutes, wrapped in a tangle of each other's limbs. Slowly my heart rate came down and I rolled over to look at him. I propped my head up on my hand, my curls in disarray as they spilled down the back of my head. He didn't seem to notice, though, as his hand wrapped around them and pulled me in for a kiss.

"I think my brain has stopped working," I said as he started laughing beside me. I nuzzled my way closer into him and listened to the beat of his heart as I drifted asleep.

THIRTY-THREE

Lennon

THE MORNING CAME TOO quickly as we rose to get ready and checked out of our hotel. I hunted down my underwear and dress from last night and stuffed everything into my bag. The ride back to Fairvale seemed to drag on forever and that little voice in my head, the one that had been telling me I'm not worthy of love since I was a child, grew louder and louder with every passing mile. By the time we pulled up to my house, I was wracked with guilt and nerves and the spiraling I was so accustomed to was beginning.

Even if I didn't want it.

He grabbed my bag from the trunk, and I led the way into my home. He crossed the threshold behind me and set it down in the entryway.

My hands fidgeted by my side. What happened next?

Like, did I say, 'thank you for the great sex, see you later?' We'd never actually discussed what this was, and the unknown had me anxious. My mouth moved before I could stop myself. "What is this, Theo?" He turned to look at me, one of his thick dark eyebrow's arches in question.

"What is what?" His eyes searched mine, looking for a sign to point him in the direction of the answer.

But there wasn't one, and I was about to ruin everything.

"Us. This. What is it that we're doing?" I started pacing the length of the kitchen. He wasn't saying anything, which only heightened my anxiety. I should have never asked. I should have kept my mouth shut, kissed him goodbye, and gone about my day. But the self-deprecating part of me was begging for answers. Begging to define whatever this was between us so I could rip it apart and analyze every miniscule part of it. Twist it up until I convinced myself I wasn't worthy of being loved again.

The feeling came out of nowhere. It wasn't supposed to go this way, but I could see the future he wanted for us in his eyes, and it made me want to run. I didn't know how to handle the love he was so willing to give me. I'd spent years refusing to get close to anyone for fear of losing the only parts of Camden I had left. Then Theo showed up and the more time I spent with him, my grief over Camden seemed to take up less space.

"Lennon, this can be whatever we want it to be. If you want to keep it casual, I can do that." His words didn't match the look on his face. He moved toward me, and my pulse ticked up a notch. "Whatever you want is what we will do, but I have to tell you." He took my hands in his, his thumb rubbing smooth circles on the back of my palm before he continued. I knew what's coming, but I couldn't stop it, and I didn't know if I was ready for it.

He loved me; it was on the tip of his tongue. I could see it every time he looked at me. Every brush of his hand, in every curl he put back into place, I could feel it. It was razor thin, ready to shred my last thread of doubt with those three words.

"I... I love you." I ripped my hand out of his as I started shaking my head back and forth. "I know it seems fast, but I can't help how I feel, and I need you to know—" he continued, but I cut him off.

"Why?" I questioned, how was it that he could love me so easily when I find most days a struggle to put myself together?

"I am just a fraction of who I was. All the good parts of me were buried with Camden. No matter what I do, I can't seem to get back to that person. Why would you want that?" I planted my feet inches from his and looked up, meeting his eyes. "Why would you want to love someone like that, someone like me?" Bright green eyes stared back into mine, and I wanted nothing more than to stop talking.

Anything more would only end in heartbreak. For both of us.

"I can't give you what you deserve. I cannot give you all of me because there will always be parts that belong to him," I choked out in between sobs. There were tears spilling over and onto my cheeks. I tried to brush them away, but he caught my hands in his and cradled my face.

"I will take whatever you are willing to give me." It came tumbling out of his mouth as barely more than a whisper, his thumbs stroking my cheekbones in feather light motions. "You can try to push me away, and you can tell me all the different reasons why you think you are not enough, but you are what I want. I once told you that no matter how far I went or how long we were apart, I would always love you. That hasn't changed. You are magnetic, Lennon, you pulled me in like gravity, and I don't ever want to leave."

I couldn't stop the tears as they flowed freely down my face. A sob ripped from my throat as I tried, and failed, to stifle my crying. Since Camden died, I had been empty. As if my very soul had been ripped from my body, leaving behind only a shell. It wasn't until after running into Theo on the street in Edinburgh that life began to return to me. I couldn't pinpoint one thing he had done that had helped pull me out of the dark, but instead, a culmination of actions and his presence that helped.

He kept showing up, and it didn't matter what version of me he was going to get. A depressed mess of a woman trying to keep herself together or an outgoing ball of energy that reminded him of what I was like when we were younger. He provided me with the security I craved so that I could strip away the layers that had been threatening to suffocate me and lay them out before him. He saw underneath the pain and fear that I had been carrying around like a security blanket, shielding myself from any further harm.

"Look at me." His voice was soft with the gentle demand. My eyes opened, and he bent down slightly so that we were resting our foreheads together and paused. "Even if what we have now is as far as it goes, even if you can't love me back, I will always be here for you. I would be happy to just live out my days in your orbit." His words echoed with sincerity.

"I can never replace Camden, and I will never try to. All that I ask is that maybe you could try to make room in your heart for me, too." The words filled the air between us, making it hard for me to think. Our life had blended unintentionally over the last few months, and I couldn't even begin to fathom having to go back to a life that didn't include his smile, his laugh, his very presence. He was more than anything I could ask for, and he loved me.

So why was it that all I could think about was Camden?

I removed myself from his hands and took a step back. "I need some time, Theo. I don't ..." I couldn't look him in the eye. I wouldn't watch while I broke his heart. "I don't know if I'm willing to make room." It was like a knife in my own chest, and I wished I could take the words back as soon as I said them, but it was too late.

I could hear as he took a deep breath, shaky and ragged. "That's okay, Lennon." Even in the face of rejection, he remained gentle with me, and I knew I didn't deserve him.

"I'm going to be out of town for a shoot next week. I'll only be gone for a few days, and when I get back, do you think we might be able to talk more?" I nodded my head yes, as I didn't trust my voice not to crack when I answered. He placed a quick kiss on my forehead and walked out my front door, taking my heart with him.

THIRTY-FOUR

Theo

WHAT KIND OF IDIOT told a woman he loved her when they weren't even a real couple? Oh, I know… the kind of person who wanted to feel their heart get ripped out of their chest.

Me, I was the idiot.

It was killing me having to keep what I was feeling inside, and while it might have been selfish to throw it out there so suddenly, I needed her to know.

It had been a week since I'd seen her, and time seemed to be moving at a glacier's pace, but my trip to Tacoma to shoot at Thornewood Castle had been a silver lining. Losing myself in my work was about the only thing I could do to keep my thoughts from spiraling. Even though she'd been adamant about not seeing me, she'd still responded to my calls and texts, and it gave me hope that the door for us wasn't sealed shut.

A bell chimed as I opened the door to Nevermore Used Books, and Mrs. Andrews greeted me from the front desk with a warm smile. I returned her good morning as my hands came down onto the counter. "Does Lennon have an order with you this week?" I asked. She needed space, and I fully intended to make sure she got whatever she needed, but I also wanted her to know that I hadn't checked out. That I wouldn't go away, even if times were hard. Mrs. Andrews pulled a small stack out from beneath the counter and placed it in front of me.

"I just got in a few of the books on her list, but she hasn't come by yet to get them." She smiled warmly at me, causing the skin around her eyes to crinkle. "You are too sweet, picking these up for her. Please tell her I said hello when you see her." I paid for the books and told her I would pass along her greeting.

I reached Lennon's house shortly after; I let my car idle as I jogged up to her front door and left the stack on her doorstep. Once I was back in my car, I texted to let her know that they were waiting for her. Before I pulled away from the curb, her front door opened. I hesitated in case it was her, but instead, I saw Abigail flying down the front porch stairs straight to my car. When she reached me, she leaned her arms on the window, sticking her head part of the way in, giving me a look that would impress even Medusa before she spoke.

"I want to be mad at you, but I kinda told you to do it, didn't I?" Color me surprised. I'd take that as an apology. "I mean I knew you had feelings, but did you have to tell her you loved her." She teased.

"I should have been a bit more subtle in my approach to telling her how I feel, but you were right. She needed to know and to make her own decision. Even if I hate the current outcome."

She let out a breath and tapped on the car door. Her face softened as she looked at me. It was sometimes hard to believe that Lennon's little sister was all grown up. I was an only child, so I never had a bond with someone growing up like Lennon had with Abby. It was a type of connection I could only dream of. The care Abby took to tend to Lennon was delicate. If you didn't pay attention, you might even miss it. She may be the younger sibling, but she would move mountains to keep Lennon happy.

"I'm sorry, Theo. She told me what she said, and while I know she'll want to talk to you about it soon, I can tell you she's a wreck over it. Please don't give up on her," she pleaded with me.

"Giving up isn't an option for me. Unless the words leave her mouth that I am not welcomed in her life, I'm here to stay. It's always been her, it will always be her, Abby."

"Good," she said before walking back into the house. It was Abby's final stamp of approval. I'd been collecting them for as long as I could remember, because you couldn't love Lennon without going through Abby first.

One of the best perks about working for Castle Architecture was that I did not have to develop my own film or print any of the shots I took if I wanted my own copies. I could send them in and have them do the work, personal or work related. After we got back from Castello Di Amorosa, I went straight back to my rental to send in the film from the trip, and I had received the notification that the photos had been mailed back and had arrived.

I ripped the package open the second I got home, taking the photos gingerly into my hands. Her smile was what caught me, her lips pulled back into a genuine smile that lit up her entire face—it was hard to look away. I had also sent in the shots of us together, and they looked exactly how I hoped they would come out. I picked up the frame I bought recently and slid my favorite behind the glass. I may not have a home that was my own, but she deserved to sit on my nightstand, regardless. The rest of the day was spent packing and shuffling about my rental, looking for things to do to kill time. Night came quickly, and I spent hours staring at my ceiling, willing the sleep that evaded me to come.

The next morning I was off to the airport with only Lennon on my mind, so I pulled out my phone as I rode in the back of my rideshare.

> On my way to Tacoma. I'll be back in three days. I miss you.

Three dots appeared instantly at the bottom of my screen, and they jumped around as I waited for her response.

> I miss you more. I'll see you when you're back. Have a safe trip.

Weight seemed to lift off of my shoulders at her indication that I would finally get to see her again. The next three days would be a nightmare to get through, but with her on the other end, it was worth it.

Thirty-Five

Lennon

My anxiety wasn't a vacation home that I went to now and then to dip my toes in the water. It was my permanent residence, and I have been rooted down here for years. I sat in my home with its rooms that contained only my thoughts, which lurked around in order to torture me. The dark ones that lived in the farthest corners of my mind and would claw their way out until they were the only ones I could hear. I lived in a constant state of panic about what could happen.

I wanted to take back what I said the moment the words left my mouth, but I was scared. Scared of defining what Theo and I were to each other, scared of having to carve out room in my heart that would leave less space for Camden. Most of all, I was scared of what it would do to me if I loved him, only to have him ripped away from me, just like Camden.

Every possible worst-case scenario flashed through my mind the second he told me he loved me. I did the only thing I could think of and told him there was no room for him.

What a lie that was.

It'd been six days since I'd been close to him. Six days, eight hours, and thirty-two minutes–but who's counting? Abby noticed Theo's car had pulled up the other day when I was deep in a pity pool party. I was face down in a floaty, drifting around, when Abby decided she had enough of my self-loathing. She stomped from the house to the edge of the pool, casting a shadow over me.

"Do you know what I would give to have someone feel and care about me the way that man feels about you?" She sounded like she was on the verge of tears as I popped my head up from looking down at the water. She towered over me in this position, it took a second for my eyes to adjust and realize she was holding a stack of books.

"What are those?" I asked.

 I was very confused about what was going on right now.

She crouched in front of me. "Theo was here. He dropped these off for you." This had my attention. I pushed myself up into a sitting position. The books clattered on the glass table when she tossed them. She kicked off her shoes and sat on the steps, dipping her feet into the water.

She took a deep breath, then looked at me. "I would kill to have someone care about me so wholeheartedly that even when you're in a disagreement, he goes out of his way to make sure your wants and needs are taken care of. That's not an everyday occurrence, and

I don't want you to throw it away because of fear." I was tired of the tears, so I clenched down on my jaw, attempting to keep them at bay.

"I wish it was as easy as just loving him, but it feels like I have to choose. And I will not give up Camden, not even a little bit, not for anything or anyone. Regardless of how much they love me."

"Is he telling you that you have to choose? I can't imagine that he would ask that of you."

"He didn't tell me to choose. The opposite, really, he asked for me to make room for him." She stared back at me blankly, then leaned back on her outstretched hands. "Do you love him?" she asked, like one question could undo the turmoil I'd already caused. My head was screaming that it wasn't that easy. I couldn't say that I loved him and have everything work out the way I wanted it to.

She got up from the steps and slipped her feet back into her sandals. Giving me one last look, she scooped the books back up and walked back to the house. "He's already waited a lifetime for you, Lennon," she stated as her hand hovered on the door handle, but before she pulled it open, she turned back to me with more emotion on her face than I had seen in years. "I know you love him. Don't make him wait any longer." She disappeared through the sliding door, and from the house, as well.

I really hoped I didn't ruined everything because, of course, Abby was right.

Abby's words had been weighing heavily on my mind. What if I could love them both, make room for both–it would be the answer to all my problems. The only issue I would have left would be ensuring Theo was willing to share. He would be back tomorrow, and I was on high alert, counting down the minutes until I could see him.

I loved him, and I needed to tell him.

He deserved to know that I never stopped thinking about him, that I was a better person to myself when I was around him. That I didn't want to spend another moment without him knowing that I was utterly and hopelessly devoted to him and to making this work. It didn't matter what happened after, I needed him to know that I was in this with him. I could make room for him the way he'd always left room for me in his life.

We could be happy, I could be happy, and I was ready to take that jump.

Cursing the lingering heat, I continued my stroll through a local farmer's market. I'd been picking through vegetables at one of the stalls, trying to decide on the best ones. The summers here are relentless and lasted so long that we barely had time for a proper fall. Today they're a striking green, tomorrow it was possible they would start fading, next they're dead and crunching beneath my feet. I grabbed a treat from the closest vendor selling something frozen and parked myself on a nearby bench.

With each scoop of the flavored ice, I relaxed further into the bench, until an older woman sat down next to me while I was lost in thought. I happened to look over at her while her eyes scanned the crowd back and forth. Her round face was aged with the type of lines that showed she's lived a life that was full of laughter.

I often wondered what Camden would look like if he were still here. Probably not much different after two years, but what about ten years in the future or twenty? I wondered if his smile lines would have deepened or if his hair would have held more gray than brown. Would his laugh still be the same, or would it have carried more happiness with the years that would have passed him? There's a small twinge in my heart at the thought of him, although it was nothing like it used to be.

She continued to move her head back and forth. I sat for a moment before my curiosity won. "Are you looking for someone?" I asked. She released an irritated sigh before answering.

"Oh, just my husband. I seem to have lost him in this crowd," she said while looking around, before her eyes landed on my face. "If you're married, I'm sure you know what I'm talking about. They're always wandering off." Her eyes crinkled as she smiled at me.

"I was, but he died a few years ago." I didn't know what compelled me to trauma dump on this poor, unexpecting woman, but the words slipped out. By the look on her face, she was already sorry she'd asked.

"I'm so sorry."

"Don't be," I said as I waved her off. It'd been a while since I'd heard someone apologize for something they had no hand in, and I was surprised to find that the sting that used to accompany those words wasn't quite as painful. "I'm currently picking out ingredients to make dinner for a man who just told me he loved me, even though I'm a mess of a human." Now, I was positive she was sorry she ever asked. There was a nervous laugh that bubbled up in the back of my throat as I apologized to her for over sharing.

She was kind when she told me not to worry about it, and we both remained sitting on the bench. I was picking at the styrofoam cup in my hand, contemplating getting up to leave and never returning in fear of running into her again when she spoke up again.

"For whatever it's worth, I believe he would want you to be happy, whatever that means for you. I don't think wanting what's best for your person stops at death. And if it were me, I would want my husband to be happy and be free enough to love again. The world is already such a cruel and unkind place, don't make it any harder than it has to be." We locked eyes for a second, before she broke contact and began scanning the crowd again. A smile pulled at her lips as she locked onto a man waving her over.

"Thank you," I managed to choke out before she got up.

"Anytime, dear."

She stood from the bench and pushed her way through the crowd towards her husband. She took the hand he had outstretched toward her, and he pulled her in, placing a kiss on the top of her head before they disappeared into the market stalls.

As a point, I never let myself think about the future. It was always supposed to involve Camden. We were supposed to grow old together. We were supposed to love and live the next however many years at each other's side. After he died, I buried all the hopes I had for what my life would have looked like.

Just for a second, I closed my eyes and let my mind drift and there's no surprise that all I could see was Theo. No one knows what the future holds, but I knew that whatever it had in store for me, I could face anything, as long as he was at my side.

My phone rang, and I sifted through my purse for a second before I was able to find it. There was a small part of me hoping that it was Theo, but when I looked down, the number scrolling across the top wasn't one I recognized. My thumb hovered over the decline button right as a buzzing sound started in the back of my head. For a split second, my stomach turned.

I hesitated, but something pushed me to the accept button, so I answered.

"H-Hello," my voice faltered.

"Lennon, honey. It's Melanie, Theo's mom."

Dread sunk to the pit of my stomach. My throat constricted, and my breaths were coming out in quick puffs as I braced myself for her next sentence. Her voice was thick and shaky as her next words cut through the receiver and lodged themselves like an ax into my heart.

"There's been an accident."

Thirty-Six

Lennon

We all possessed the natural instinct of flight or fight. When something goes terribly wrong or when we are presented with horrible news, one or the other always kicked in. But there's also a third response—freeze.

My feet stuck to the ground, my arms hung limp at my sides, and my phone dangled precariously between my fingers as her words registered in my mind. There were people moving around me, but I couldn't see their faces through the tears that blurred my vision. My phone dinged, and Melanie had sent the hospital details.

There was an accident.

It echoed in my head. Growing louder and louder until it was the only thing taking up space in my brain. The air I was pulling in wasn't getting to my lungs. It was stuck in my throat, causing me to choke on nothing.

There was an accident.

My mind flashed to Camden, and I was pulled back in time for a moment. The last time I answered an unknown caller, I was told my husband was dead. The parallel between that day and now was uncanny, and a feeling of déjà vu swept through my senses. It crawled through my veins, making itself known to every molecule in my body.

Fifteen seconds was all I allowed myself. I fell apart for fifteen miserably long seconds before I flew into action and finally reached my car. I pulled out of the crowded parking lot, and for once, I was thankful I lived close to a major city. Sacramento International Airport was about forty-five minutes away, but I made it in under thirty.

With nothing but my purse, and I couldn't tell you where I parked, I raced inside. The sliding doors parted and I booked it towards the nearest counter and asked for a ticket on the first plane to the Tacoma/Seattle airport. My first sigh of relief came when the employee told me there was a plane leaving in forty-five minutes, which gave me fifteen minutes to make it through security, onto the tram, and to the correct gate. I sent up a thank you to whatever God and patron saint I could think of, since I'd only seen people buy a last-minute ticket at the counter in movies and wasn't exactly sure it was something done in real life.

When I reached my gate, I slipped into the last spot in the line of people. I handed over my crumpled ticket to the flight attendant while I was doubled over, trying to catch my breath. She threw me a sideways glance, probably wondering if I should even be allowed in, then told me to have a nice flight.

Taking my seat, my hands trembled, causing the buckle to miss the slot a few times before I could click it into place. Ninety minutes—wheels up, wheels down—before I get there. The adrenaline pumping through my system had me on a high, and thankfully, was keeping the spiraling anxiety at bay.

When the plane touched down, I switched on my phone and proceeded to order the closest rideshare before I started the second leg of the apparent track race I was in. When I reached the pickup area, my ride was pulling up, and I ignored every rule about getting in cars with strangers after barely confirming he was here for me before I was begging him to drive as fast as he could to St. Clare Hospital.

Something or someone was on my side–fate, the universe, divine intervention. I could feel it as traffic opened up on the freeway and we hit every green light on the way. I made a mental note to look into going to church once this was all over.

Fate brought me Theo, surely, it wouldn't take him away.

I hadn't heard much from Melanie since she called me, only that he was brought in with a head injury and had been unconscious since then. My stomach lurched at even the slightest thought that he might never wake up. He had to wake up. I wouldn't accept anything less, and I refused to put another man I loved into the ground.

When we pulled up to the hospital, I jumped out, shouting to my driver that five stars and a hefty tip would be on its way. The glass doors to the hospital slid open before I crashed into them, and made a beeline for the nearest nurse counter.

"I'm looking for Theodore Beckett. He was brought in by ambulance," I gasped out.

There was a pretty young nurse on the other side of the desk who gave me the once over before responding. "And your relationship with the patient?" I realized she was doing her job, but I was so past my breaking point I wanted to scream at her to just tell me where he was.

"I'm his wife." I answered in desperation.

It slipped off my tongue so effortlessly that anyone listening in wouldn't have cause to doubt me. I'd say whatever it took, not willing to risk not being able to see him. She glanced up at me, and for a second, I thought she was going to challenge my answer. The feral look of desperation in my eyes must have been enough because a few seconds later she plied me with his room number and quick directions on how to get there. Before I could push myself away from the counter, she told me not to be alarmed if he wasn't awake. The knot that formed in my stomach when Melanie called me tightened slightly.

My shoes squeaked against the linoleum floor as I sped down the deserted halls. Within minutes, I was standing in front of his door. My hand hesitated as it reached for the handle. Behind the door was the man I loved, a man that I wanted to make a life with, but for some reason I was once again faced with the idea that I might have to live without him. I drew in a breath and attempted to brace myself for whatever was on the other side.

Pushing the door open, my senses were assaulted by the sterile smell of the room. My knees threatened to give out and send me crashing to the floor as I took my first steps inside. Time froze as I approached his bedside, only the sound of his heart rate hung in the air. My heart thrashed around in my chest while I registered his battered appearance.

His arm was in a cast. Bruising lined both of his eyes, and there were fresh stitches bordering his hairline. His brown hair hung in limp curls until I reached out to push them off his forehead. He almost looked peaceful despite the damage to his body. But he needed to wake up. I needed to see the green in his eyes more than I needed my next breath.

My legs finally gave out, and I collapsed into the chair by his bedside as a heart-wrenching sob tore through the room. Hot tears poured from my eyes and down my face, and I made no move to wipe them away.

For the second time in my life, I pleaded with him to not to leave me.

"Theo, please do not make me do this again. I will not make it this time." My voice thick with desperation. "I haven't had enough time with you. I'm a selfish person, and I am telling you it was not nearly enough time together. You need to wake up," I demanded.

"*Please.*"

There was nothing delicate about my request. It was full of agony and bordered on hysteria. But that didn't matter. I would scream into an empty void for the rest of eternity if it meant he could hear me.

My head fell backwards as I turned my eyes and pleas towards the ceiling. "You cannot have him," I begged. "Please don't take him too." If I had to be honest, I don't know what I believed in, but I could not fathom there was a God that would put me through this twice.

The steady beeping of the machines accompanied my crying as I gently took his free hand into mine. "I haven't even had the chance to tell you I love you," I said as I placed a kiss on his hand. My head rested on the edge of the bed and finally I allowed the tears to overcome me.

I wept beside him, unashamed, heartbroken and unaware of how much time had passed.

"I knew you'd come around." His voice broke through my cries, causing my head to shoot up. He turned his head slowly to look at me. "Hi, Lenny." A soft smile tugged at his lips and it was possibly the most beautiful thing I had ever seen.

"I love you," I blurted out, unable to keep my voice quiet and his eyes softened at my words. He shifted like he wanted to sit up, but even the smallest of movements caused him to suck air between his teeth.

"When you told me how you felt, I didn't know how to handle it, so I pushed you away, and I'm so sorry." I dragged my hands through the wetness under my eyes. "I thought... I thought you were dying, and the only thing that ran through my mind was I never got the chance to say it back." He motioned to me to sit on the bed facing him, and he gently took my hands in his. He chuckled over my fretting as I tried not to bump him or crush any of the IV's that he was hooked up to.

Then he looked up at me, and in those green eyes I was so desperate to see a minute ago was a look that I wanted to remember forever.

"I want you to know that I will never make you choose between being with me and loving Camden. I want you just the way you are, even if you think you're broken, even if parts of you belong to him. I just want to love you exactly how you are," he said, and every single broken piece of me was stitched back together.

Another sob escaped, but this time fear wasn't the driving force. He loved me and finally he knew that I loved him.

He gave me a rundown on what happened, and I made him promise to never climb a tree again, no matter how good the photo might be. Nurses came in and out of the room to check on him and let him know they'd send his doctor over that he was awake.

When my adrenaline wore off, I laid my head back on the bed close to his hip while we waited for the doctor, his fingers threaded through my hair as I drifted in and out of sleep. When the door opened next, I made no move to get up. The nurses had been working around my new permanent position with no issues. It was only when I got a whiff of perfume that I lifted my head up to see who the newcomer was.

"Mrs. Beckett," I exclaimed as I popped up from where I'd been seated. My eyes darted around frantically before she waved me back down and dragged a chair over to Theo's other side.

"What did I tell you about that? You can call me Melanie, seeing as I hear you are the newest Mrs. Beckett," she said with a sly smile.

"Mom!" Theo exclaimed from his bed as his eyes bounced wildly from me to his mom back to me. I burst out laughing and dropped back down into my seat, thankful for the break in the atmosphere. Theo continued to wait for an explanation as I worried my bottom lip.

"I may or may not have told the nurse I was your wife in order to see you. Sorry," I said as I shrugged my shoulders nonchalantly.

I wasn't sorry.

His shoulders relaxed as he took my hand again, his fingers absentmindedly rubbing over the spot where a ring would be. "Feel free to use that line to gain access to me at any time."

"Don't worry, I will." I sat forward and brushed a kiss against his temple.

Six months later

"It. Won't. Fit," I grunted out, as I yanked on the zipper to my suitcase, trying to force it closed as Theo walked through our bedroom door.

"Well, you have about five jackets in there. What did you expect?" he laughed out as he took over zipping while I sat on my luggage.

Theo was discharged from the hospital two days after I got there, we stayed in a hotel for about a week before he was cleared to fly. On the flight home, I told him he would be staying at my house once we got back. Not quite a demand—he could have gone to his parents', of course—but he agreed.

About a month after his accident, he started taking on assignments again from work, still staying semi-local, and I would join him every chance I got for a long weekend getaway. Today, though, we were getting ready to head back halfway across the world. Theo had a meeting with Archie in Scotland, then we were off to France, where Theo was doing a shoot in Mont Saint-Michel, the abbey that sat on an island off the coast of Normandy.

"I have to bring this many. It's going to rain practically the whole time we're in Scotland and France," I whined at him. He pressed a kiss to my lips before taking the suitcase out to Abby's car.

I took a look around our room before heading out. My closet was empty of Camden's clothes, with Theo's shirts hanging in their place, and the spot that once held his catch-all dish had been replaced by the photo of Theo and I from our trip to Castello Di Amorosa. I swiped the photo the day I took Theo to pack his things at his Airbnb. Once we got back to the house, I marched straight into my room and placed it on the nightstand I call his. There were no objections on his end.

I'd be lying if I said making the changes didn't hurt, but I finally realized that holding on to Camden's things wasn't the only way to keep him close. And Theo deserved his own space in my life, no matter how trivial it might have seemed.

Abby honked from the driveway, and I rushed to lock up and then hopped into her car. "Ready, you two?" she asked with a smile.

"Ready," we replied in unison.

We made it to the airport, and Theo got out to grab our bags from the back. Abby leaned across the console and grabbed onto my hand before I could exit. "I am so happy for you, Lennon. This is what I've been wanting for you, someone who just makes you happy." I tugged her in for a hug before jumping out and helping. I took a deep breath as I linked my hand with Theo's, and we walked through the airport doors as one.

When Camden died, it felt like the air was stolen out of my chest. Every day was a constant battle to keep myself alive. I was breathing, but as if only through a straw. Just enough air to keep me alive, but not nearly enough to live.

Loving Theo, though, that was like learning how to breathe again. He was slow, tentative sips of air that would settle into the deepest parts of my lungs, causing them to expand further and further the longer I was around him. Months passed, and I realized the small inhales I had been living on for so long were deep breaths, bringing me back to life.

There were still days where it was a bit harder to breathe, and there would always be a constant ache in my chest, but I was learning to embrace the fact that it would never fully disappear. Because there would always be a part of me that would never stop loving Camden.

It was who I was, and I was okay with that.

I turned to Theo as we approached the security line when he pressed a kiss to the back of my hand. "So, my love, do you think we will have time to see some of the castles we didn't get to during our first trip?" I asked, bumping my hip into his. He turned to look at me and uttered my three favorite words.

"Anything for you."

THIRTY-SEVEN

Epilogue

Theo — Two years later

"Did you know that it's the inspiration for the Sleeping Beauty castle?" Lennon quizzed me as she stared down at the viewfinder of the Pentax camera. She'd been supplying me with endless facts about this place since we got here yesterday.

"Do you have a book with all this information? How do you know all of this?" She looked up briefly and stared at me before adding that it was also rumored to be the Cinderella inspiration. I laughed when she rolled her eyes and went back to what she was doing.

We were currently on my assignment at Neuschwanstein Castle in Germany for the week. A few months after my accident, I had a meeting with Archie and let him know I'd be staying in the States.

I was prepared for him to push back, but instead, he told me that the magazine was expanding into estates, as well, opening up the market for more work in the States. More than enough to carry me along for years.

About twice a year, though, I picked up an assignment in Europe and took Lennon with me.

Any assignment she came on with me were always infinitely better than the ones I did on my own. Sometimes she lounged around in the area I was shooting, others she was off exploring the site, but my favorite would always be when she pulled out the Pentax she bought me all those years ago and captured what she deemed worthy. Being able to see these places through her eyes had been a gift that I never wanted to give up.

And today, I planned on telling her I wanted it to be for a lifetime.

I fiddled with my camera, trying to calm my nerves as the tiny box in my pocket weighed me down.

When I told Abby that I was planning on asking Lennon to marry me, she screamed so loud it felt like she busted my eardrum. She jumped up and down like I told her Santa brought her the gift she had been asking for all year, then peppered me with a million questions.

Could she help pick out the ring?

Where would I do it?

Could she be there?

I told her yes to the first, but no to the last. I knew I wanted it to be on one of these trips, just the two of us.

She slid the viewfinder as she pointed the camera out across the trees where Neuschwanstein stands, then smiled. That was how I knew she got the shot she wanted. My stomach did backflips, and my hands seemed to drip with sweat as I walked over to her and took the camera from her hands. She looked at me, confused, but didn't protest as I sat down.

Everything faded away when I looked into her blue eyes.

"Lennon," I started, as I took both of her hands in mine. "Decades ago, you wove yourself into the very fabric of my life, and since then, I have been covered in you." She said my name, her voice was barely more than a whisper as her eyes swam with emotion.

"Please, let me get this out. I feel like I might actually pass out if I don't get to say this to you." She nodded her head reluctantly at my request, and I sucked in a breath. I had so much I wanted to say to her. We could spend the rest of our lives together and still only scratch the surface of my feelings for her.

"For years, I wandered this Earth going from country to country, filling my days with some of the most beautiful sites this world has to offer, but I knew something was missing. It wasn't until Scotland that I realized that what I was missing was you. The moment you left, I decided that I didn't want to spend another day away from you." I reached into my pocket and pulled out a black velvet box before stepping back and getting down on one knee. Her hands came up to her mouth and tears spilled over.

"You have been, and always be, everything I want in this life. I love you with everything I am, and what I want most is to spend the rest of my life making you, and keeping you, happy." I opened the lid, exposing a solitaire diamond that sparkled in the afternoon light coming through the trees.

"Lenny, my love, will you—"

Before I could finish my question, her arms were around me, pulling me into a soul-crushing kiss. I pulled her in tighter and made no attempt to hold back my own tears.

"I take that as a yes," I said, and I stood up to remove the ring from the box, sliding it onto her finger without waiting for her to confirm. She beamed at me. Her face was like the sun overhead, bright and warm. It poured into my soul, filling me to the brim with happiness.

"Yes. How could it be anything other than yes?" She looked at me with a face that held promise. A promise of her heart, her love, her forever, and it was the greatest sight I'd ever witnessed.

"Finally," I said, pressing my lips into hers.

Years after leaving her, even if we both knew it was for the best, something brought me back to her. An undeniable force that was impossible to ignore. Before Lennon, I didn't believe in much, let alone fate, but if she had taught me anything, it was that you couldn't escape what was meant to be. Because even if Lennon was meant for Camden, I knew that I was always meant for her.

Acknowledgments

I'm still trying to wrap my mind around the fact that I wrote a freaking book. Not only wrote a book, but followed through enough to get it out into the world and into your hands!

Even if just one person reads and enjoys this book, it would be enough. Whoever you are, wherever you are, thank you. Thank you for taking the time to step into my mind while I let it run wild. Thank you for taking a chance and opening a book written by someone you've never heard of but had a story to tell.

Sarah with Indie Proofreading. Thank you for taking my jumbled mess of words and making them coherent. For being able to see the direction I was trying to take with this story and helping me get there.

I believe soulmates are not limited to being only our lovers. They take on various forms in the people we surround ourselves with - friends, family or even that person who drifted into your life when you were young and showed you what it was like to fall in love for the first time. No matter how fleeting or permanent they may be, they all serve the purpose which is to make the life we have one worth living.

To my soulmates Brooke, Lily, Elijah and Eric, each of you make my life exponentially better every day and, without a doubt, one worth living. You pushed me into bringing this book to life, and I'll never be able to thank you enough.

For my sisters, I hope when you read this story, you see a glimpse of us in Lennon and Abigail. Just know the love they have for each other is only a fraction of what I hold in my heart for you both. Whether you're one mile or a hundred and fourteen miles away, even if you can't see it, I hope it's something you will always feel.

To my mother, who is someone I am constantly and immensely proud of. Your sobriety gave my pain meaning and a purpose and it's a price that I will forever be willing to pay. Without it, I wouldn't have been able to put words to the feelings I had harbored or been able to use them to create something beautiful. Out of all the books I've read, your redemption arc is by far my favorite story.

Finally, there is no one more deserving of my gratitude than my husband. Thank you for always being the loudest in my cheering section. For supporting every spur-of-the-moment dream I've been able to concoct without hesitation but with so much enthusiasm that failing never seems like an option. Because of you, I feel like I can do anything in the world, even become an author. There are not enough words to describe the amount of love my soul holds for you, but I love you to the very edge of the universe.

About the Author

Brittney is a Northern California native who spends her nights crafting love stories. When she's not writing you can find her amongst friends deciding which game to play next, performing Taylor Swift songs to her unsuspecting husband, and binge watching period romance movies.

Instagram – @brittneylaurenwrites